Riggs Park

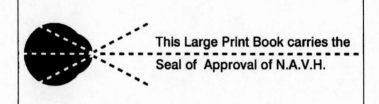

This Large Print Book carries the
Seal of Approval of N.A.V.H.

Riggs Park

Ellyn Bache

Thorndike Press • Waterville, Maine

Published in 2006 by arrangement with Harlequin Books S.A.

Thorndike Press® Large Print Americana.

The tree indicium is a trademark of Thorndike Press.

The text of this Large Print edition is unabridged.
Other aspects of the book may vary from the original edition.

Set in 16 pt. Plantin by Minnie B. Raven.

Printed in the United States on permanent paper.

Library of Congress Cataloging-in-Publication Data

Bache, Ellyn.
    Riggs Park / by Ellyn Bache. — Large print ed.
        p. cm. — (Thorndike Press large print Americana)
    ISBN 0-7862-8223-1 (lg. print : hc : alk. paper)
    1. Female friendship — Fiction.   2. Cancer — Fiction.
3. Middle-aged women — Fiction.   4. Large type books.
I. Title.   II. Thorndike Press large print Americana series.
PS3563.A845R54 2005
    813'.54—dc22   2005027317

For my favorite breast cancer survivors,
Brooks and Carol Ann.
And for Barbara,
whose brain tumor in no way diminished
her great and wonderful brain.

As the Founder/CEO of NAVH, the only national health agency solely devoted to those who, although not totally blind, have an eye disease which could lead to serious visual impairment, I am pleased to recognize Thorndike Press* as one of the leading publishers in the large print field.

Founded in 1954 in San Francisco to prepare large print textbooks for partially seeing children, NAVH became the pioneer and standard setting agency in the preparation of large type.

Today, those publishers who meet our standards carry the prestigious "Seal of Approval" indicating high quality large print. We are delighted that Thorndike Press is one of the publishers whose titles meet these standards. We are also pleased to recognize the significant contribution Thorndike Press is making in this important and growing field.

Lorraine H. Marchi, L.H.D.
Founder/CEO
NAVH

* Thorndike Press encompasses the following imprints: Thorndike, Wheeler, Walker and Large Print Press.

From the Author

Dear Reader,

It seems incredible to me now, but I once was horrified by the idea of someday becoming an "older woman." Why would people over fifty want to go on? They looked awful, and their lives seemed unbearabley dull.

What on earth was I thinking?

Happily, I have been lucky enough to become an "older woman" myself, with all the joys and turbulence that implies. Only the "older" woman can know the irreplaceable preciousness of a fifty-year friendship . . . a long career . . . grown children . . . loves and losses she finally has the maturity to understand. Only the "older" woman can view the world through the lens of her own history and see how its difficulties, as much as its triumphs, have contributed to the fullness of her life. I wrote *Riggs Park* to celebrate that "older-but-not-yet-old" time, in all its richness. I hope you enjoy it.

Ellyn Bache

CHAPTER 1

Wrightsville Beach, NC

October 2000

Until Marilyn called, I had no thought of being flung back into the warm and rushing stream of my own youth. I was having enough trouble with the present. Staring out at the sea without really seeing it, I had spent the last hour mentally snatching petals from a daisy — he loves me, he loves me not. Subtract fifty years, add an actual flower, and I might have been eight. I hardly heard the phone. Two rings. Three. The answering machine could take it. Then I got curious and picked up.

"Well, it's back," Marilyn announced. Pert and casual. Not even a hello. Her same peppy self.

"What's back?" As if I didn't know. "The decent fall weather's back?" My heart always skipped a beat or two when I lied, but as much as it scared me, I fibbed on. "Washington's always pretty in the fall."

"No, no. Not the weather. The beast."

Slay the Beast had been our motto.

"Oh, Marilyn, no. When did you find out?"

"They told me for sure this morning. I swear, I always get cancer on Thursday and then I have to wait the whole damn weekend for the test results."

"But *Thursday!* That was a week ago yesterday. Why didn't you call me?"

"I wanted to. I just couldn't." The cheery tone drained to a whisper. "Don't be angry, Barbara. It was such a seesaw. The doctor found the lump on Thursday, they did the mammogram Friday, all weekend I was catatonic, and on Monday they told me it looked suspicious. Tuesday they did the biopsy. I kept hoping they'd say it was a false alarm and I'd be able to call you and we'd have a good laugh about it." She ran out of air, took a long breath. "Then I got the diagnosis this morning."

I opened my mouth, but my voice had left me. I willed it back. "It must have been a nightmare," I rasped. "I hope Bernie was with you. I hope he held your hand through all this."

"You kidding? My paramour and protector? He wouldn't have missed it. My sainted husband says —" Marilyn imitated his low growl " '— You beat it before, so

10

you'll beat it again.' "

"Well, he's right. You did and you will. I bet you already have a plan."

"I do. For starters, I want you to come up here."

"Sure. Done." I spoke without thinking. A trip to Washington? Now? No possibility. "Are you going to have —"

What was left? Marilyn had had surgery; she had had chemo. The drugs had made her sick and thin and bald, but after three years we were convinced the poisons had done their job. When Marilyn's hair had begun to grow back, I had driven up from North Carolina to help her celebrate, if you can call it celebrating when you accompany someone to her first Hadassah meeting in a year.

"Look how much the treatments have aged me," Marilyn had complained then. "Look at these jowls!" But though Marilyn's jaw seemed a bit fleshier than before, I thought she looked marvelous. On the day of the Hadassah luncheon, Marilyn's fine new cap of hair (mostly chestnut, not much gray) had been slicked flat, a fashionable inch and a half long all over her head, accented by long silver earrings and a formfitting navy suit that glided over her slimmer figure. Neither of us had ever been a great beauty, despite the plastic surgery we'd believed would transform us. But Marilyn had sometimes felt like one, after her charms had captured Bernie Waxman's heart when we were only fifteen. Marilyn still swore she didn't return Bernie's affection for another five years, but his love, from the beginning, gave her the confident, radiant loveliness only a sea of caring can confer. If some of that early luster dimmed as we aged, we told ourselves looks didn't really matter anymore — a maxim neither one of us believed.

Lord, no! Women of our generation knew from toddlerhood that beauty was the coin of the realm; women of our generation never recanted even after the world declared us "liberated." So when Marilyn and I stood in the ladies' room outside the Hadassah meeting, two ordinary women in our midfifties telling ourselves once again that psychological well-being rather than comeliness was the issue, we were nevertheless applying lipstick and combing our hair in preparation for the kosher lunch.

A white-haired matron in an expensive suit emerged from a toilet stall and planted herself beside us at the sink. "So, Marilyn. You really like your hair that short?" Flaring her nostrils, wrinkling her nose,

12

the woman signaled unspeakable distaste.

Unfazed, Marilyn flashed a brilliant smile. "Mrs. Katz, this is my friend Barbara Cohen."

Mrs. Katz nodded without diverting her attention from Marilyn.

Marilyn regarded herself in the mirror, ran her hands all over her head to smooth her new coif, preened in an exaggerated way. "It's the style. You don't like it?"

Mrs. Katz shrugged.

"Well, it'll grow," Marilyn said.

Bursting with merriment, Marilyn and I contained ourselves until the woman ambled out, then let loose with uncontrollable laughter — absurd laughter, uncalled-for laughter, very nearly hysterical. Marilyn had faced the fire, survived her ordeal, and the old buzzard was none the wiser. Tummy-tucked (to provide tissue for the breast), breast-reconstructed (no nipple yet; that would come later), she was back among the living, working part-time, eating without throwing up, going to Hadassah. Victorious!

But cured? We didn't know, and pretended not to care.

Now, three years later, I clutched the phone with sweaty hands while Marilyn posed my unspoken question. "Am I going

13

to have more chemo? Right now I'm still looking at options." I cringed. Marilyn adopted her spunkiest tone. "The last couple of years we've been at the age of dying and hardly knew it, did we?"

"Don't talk like that. What about a macrobiotic diet? What about acupuncture?"

"No. I think you have to believe those things before they work. Listen, when can you come? You can't refuse a dying friend."

"Stop that, I said!"

"And I have things to tell you. Things I don't want to take to my grave."

"One more morbid comment and I'm hanging up."

"I'm serious, Barbara. I don't want to discuss this on the phone."

"You think my line is tapped? You think you can't trust me unless you whisper it personally into my ear? This is Barbara Cohen you're talking to. We've known each other over fifty years."

"Good grief, we have, haven't we?"

The fact hung in the air between us, rendering us momentarily speechless. In the spring of 1946, at the age of four and a half, I'd moved to the corner of Washington called Riggs Park, two doors away from Marilyn's house, and we'd been inseparable ever since. More than half a century ago! On that first day, my mother, Ida, had scoured the neighborhood for playmates for me and my older sister so she could unpack knickknacks in peace. I vividly remembered the gray weather outside and satisfying bright colors within: the smell of new pink paint on the walls of the first bedroom I'd had all to myself, and the satisfying presence of this cheerful, ginger-haired girl who didn't mind what game we played or what we ate — peanut butter sandwiches, Oreos, warmish milk — and who from that day on would be my undisputed best friend.

"We might have known each other forever," Marilyn said now, "but that doesn't mean I've told you everything." Her voice dropped a notch. "It's about Penny."

So, of course, I had to go.

The door slammed just as I hung up the phone, and a moment later Jon appeared — the source of my current troubles — tanned and fit from the too-long summer, his hair a white tangle from the humidity. He put down two cups of coffee from the convenience store and pulled his damp shirt out from his chest, clowning. "I hope you appreciate this. Only a prince would

15

go out in this sauna for the love of his woman."

"Some prince! *You* were the one who wanted coffee. Me, I use the coffeemaker in the kitchen."

My words were light, but my manner must not have been, because Jon noted my hand still touching the phone and frowned. "What's wrong?"

I shook my head.

"Barbara? Lose a job? What?"

"Too early in the year to lose a job." I did academic research for professors and students at the University of North Carolina at Wilmington, which meant that I never got busy until well into the semester. "Just midafternoon slump."

"And that accounts for the pale face? The oyster-shell countenance?"

I forced a smile. "Probably those fried-egg sandwiches you made for lunch."

"Don't let the cholesterol lobby fool you. Eggs are healthy." He handed me one of the coffee cups, let his fingers linger on mine just long enough to call up a stab of desire low in my belly, something that still embarrassed me after more than two years. "This will fix you right up."

I took a sip. "Perfect. Thanks, Jon."

"You're really all right?" A furrow of

concern appeared between his ebony brows.

"Yes, fine."

"Who was on the phone?"

I inched my free hand away from the receiver. "Jealous?"

"Absolutely."

"It was just Marilyn."

A flicker of a question passed across his face, then vanished. Six weeks ago, a month ago, he would have quizzed me about Marilyn's welfare, would have kept at it until I told him what was wrong. Now he let an opaque curtain of distance settle over his features, as it did so often lately, and picked up his coffee. "Back to the taskmaster," he said.

Suddenly wanting to hold his attention, I asked quickly, "Trouble with the new chapter? It must be a humdinger, judging by the shocking number of trips you make to the store to escape it."

His eyes cleared, brought him back. He grinned. "*You* try writing a book." It was a collection of his articles, plus interviews with athletes who'd been caught in the riptides of politics and power — athletes, he'd said in happier times, who'd been *dissed.*

"Isn't this the chapter with Zeke Jones?" A false, annoying brightness invaded my voice. "Cheated out of the World Freestyle Wrestling Championship in ninety-five?"

"You remembered."

"I never believed I'd know the names of sports figures," I said. "Much less wrestlers."

"Shows what broadening your background can do." The grin died on his lips. "If you don't feel well — If something's bothering you —"

"I'm fine." My practiced smile sent him down the hall to the bedroom he used as his office, a man of such physical and psychological impossibilities that I wondered why I'd ever thought I knew him: the shoulders far too broad for his long, slender legs, bushy brows far too black for the thick white mop of hair on his head, moods as unpredictable as the coastal weather, a man of such paradoxes and secrets that I had no right to go to Marilyn until I unmasked them. And no right not to.

Oddly, I hadn't once mentioned to Marilyn how strange my relationship with Jon had been this past month, and I was glad of that now. Marilyn wouldn't have asked me to come to Washington if she'd known we were having difficulties, wouldn't have wanted me even if I'd offered. "After twenty years alone, now you finally have someone you care about and you're going on a trip instead of sorting out your troubles? What's wrong with you?" Ever the pragmatist, she'd insist that if I was embroiled in a stormy romance (at our age, did the term *romance* apply?), my first obligation was to see it through.

And considering my storybook beginning with Jon, maybe it was. Jon and I had not been in touch since we were in our twenties. Then, after more than thirty years, he caught sight of me during my one and only appearance on national TV, cleaning up my yard in Wilmington after Hurricane Bonnie in 1998. A sports journalist who spent most of his time on the road, he'd dropped everything and come to North Carolina to find me. Imagine! Seeking out a woman in her fifties! On the pretext of seeing how she'd fared in a storm!

"You needn't have worried, Bonnie only grazed us, it was nothing compared to Hurricane Fran back in ninety-six," I'd babbled when he first arrived, loose-tongued and stupid from the heady brew of surprise and flattery and disbelief. "My phone didn't go out at all, and my lights were back on in twenty-four hours. That's the worst. No power, and hot as hell, and . . ."

With the most extraordinary tenderness, Jon lifted a tanned, elegant finger toward my moving lips, and touched them into silence.

We'd been together ever since.

And even with the recent gloom that had settled over him, ours was still no tame "companionship" — though I often hoped my daughter, Robin, thought it was. Grown children should not be subjected, I believed, to the embarrassing fact of their parents' continuing sex lives.

Not that I'd expected to have a sex life! Certainly not! By my midfifties, I'd felt myself finally cooling and calming after an all-too-fevered youth. I was genuinely relieved. Too much of my early life had been spent in thrall to sex. Sex had permeated my every thought, made me sleepy, spoiled my moods, played havoc with my disposition. When I was in labor with Robin, I'd heard myself grunt as I pushed — and found it such a bestial, involuntary sound that in the midst of my pain and concentration I couldn't help thinking how much the insistent, animal nature of birthing resembled the incessant demand of mating. When middle age finally freed me of it, I felt as if I'd come out of a fog into open air, or outgrown a pesky allergy.

Then Jon appeared, looking better than he had a right to, and in an instant I was caught up once more in all that animal yearning. If it was foolish at that point in life — of course it was! — I no longer cared. After a year of passion far too heated for couples our age, we pooled our resources while real-estate prices were depressed from Hurricane Floyd in 1999, and bought our house across the drawbridge from Wilmington on trendy Wrightsville Beach. A risk, on that storm-tossed barrier island, but a commitment, too. After we cleaned up the flood damage, the place was everything both of us wanted: love nest, workplace, home. Jon stopped traveling and signed the contract for his book. Each of us set up an office in a spare bedroom. We awakened to the ocean sunrise and had coffee together before parting to our separate work areas. At noon we met for lunch on the oceanfront deck, where we watched dolphins arc in and out of the water. We lingered over sandwiches and told each other about our mornings. Tide-besotted and grinning with middle-aged infatuation, we were both — I believed this, truly — as happy as we'd been in our lives.

And not just because of the sex. There was also the luscious sense, after tossing alone in the world for far too long, of being once again mated. I'd been divorced nearly twenty years; Jon had been married only briefly. We reveled in the long-lost pleasure of touching shoulders as we passed in the hallway, of worrying together about the dripping sink, of reaching at the same moment to switch off the radio, of having someone always available for dinner, a movie, a visit with friends. Coupled and comfortable, we even went sometimes to Friday-night services at the Temple of Israel in downtown Wilmington, where I loved being regarded as half of just another ordinary middle-aged pair.

From his office, Jon's fingers clicked on his keyboard, then stilled, stopped. I held my breath, waiting for the comfort of renewed sound, activity, ongoing life. Out on the beach, two late-season tourists splashed in the shallows, bumping hips, laughing so easily that my eyes welled with sadness and envy. For weeks, I'd been trying to pinpoint the moment when Jon and I had lost that sweetness, when we had begun to feel ragged and old.

Certainly it was after Labor Day. We'd

eaten breakfast on the deck that holiday morning, Jon in shorts and a blue golf shirt, me teasing him about the curly white hairs peeking out of his open collar. "Oh, you think it's an imperfection!" Jon had joked, and I'd replied, "Yes, terrible! Like a chest wig to show your masculinity," to which Jon had huffed, "Huh! I'll show you masculinity!" and had chased me into the house. On Labor Day — no question about it — we'd still been happy.

So . . . when? Later that week, my daughter Robin had called to say she was coming to Wilmington for a film shoot, and I'd been happy then, too. A first assistant director, Robin worked at Wilmington's film studio once or twice a year. This time, I'd been especially glad to hear from her because she'd recently separated from her husband and seemed truly distraught.

"Most of the crew is staying in one of those cute bed-and-breakfasts downtown," Robin said on the phone, "but, Mom, the thought of hanging around with them right now gives me the willies. Think you could put me up?"

"Of course! Do you even have to ask? We'd love it!"

"I'll only be there two weeks before we leave for location."

"Robin, stop apologizing! I'll even do your laundry. This is wonderful!"

And Jon had seemed pleased, had sounded cordial — although the very fact of Robin's existence, I sometimes thought, made him sad. His short marriage had produced no offspring, and he regretted never having been a father. Much as he seemed to like Robin — and I was sure they genuinely enjoyed each other — I sensed she reminded him of what he had missed.

Yet the offer he made two days later puzzled and disturbed me. "I have some interviews to do out of town," he said. "The logical thing seems to be to schedule them during Robin's visit."

"Oh, honey. It's your house as much as mine. Robin knows we're a couple."

"Yes, but she's never stayed with us before."

"Only because she thought she and Bob would put us out. Now that she's alone —"

"As I recall," Jon said with a wink, "she told you she didn't want to disturb 'your little love nest.'" And then, seriously, "I think I make her nervous. I think she'll be happier if I go."

"Don't be silly. She doesn't want to stay with the crew because she's afraid they'll feel sorry for her now that Bob's gone.

That's what makes her nervous."

"With me working here, you won't have any privacy at all."

"Robin won't care. She works six days a week until God knows what time. We'll hardly see her." I tried to quell the note of irritation in my voice. "On Sundays all she'll want is sleep."

"She's young. She won't sleep that much." Impatiently, Jon fiddled with a pencil he'd tucked behind his ear. "I have to do those interviews sometime. This will give you time together."

"You make me feel like I'm kicking you out."

"Of course not."

"Maybe you're looking for an excuse to get away." I meant it as a joke, but my voice shrilled in my ears.

"Don't be paranoid, Barbara."

"Paranoid!"

"What else would you call it?"

"Oh, fine. Now I'm the loony little woman."

"Listen to yourself!"

"Listen to *you.*"

Stunned into silence, the two of us stood face-to-face and numb, aware that in our two years together, this was the closest we'd come to a fight. I wanted to pluck my words out of the air; I watched Jon's eyes grow dark with sorrow. "I'm sorry," we both mumbled.

Jon opened his arms, swept me in, held me close. "You're right," he whispered. "If I go, it'll send the wrong message. I don't want her to feel unwelcome."

He stroked my hair. I was convinced. But maybe — certainly — that was the beginning.

The day Robin arrived, I declined Jon's offer to drive me to the airport. I always liked to be alone to relish the sight of my daughter after a long absence, to bask in what was a perennial surprise and delight: her large eyes and prominent nose; the ripe, wide mouth; the erect bearing that made Robin seem so regal. Yet when the plane arrived, I wished Jon were there to soften my shock at seeing the weary young woman who shuffled through the gate, face the color of talc, pale hair wiry and wild, clothes hanging on a spindly frame. Even with Robin's divorce, I hadn't imagined such all-pervasive wretchedness. I rushed forward blinking back tears, and closed my arms around my daughter's knobby shoulders, feeling called once again to protective motherhood, yet helpless, too. What could a mother, herself long divorced and now living in what was once called "sin," do for a grown but aching child?

"Can you believe I waited so long to get married and then got snookered?" Robin said wryly as we waited for her luggage. "Thirty years waiting for the right guy, and then to get left for an actress."

"Stop kicking yourself, honey. You couldn't have known it wouldn't work out."

"Huh!" Robin snorted, spotting her suitcases on the carousel and rushing to get them. In the car on the way to the beach, she slumped in her seat and gazed so aimlessly at the summer-weary landscape that I had to restrain myself from pulling over and taking her in my arms, which she would have hated. Like Wells, her father, Robin had always been embarrassed by what she termed "gushy shows of emotion." Yet she'd always come to me when she was troubled. Not for hugs, not even for advice. Simply to nest, to be near a fixed point in her universe until her spinning stopped. I was glad she'd come to me now.

But I was horrified, over dinner that night, when she confessed to Jon and me that she'd been two months pregnant when Bob left and had miscarried, at home, alone, the morning after he moved out.

"Oh, Robin!" I cried. "Why didn't you tell me?"

"I didn't tell anybody," she said woodenly. "I was — I don't know. I felt like such a complete failure, I didn't tell anyone."

"But I'm your mother!"

"You should have come to us right away," Jon added, his voice gruff and wounded.

Robin smiled sadly. "I'm a big girl."

"You could have come to us," Jon said.

Stricken, I shot Jon a glance of gratitude for taking her side. But the discussion didn't end there. It went on and on, Jon sounding so troubled that finally even Robin seemed embarrassed. I raised my eyebrows at him quizzically. What was he trying to prove? On previous visits, he and Robin had talked about nothing more personal than movies and sports.

"Bastard," he muttered when Robin left the room. "What a bastard."

"She'll be all right."

"I hope so. We'll see."

A jab of irritation canceled out my concern. After wanting to go off to do his interviews, how much could he care? Much as he seemed to regret not having children, he'd never struck me as particularly fatherly, either. "You don't know Robin," I said. "She's resilient. Amazingly so."

"We'll see."

As if I didn't know my own daughter! But, of course, I did. By midweek, Robin was immersed in the intense business of filmmaking, and by the weekend, she'd actually cheered up — not that we saw her enough to know what was going on in the depths of her soul. When after two weeks Robin left for location in the Pennsylvania mountains, her color was good, her appetite restored. It had been a stupid marriage in the first place, I reasoned. A relief to have it over with. Robin was on her way to recovery.

But Robin's departure also ushered in those soggy days of waning summer when Jon began to retreat into the private corridor of sorrow I could neither understand nor penetrate. "When they're at that age," he said in a tone of immense weariness, "you wish you could somehow make it all right."

"You can't. Not when they're grown. But it *is* all right. Or will be."

"Yes, of course. I know that."

But except for lip service, Jon stayed locked in his fortress of thinly masked grief. He took to wandering from his office to the kitchen for ice water, shambling back again, staring out the sliding glass doors at the ocean, so preoccupied that I began to dread working in the same space with him, even such a space as this, lovely and sprawling, with its view of the marshes and the sea. He was not ill-tempered, not inattentive. But a subtle, brooding quality crept into his manner, which he tried to hide with a false, jovial air that set my teeth on edge.

To escape his moods, I took long walks on the beach — not that they helped. Outside the air was hot and gummy. The exquisite clear sunshine of July and August had given way to a burning September, an unseasonably hot October. The warm Atlantic waters refused to cool; the autumn fish stayed away; the festive red gaillardias put on a second season of wild red bloom in the sand. How was it that fall had come to the entire country except the Carolina coast? I longed for crisp air and brisk nights. My lungs felt flaccid from too much humidity, my skin parched from too much sun. Why, I was nothing but a crone who'd faced the millennium with a closer view of sixty than fifty! What made me think I could still hold a man? I was healthy enough (at fifty-eight, I wasn't *old* yet, was I?) but in the eyes of the world (Jon's eyes?) I must be fading. For me, that autumn on the sweet coast of North Carolina held such a damp core of sadness that even on the days when the water turned velvety blue-green in the slanted light and made my throat ache just to look at it — even then melancholy persisted in the soft air and ruined everything.

One day I returned from my walk to find Jon staring at a picture I thought I'd thrown away, of me and my ex-husband, Wells, on a woodland hike early in our marriage. Jon looked up so guiltily that I might have found him with another woman.

"Regretting you didn't claim me first, during your treacherous youth?" I asked, trying for levity.

Jon ran his hand up my arm, barely grazing the skin, and I was at once touched and annoyed by the physical effect he had on me, which seemed as out-of-season as the weather. "I'd give a lot to live my treacherous youth over again," he said.

He lifted a finger to my face, traced the line of my cheekbone. I didn't want to think about lost youth; I was more worried about what we seemed to be losing now.

"Be serious, Jon. What's bothering you?"

"You think I'm sulking, don't you?"

"Well, aren't you?" I asked, remembering his silent morning.

Deliberately dramatic, he flung the picture into a drawer, closed it with a flourish, turned to me with a manic grin. "I hope not."

"Jon, don't."

He moved close, studied me. "You know how you make me feel?"

"How?"

"You make me feel lucky. I haven't felt lucky in a long time."

He kissed me on the forehead, leaving me disarmed, but none the wiser, and retreated into his office.

If I could have confided in Marilyn, I might at least have taken comfort in having an ally. But my troubles seemed too humiliating, somehow. I would work through them, *then* confess. In the meantime, I invented endless explanations for Jon's moods. He was grumpy because he missed traveling. He preferred working alone but didn't want to say. He was worried about his book. *That,* at least, was true enough. The book was massive, so different from writing short pieces that naturally it took its toll. I'd seen how engrossed he was, working on a chapter about swimmers who'd been denied their chance for greatness when Jimmy Carter had withdrawn from the 1980 Olympics. Caught powerless in a whirlwind of politics, some had put the disappointment behind them and gone on to other successes. Many had not. It must be hard to write, day after day, about such young promise being dashed. Jon had once been a fine athlete himself. A teenage mishap had ended his budding career. Maybe it grieved him to remember. Maybe the memory of his youthful disappointment spilled over to the collapse of Robin's marriage: failure one generation later, still hard to watch. I was full of theories.

Or maybe it was just that he no longer loved me.

But no! I didn't believe it. Not after we'd come this far.

Feeling exiled at the beach these last few weeks, breathing the sticky air, I'd vowed stubbornly to hang on to the vestiges of our new life. I would endure Jon's silence, wait him out. Offer him, if nothing else, my presence. I had no right, just now, to be anywhere but in my own troubled household, in the flat heat of a muggy North Carolina autumn.

So how was it that, when Marilyn had

called, I'd said I would go to Washington?

Because there was no choice.

Because stronger even than my feeling for Jon was the lesson only treachery and its consequences could teach: Life is not that long. You will love only a handful of people. When all is said and done, you will be able to count them on your fingers. It will not matter if they are worthy or deserving. Don't take them lightly. Don't let them down.

After more than fifty years of friendship, there was really no question who had the older, the greater claim.

Outside, the beach had emptied. Only the screeching, circling gulls and the brown pelicans remained, diving into the surf for their supper. Swallowing my apprehension, I strode into Jon's office and announced that Marilyn's cancer was back, that Marilyn wanted me to come.

Jon rose from his desk, roused as if from a trance. "Of course, you have to go. Why didn't you tell me before?" He seemed genuinely hurt.

He crossed the room and engulfed me — such a solid man, so broad-shouldered and narrow-waisted, that I grew breathless simply being near him. "I have those interviews to do. We should both go at the same time. That way we'll be apart as little as possible."

Apart as little as possible.

"This is a nice thing you're doing," he muttered.

"Not nice. Just necessary."

He rubbed my neck, stroked my hair. "Nice, too. Kind."

I disentangled myself, feeling no easier than before, and fled to the beach. From the window it had seemed a paradise of sand and shells, water that changed color with every play of the light. Outside it was unnaturally still, the sun amber and ancient at the horizon, the kind of weather that always heralded the last, tired gasp of summer, when the wind died and the shoreline turned from heaven into a hell of insects, its pale sands swarming with black flies. They lit on my skin the moment I crossed the dunes, bit and stung and clung, no matter how I batted them away. It was impossible to stay outside if you weren't going to escape into the water. I turned and ran back to the house, once more wanting Jon's closeness, the familiar smell of him: Dial soap, Right Guard deodorant. That snowy hair above the ebony brows, the fine olive skin etched with lines. How could I leave? There had been such tenderness in his voice, as if he already missed me.

But I thought there was also, unmistakably, relief.

CHAPTER 2

The Old Neighborhood

I threw clothes into my suitcase, more than I needed, not allowing myself to dwell on Marilyn's cancer or my troubles with Jon. I would pretend, as Marilyn had, that we were mainly concerned about Penny. After all, Marilyn and I had protected her, discussed her, analyzed her, searched for her, from the time we were children. Marilyn and I had spent most of our lives searching for Penny, even before she'd disappeared. It was still a central fact of our lives. This, I kept telling myself, was the reason for my trip.

From the beginning, Penny had wandered. In her head — later on, yes of course — but in a pure, lonely, physical way at first, up and down the streets of the old neighborhood, Riggs Park. Climbing, at four years old, the steep hill of Oneida Street as far as New Hampshire Avenue and the traffic, alarming the neighbors until they realized it was just a neighborhood phenomenon, expected and unremarkable. Mostly she didn't venture far.

All you had to do was remind her to go home for dinner and she would. She had no desire to get lost, and certainly none to run away.

"Oh, well," neighbors would recall later. "You remember how the boys teased her. You remember how wild she was when she got older." They'd forget the aimless roaming started before all that, before we went to school and the boys became an issue. In the early days, Penny wandered from simple neglect and despair. She wanted someone to find her.

And my mother, Ida, did.

Returning from a rehearsal at dusk one evening, walking down the hill with her clarinet case under her arm, my mother spotted a small, red-haired girl with skin so white it was almost blue in the fading light, wearing a sleeveless pinafore with no blouse underneath or sweater on top.

My mother knew who Penny was. The Weinbergs had moved in a few months before, and in an odd way, they had a connection. Like my mother, Penny's father Sid was a musician, not classically trained like she was, but nevertheless a trumpet player in the navy band. He was said to be five years younger than Penny's mother, who had been a widow with two children when they married. Only Penny and her next-oldest sister, Charlene, were the issue of this second marriage. It was quite a story.

"You must be freezing," my mother said, looking down at the white-skinned child.

"You like it?" Penny twirled to model her outfit, toothpick arms covered with goose bumps. "This is Mom's favorite. My shoes, too." On her feet, she wore black patent leather Mary Janes, not meant for playing outdoors.

There was something diaphanous and otherworldly about Penny even then, something that in her most focused moments, simply wasn't there. My mother thought Penny didn't follow what she was saying. "Come on, I bet your family's worried sick," she said, and took Penny's hand to lead her home.

When Helen Weinberg opened the door, she did not wrap her daughter in her arms to warm her. She frowned and said, "Oh, Penny, what have I told you about going out without a sweater?" Fixing my mother with a fierce expression, Helen said, "I'm forty years old, Ida. Too old to be chasing a four-year-old. I have three other children at home. You'd think this one would have some sense."

After that, my mother and Marilyn's included Penny in all our activities, instructing that we were always to play at our two houses and not Penny's, which was far too small.

"But it's bigger than ours!" Marilyn protested, keen on logic even then. In that cookie-cutter subdivision of what today would be called duplexes, Penny's house was one of only a handful built on such a precipitous slope that the backyard was two stories below the street, allowing not only a regular basement but a subbasement, as well — a horrid, dank, subterranean place — with several extra rooms.

"It's a little bigger," Marilyn's mother agreed, "but in our family and Barbara's there are only two children, and in Penny's there are four. It's too much to ask Mrs. Weinberg to keep up with all those daughters and have friends over, too."

That was certainly true. From the moment we first knocked on Penny's door, we sensed that Helen simply had no room in her heart for more little girls — certainly not us, and maybe not even Penny. Nobody else in Riggs Park had four children. Very few had even three.

"And those were the ones who kept trying for a boy," Marilyn reasoned later on. "Ira Schimmel had two older sisters, but once Ira was born they stopped. Same with Mel Eisenberg. The Gerbers and the Weinbergs weren't so lucky. They kept getting girls."

"Marilyn!"

"Well, think about it. Even their names. Stephanie Gerber was supposed to be Stephen. And Penny —"

"It was a different situation. The first two had another father."

"Even so."

There was no point arguing. Penny's two older half sisters were Rochelle and Diane, feminine-sounding girls who were nearly adolescents by the time the family moved to Riggs Park. But Penny's full sister, Charlene, would have been named Charles if she'd been male, and Penny's real name was Davidina, which in other circumstances would have been David. Sid made no secret of the fact that he'd wanted sons.

In second grade, the boys at school took notice of Penny's masculine name and dubbed her Davey, which she hated. Encouraged, they decided an even more effective form of torment would be to call her Red because of her hair. It was wild and carroty then, framing a moon-pale face dotted with freckles. One day, teased

41

beyond endurance, she stormed off the Keene School playground in the middle of recess and disappeared before any of the teachers noticed. A frenzied search soon began — what if she were lost? — but Davidina had not gone far. Trembling with cold, her jacket lying in the dirt beside her, she was huddled against the cream-colored brick wall of the Chillum Manor apartments next door, her face swollen from crying. A gentle nurse wrapped her in blankets and led her back to school, but she remained inconsolable until her mother picked her up. She didn't return to class the rest of the week.

Finally our neighborhood guru Essie Berman stepped in, because after all, a child could not drop out of school forever. Essie was a six-foot-tall woman with kinky salt-and-pepper hair that snaked out around her face like a Brillo pad and such a fierce countenance that she might have frightened us if she hadn't been such a normal part of our landscape. She lived alone in a house up the block and had served, as long as we could remember, as an extra parent or aunt to all the kids in the neighborhood, concerned and loving, but rarely gentle.

On Penny's behalf, Essie invited Wish

Wishner and Seth Opak — that year's leaders of the pack — to her house to lend them a signed baseball she'd acquired. She wanted their fathers to inspect it in case it was valuable. She poured Cokes. She mentioned with her usual brusqueness that she had heard the boys were calling Davidina Red and wondered how they could be so stupid. Davidina's hair wasn't red at all, but more the color of a penny (which it very clearly wasn't, though years later, after the carroty orange deepened and mellowed, it would come closer). "If you're going to call her something, at least be accurate," Essie admonished.

The boys considered this. They were intrigued by the idea of hair as money. They abandoned the names Davey and Red and adopted the moniker they thought would provide a more original, even clever, form of torture: Penny.

Essie invited a furious Davidina over to make chocolate-chip cookies. "The boys call me Penny now," Davidina confessed in a shower of tears.

"So? You don't like it?"

"Of course not!"

"Well, I do," Essie said. "Penny sounds coppery and bold. Think of a new-minted penny standing out in a heap of dull old coins. What's wrong with that?"

Essie handed Davidina a Kleenex.

"It's a bright, snappy name if you ask me. Cheerier than Davidina and more accurate than Red. Imagine the color of a penny. Imagine how it shines. That's how your hair looks. It's beautiful." This was an exaggeration. But Essie's powers of persuasion were legendary. From that day, Davidina answered only to Penny.

Maybe it was the boys' teasing that left her hypersensitive, or maybe she had always been that way. Marilyn and I were never sure. When my father took us to the monthly Sunday night concerts at the National Gallery of Art, where my mother played second clarinet in the gallery orchestra, Penny often burst into tears, suddenly but briefly, and sobbed as if her heart would break. Even at seven, I thought I knew all about the emotional power of music, but I never fully understood what to make of Penny's outbursts. Maybe she was upset because she rarely got to hear her own father's concerts. Sid was often on the road. Or maybe it was something else entirely. Dutifully, Marilyn and I put our arms around Penny and led her out of the chilly marble atrium, down the hall toward the Impressionist room, where we looked at the colorful paintings until her strange mood passed. We didn't mind, not really. When a child is not cherished early on, you can't expect her to be predictable. I think we knew that even then.

Houses in Washington weren't air-conditioned in those days, and the gluey swamp-heat that descended on the city sometimes lasted for months, so thick and humid that even our parents grew testy. To take the pressure off them for a few hours, Essie Berman sometimes piled three or four children into her rusty old Plymouth and drove us to Rock Creek Park to watch the fireflies at nightfall. There were fireflies everywhere in the city, of course, but nowhere so many as in one particular location off Military Road. A grassy bank dropped down to a wide mowed field, and in the distance a tree line served as a backdrop to the drama.

As dusk turned to dark and the trees blackened, flickering spots of light began to float on the air, dozens at first, then hundreds, thousands, until we felt surrounded by a dance of stars. We scattered among them, carrying jelly jars with air-holes punched in the lids, less to capture than to marvel. How, after all, could any creature be its own source of light? We could be observers, Essie instructed, but not murderers. We should look, then set them free.

But one night — we must have been eight or nine and had been catching fireflies for years — Penny balked.

"I'm not going to do this anymore," she said. "You shouldn't, either. It's mean. It's like putting them in jail."

"Only for a few minutes," said Marilyn. "We always let them go."

"It doesn't matter. How long do fireflies live? Only a day or two, I bet. A few minutes to them is like years for us. Like being in jail for years. It's wrong."

"They're so slow they probably don't even know they're captured," said Rosalie Shiffman, another girl who had come along.

"Of course they do! You always know when you're trapped!"

"You're making it sound like they're people, not bugs!"

"Just because they're bugs, that doesn't mean they don't have feelings," Penny asserted.

"Feelings. Sure. Lightning bugs?"

"You don't know." In the darkness, Marilyn and I couldn't see the red anger rushing to Penny's face, but we could feel it as if it were churning under our own skin. It never took much to make Penny blush.

"Leave her be, Rosalie," Marilyn ordered. We didn't like Rosalie, anyway. In the distance behind us, sitting on the bank, Essie smoked a cigarette and watched the glittering night. Even if she were aware of our bickering, she wasn't likely to interfere.

"Well, I'm catching them," Rosalie said. "You can do what you want." In defiance, she caught a firefly not in her jar but in her hand and let its light flicker there for the longest time.

"Let it go," Penny ordered.

Rosalie walked away, her fingers turning alternately dark and golden. Penny followed. "Let it go, I said!"

Instead of obeying, Rosalie clenched her hand into a fist.

Penny screamed as if she were mortally wounded. "What are you doing? You killed it! Are you crazy?"

"You're the crazy one!" Rosalie shouted.

"Murderer!" Penny yelled.

"You think so? Look." Rosalie opened her hand to reveal that there was nothing inside. No squashed bug, no streaks of blood or guts. "I let it go. One firefly, big deal."

But it was too late. Penny had dissolved into hysterical tears. She shook her fist at Rosalie, then let me and Marilyn circle her, hold her close.

It was not an unselfish gesture, not really. Taking care of Penny was second nature by then. Everybody needs someone with more troubles than they have. Protecting Penny made us feel normal, sane. But from that night on — Marilyn felt it, too — Penny also scared us.

Because that night it had become clear, somehow, that Penny had viewed the liquid flow of lives through the sieve of time as most people did not; that to Penny fireflies and people were equal: fragile lives pulsing, flickering, vulnerable as candle flame and no more powerful. From that time on, Marilyn and I saw our own impermanence, like the impermanence of fireflies, reflected in Penny's eyes. It frightened us, right from the beginning.

Nearly fifty years later, trying to close an overflowing suitcase for my trip to Washington, I actually shuddered at the memory.

CHAPTER 3

On the Road

I didn't regain my composure until I was more than halfway to Washington. The struggle to zip most of my wardrobe into a single piece of luggage had very nearly gotten the best of me before Jon tiptoed in, silently pressed down on the bulge of clothes and closed the zipper. Then he kissed my neck so softly, in such sweet prelude to what would be a touching night of goodbyes, that I slept better than I had in weeks. So when I left the next morning, I was surprised at the raw fury twisting up again in my gut — until I realized it was directed not at Jon, not at Penny, but at Marilyn. How could she possibly be sick again? She was supposed to recover! She was almost there. Half in jest, we'd always reassured ourselves that our Coolidge High School class of 1959 had endured enough youthful trauma to earn the survivors immortality, or at least good health until eighty-five. We pretended it was a joke, but secretly we believed it.

Truly terrible things had happened to

some of us. One of our class officers was felled by the chop of propellers while he flagged in planes at National Airport. A disease called scleroderma claimed a shy, lovely girl named Linda, freezing her porcelain skin into a rigid and unbreathing mass. A handsome, witty classmate died in a bizarre auto accident. And all this was in addition to the dark, incomprehensible events that touched some of our Riggs Park friends and altered forever our memories of our childhood home. At the time, we felt vulnerable, and maybe jinxed.

Then one day when we were about thirty, Marilyn said to me with a kind of dumb astonishment, "Do you realize that not a single one of us died in Vietnam? Not a single one."

It was true. Instead of going to Southeast Asia, the boys had either married or gone to graduate school, pushed by parents who'd survived the Depression and wanted, above all, a good education for their children. We girls had also finished college, married well, borne healthy children. Except for Marilyn's older brother, Steve, whose songs had climbed the charts and made him a household name, none of us became famous. But most of us were so comfortable — doctors, lawyers, scientists

— that the specter of our haunted youth faded like the memory of bad dreams.

Maybe because of that — and in spite of the rash of early deaths — I'd never considered that our whole generation would one day die off. Until now, I'd believed the world held me in the cup of its hand and would shelter me there — a dangerous notion, I realized, that invited the fates to show me just how indifferent they could be. But to begin with Marilyn? No! I wasn't ready to be traveling north to a deathwatch for my best friend — not now, not ever.

I clutched the steering wheel so hard my knuckles hurt — until, after an interlude of near-panic, I saw that morbidity would be a difficult emotion to sustain for the full seven-hour drive. By the time I turned north onto I-95 and opened the window, I saw I'd climbed out of the pocket of damp coastal air into a dry, pleasant day. Switching on the cruise control, I coasted toward Richmond, crossed the James River under a sky pewter with clouds, and eased into a rest stop to eat the sandwich I'd packed. Somehow my black mood had vanished along with the humidity.

Nibbling a pear, letting my eyes rest on the peaceful green of rolling hills, I suddenly felt completely normal, which was probably unbalanced in its own right, but comforting. Even my sense of humor began to return. Recalling my packing frenzy last night, during which I'd piled wools on top of cottons (wools in D.C. in October?), I'd prayed for cool as fervently as I had in high school, when Marilyn and Penny and I had spent Rosh Hashanah afternoons lolling on the steps of B'nai Israel Synagogue on Sixteenth Street, sweltering in new woolen shul outfits that we wore whether the temperature was sixty degrees outside or ninety. Adolescent lunacy. Almost nobody from Riggs Park belonged to B'nai Israel or went there except to dances in the social hall, but somehow great numbers of us gravitated there on the high holidays. After a few minutes indoors worshipping God, we came outside to worship each other, praying not for forgiveness, but that our deodorants would hold and not leave us exposed to the world with circles of perspiration under our arms. Sitting at the rest stop, I was suddenly — finally — amused by the realization that my recent yearning for crisp autumn sunshine had the same childish intensity it had had during that annual high-school mating ritual.

I threw my trash away and braced for the rest of the trip. After so many years living out of town, I was never prepared for Washington's traffic, neither the inevitable tie-ups north of Quantico nor the gridlock I was sure would one day grip the beltway traffic entirely.

Although I always told people I was "going to Washington," as if that meant the city itself, the only person I knew who still lived there was Seth Opak, who'd grown up with us in Riggs Park and liked to boast he was the sole holdout who'd never abandoned the city even during the white flight of the sixties and the growing crime rate in the years after that.

Everyone else had long ago moved to the Maryland suburbs or northern Virginia. In their final years, my parents had lived in Silver Spring. My sister, Trudi, had owned a condo in Alexandria before relocating to Florida, and Marilyn and Bernie were still in White Oak, in the same big house where they'd reared their two sons and at least a dozen dogs. The house was now much too big for them, they declared, but far too precious to sell.

Engrossed in driving, I didn't notice until I got off the beltway that the trees were changing color. And it wasn't until I got out of the car at Marilyn's that I realized the late-afternoon air was not just cool but almost cold. Delicious!

Marilyn flung open the door just as I started to ring the bell. After a long trip, it would usually take hours to shake the feeling I was still moving, but even in my fuzzy state of mind I registered Marilyn's manic energy. "You're here!" she shouted. Perfect spots of color circled her cheekbones. Excitement? Fever? Makeup?

How could she be dying?

I moved forward for a hug, and astonished myself by bursting into tears.

"Sentimental fool," Marilyn whispered, gathering me close, and I knew from her shaky voice that she was crying, too. We clung to each other and wept, cocooned inside such a close, damp embrace that I sensed the truth of everything I had only feared on the phone: that Marilyn had come through a forest of pain and did not want to go back again. That Marilyn saw herself drifting toward shadows and darkness, and could not help it any more than she could help breathing. Knowing what we knew, the two of us held tight, wept for our current solidity and the vapor we would become, the loss of ourselves and the sheer horror of it; our belief and disbelief. We wept until we had purged ourselves of feeling and heard the startling excessive noise of our own snorts and sobs. Then we began to laugh, to giggle like children even as we hiccuped and sniffed, making the sound even worse. At long last we pulled apart, slightly mortified, and pointed to each other's reddened, mascara-streaked, swollen faces.

"Ten minutes," Marilyn rasped, wiping a tear from my cheek. "Ten minutes to freshen up so we can stand to look at each other."

Marilyn showed me to the guest room (as if after all this time I couldn't find it myself) and told me I had just long enough to wash my face. Then — dry-eyed, smiling, fully in command of herself — she dragged me downstairs to the kitchen. "Wine or tea?" she asked.

"Better make it tea. Wine'll put me out in a minute."

"Wine for both of us," Marilyn said, as I knew she would, and retrieved a bottle of Chardonnay from the refrigerator. "Bernie'll be here any minute." Moving at approximately the speed of sound, she plucked a corkscrew from a drawer, opened the wine, poured it, shoved a glass in my direction. Marilyn's frantic activity always frightened me. It could be a sign of fear as easily as of high spirits.

"Okay. I've decided what to do," she said at last. "At least for the immediate future."

"What?"

"Did I tell you this is a new cancer? Not the old one spreading? I found out after I talked to you. That means there's less urgency to do something about it in the next five minutes."

"So — ?"

Marilyn sipped her wine, caught her breath. "I'm looking into two new treatments. They're not mutually exclusive. I'll probably do them both. One's a vaccine. One's experimental. It doesn't make you bald." She touched her hair, which was as long as I'd ever seen it, curling halfway down her neck. When the cancer had struck, when she'd had to have chemo, the hardest part, Marilyn claimed, had been losing her hair.

"I've never loved the way I looked," she'd said. "But if there's one thing I was always satisfied with, it was my hair." Until then, I hadn't thought Marilyn's hair was anything special. She'd always worn it short, even in the sixties when everyone else was growing it down past their shoulders. But the point was, it was always *all right:* its rich, gingery color, the wave that was never too little or too much. There had never been anything wrong with Marilyn's hair until she hadn't had any.

I felt guilty about my own thick locks the whole time Marilyn was sick. My hair had always been bushy and wiry, not straight and shiny as I would have liked, but so pale it was almost white. In a neighborhood where darkness was the norm, my sister Trudi and I had been called "the blondes," and it had been a term of respect. But to be bald? Unthinkable. So I understood why, in late middle age, Marilyn was enchanted with length.

"Spare the Hair, that's my new motto," Marilyn said.

"What about Slay the Beast?"

"That goes without saying."

"So this experimental treatment —"

"It doesn't start for another month. All I know is, the doctors are excited about it." Marilyn flashed a smile that didn't extend to her eyes, and occupied herself swirling the wine around in her glass. "Or — hell, it might not work at all. I don't even want to think about that." She lifted her glass, took a long sip. "Which is why I'm also doing the vaccine thing. And why I've decided on plan B."

"Plan B?"

"The reason I lured you up here."

"You mean the real reason instead of the 'secret about Penny' reason?"

"Penny later. This first. Promise you won't laugh."

"Tell me," I said.

"I'm going to have a face-lift."

"A face-lift!"

A tremor of alarm shot through me. What did this mean? Marilyn was not the same person she'd been before, not that ordinary, vain woman who thought the most important thing was to have a normal shape, to have matching nipples. After two failed grafts, Marilyn claimed she didn't care if she ever had nipples again; and the tummy tuck to provide her with reconstructed breasts had been a mistake, so painful; people had no idea. And now a face-lift? I didn't believe it.

But Marilyn was suddenly radiant. "You remember what I always said. When my face got to looking like my mother's, I'd do it."

"Marilyn!"

"Anyway, I needed you here for moral support. Bernie's opposed. And he's no good at being a nurse."

Which was completely untrue, because

after Marilyn's surgeries he had changed her dressings, chauffeured her to doctors, been a saint. When they'd first removed the bandages from her chest, Marilyn had confided, Bernie had never flinched or looked away.

"I go in on Monday. Lifts have become so routine they do it as outpatient surgery. I come home the same day."

"Monday! But today's already Saturday."

"Correct. Sometimes even the busy surgeons recognize that time is of the essence." She put down her glass. "Look." With thumb and index finger, Marilyn grasped an inch of flesh where her jaw met her ears, and pulled up: lifted her jowls, tightened the crepey skin on her neck. "What do you think? I'm going to be gorgeous."

"You're already gorgeous! A face-lift is crazy. You look fine." A chilling memory assailed me of a comment my mother had made when a great-aunt, recovering from a broken hip, had slipped into senility. "At a certain point you have only so many resources," she'd said. "The body heals, but the mind doesn't." And I wondered now if Marilyn, in her effort to heal her cancer-battered body, was also losing her mind.

But she smiled, pulled the skin on her

neck tighter, waited. And looking at her taut face, momentarily youthful, I began to understand. Of course she was afraid of the surgery; of course a face-lift was impractical. At the same time, it was the ultimate expression of hope.

I stood up, walked around the table, folded Marilyn into another hug. "Ever the optimist," I whispered.

She shrugged me off, trying not to show emotion. "It's the season for optimism, don't you remember? We were always upbeat in the fall."

I recalled then what the two of us had believed the whole time we were growing up: that in Washington in autumn, when the great humid weight of summer finally lifted, when the skies cleared and the mid-Atlantic haze blew off, leaving Riggs Park and the whole of the city fresh and clean and sparkling, we were privileged to witness, instead of death and wilt, the astonishing beginning of the world.

In retrospect, it seemed pretty childish.

When Bernie arrived, he had the grace to kiss me on the cheek, ask a few polite questions, and then profess a hankering for pizza, which he promptly went out to buy before disappearing to the bedroom to watch a rerun of *The Godfather* on TV. Left to ourselves, Marilyn and I stayed up past midnight, honoring an old tradition of sipping wine and catching up.

Marilyn filled me in about her sons; I spoke about Jon briefly and cheerily and deceptively, wanting to spare her my recent tale of woe.

"So tell me," Marilyn sighed. "After all this time, is he the true love of your life, after all?"

"I think he is," I whispered.

Marilyn cocked her head and waited for more, but I talked instead about Robin's frenzy of work and how it had restored her spirits.

"There's a difference between *happy* and *hyper*," Marilyn noted — and might have been speaking about herself.

"Yes, but I think Robin was better when she left. Truly. Or at least getting there."

Marilyn's sharp gaze blurred. She was on her fourth glass of wine, maybe her fifth. "Bob was a schmuck anyway."

I raised my glass in a toast. "To being rid of schmucks."

We clinked glasses so energetically that mine sloshed over.

"I'll tell you," Marilyn confided as she refilled it to the brim. "You're lucky you can work at home. Don't have to face the competition. Otherwise they come after you." Always quick to claim she wanted only a job, not a career, Marilyn had nevertheless worked part-time on Capitol Hill for years, and loved being a political insider more than she admitted.

"Come after you how?" I slurred. "You've been hearing too many political intrigues."

"No I haven't." Marilyn shook her head emphatically. "Every pretty little college grad in the country comes to D.C. and wants your job. A bunch of ambitious little Monica Lewinskys. They check you out, and you can see just what's going on behind those glossy young eyes. They're thinking, 'No problem, I've got her job inside of six months, that babe's over the hill. I'm the future and she's the past.' "

"Oh, Marilyn!"

"Well, it makes me mad as hell. I hate those kids. I do." Marilyn put on a fierce expression and emptied her glass. "Then one day one of them came into the office and you know who it was? Andrea Grossman."

"Who?"

"Remember Joan Engle and Larry Grossman? Got married right out of high school? This is their daughter."

"Oh." I shook my head to clear the buzz. I couldn't picture Joan Engle at all.

"So I realized who's coming after us," Marilyn went on. "Our kids. How much can we hate our own kids?"

I laughed, which seemed the only alternative to weeping, clearly not the protocol of the evening. "Here's to staying *on* the hill, politically and personally," I said, raising my glass for another toast.

"Hear, hear," Marilyn agreed, and drank.

Then, through the blur, I remembered. "So what's this about Penny?"

Marilyn shook her head. "Too drunk," she said. "Tomorrow."

In the morning, I woke up with the expected headache, but meant to get out of bed anyway so I could run one errand before Marilyn roused herself: visit my parents' graves.

I couldn't make myself budge. The weight behind my eyes and the warm quilt tucked over my shoulders seduced me into another hour's sleep. Then I opened my eyes to too-bright sunshine and a head clear enough to admit a couple of new, niggling worries: Why would Marilyn make me come all the way to Washington to tell me she was going to have a face-lift? Why not say that on the phone? Why lure me up here on the pretext of secrets about Penny and then not reveal them? None of it made sense. I forced myself out of bed and into some clothes, and wandered groggily into the kitchen.

Bernie was sitting at the table, reading the Sunday *Washington Post.* "Sneaking around at dawn?" he greeted me.

"Hardly dawn."

After plugging in the coffeemaker, I gulped two glasses of water, took two aspirin, and watched the black liquid seep into the pot.

"Marilyn's still sleeping?"

"She's pretty tired lately." Bernie studied the paper, rubbed his stubbly chin. Even as a teenager, he'd had such a heavy beard that he had to shave twice a day. Then, the ever-present black shadow had made him look older. Now the whiskers were white, he was twenty pounds overweight, and in his baggy gray sweatpants and sweatshirt, he looked not just "older," but *old.*

I poured coffee when the brewing stopped, and slid a cup across the table to him. "Why does she really want me here, Bernie?"

Shrugging, professing innocence, he finally looked up as he shook a packet of Sweet'n Low into his cup. "She's lost her mind is all. Or maybe I have. Either the face-lift is crazy or Bernie Waxman is crazy. Which?"

My worrisome idea of the body healing at the expense of the mind threatened to surface again, but I suppressed it. "So you think she just wants me here as defense against your poor attitude? For moral support? That's what she told me. I don't believe it."

"For moral support she could call Andrew," he said, speaking of their younger son, a luminously sweet child who'd grown into a kind and generous man. Bernie sipped his coffee, then put down the cup, but kept his eyes on me, his round, stubbled face etched with worry.

"The face-lift will be all right," I assured him. "Weird, but okay. The idea of it cheers her up." But it doesn't cheer *me*, I thought. "We've always been women who believed in plastic surgery."

"I don't understand it."

"She's not doing it because of the way it will make her look on the outside. It's for how it will make her feel on the inside. Especially right now."

"She'll feel like shit. She'll be bruised and swollen and have to take three naps a day."

"Not forever," I told him.

But I was worried, and all the more because I knew the genesis of Marilyn's decision. During Easter vacation our junior year of high school, the two of us had had our noses done. We'd shared a room at the Washington Hospital Center and scheduled back-to-back operations so we could commiserate, in case it turned out to be worse than we thought. Despite the evidence of friends who'd survived, both of us had been terrified.

For a long time I believed we'd subjected ourselves to the ordeal mostly because in Washington, D.C., in the fifties, if you were Jewish and your nose was not perfect like Penny's or my sister Trudi's, having it surgically altered was simply what you *did.* Years later, a truer, darker motive occurred to me: that we had been living under such a deep cloud of misgiving about ourselves that it was stronger even than our fear. If we didn't go through with it, what kind of lives would we have? Who would want us? If we didn't marry, we'd end up as old-maid secretaries or teachers, not administrators like our brothers. Being desirable was smarter.

Yet there we were, on the threshold of womanhood, our faces imperfect, our figures too round, failings we'd discovered while poring over the pages of Seventeen. If recent history meant anything, there were even places in the world where our Semitic noses would have doomed us to the gas chambers. Why take the chance? Without plastic surgery, we would never look quite as the world thought we should. Our disfigurement would stay with us all our lives.

In retrospect, that seemed a shabby way of thinking — and if we'd been born seven or ten years later, we might have been braver. Might have scorned makeup, felt free to spurn marriage in favor of careers, bed down with anyone we liked. But we were children of the fifties, living on the cusp of a revolution we would never fully embrace. At sixteen, we knew we'd better start correcting our flaws.

My mother very nearly forbade it. Ida said the quality of my life would be determined by my character and not the shape of my nose. I didn't believe it, or at least wouldn't admit it. An electric tension vibrated between us for weeks. Finally Ida blurted out in frustration, "There's nothing wrong with your nose!" and I replied, "That's just pure bullshit!" — an unheard-of retort to a parent in those days, so astonishing that my mother almost slapped me, but lowered her hand just in time. I burst into tears, ran to my room. Nothing wrong with my nose! Of course there was. It was too long and too high-bridged for my face. Anyone could see that. Period.

And Marilyn's was worse, a true hook. On that point even my mother and I agreed. Years later, when the movie *Patton* came out, Marilyn claimed that George C. Scott had the exact nose as her own original. And damned if Marilyn wasn't right! By then we had some miles on us and could laugh about it; and later we would wonder how our children (my daughter Robin and Marilyn's elder son, Mike) had inherited our noses and looked just fine, when on us they had seemed so hideous. But at the time we saw no choice but to change them.

Parental permission secured, we went to Dr. Arthur Dick, Washington's Michelangelo of rhinoplasty, known for customizing his work to the face in question so that the results always looked natural, never "done." In addition to his technical genius,

Dr. Dick had a genuine affection for his patients. He did not believe plastic surgery was an act of vanity. He thought it was a sign of mental health.

But despite his gentle manner, we were not reassured — especially when we learned that, during the procedure, *we would be awake.* "That's so if you swallow any blood, you can cough it up more easily. You'll get some sedatives, then a local anesthetic." Shots! In our noses! This was almost too horrible to imagine. We dug fingernails into our fisted palms to keep from fainting. We might have fled except that we were sixteen and our very futures were at stake. Others had lived through it. Maybe we would, too.

No one told us we'd be given so much Demerol before surgery that someone could have said, "Okay, we're cutting you open from neck to navel now," and we would have smiled lazily and murmured, "Have at it, guys," before peacefully dozing off.

I remembered very little. A white operating room, robed nurses handling silvery instruments, surgeons wearing what looked like shower caps over their hair. For a while I heard a hammering sound but had no sense that what was being hammered was *me.* Once, I woke up to cough. The next thing I knew I was being wheeled back to our room.

Later that day, after we'd slept off most of the sedatives, we inspected ourselves in the mirror. Great white bandages swathed our noses, reached up onto our foreheads, clung to our disarranged hair. Our eyes were blackened and bloodshot, our faces so swollen our cheekbones had disappeared. Luckily, we felt better than we looked. We admired the spray of flowers that arrived from some of the girls in our sorority. We oohed and aahed when Bernie appeared with a giant teddy bear for Marilyn. And then Penny tiptoed in, tentatively, with our other friend, Francine Ades. Penny took one look at us and ran out of the room.

"Do you think we made her sick?" Marilyn asked.

"Probably. You know Penny." Francine sounded long-suffering and impatient, but she went out to see what was wrong. When they returned a moment later, Penny was wiping away tears, her freckled white face splotchy from crying. Francine held her elbow and guided her to the foot of my bed.

"Look. Barbara is the blonde." She

tugged Penny's elbow and faced her toward the second bed. "The other one is Marilyn."

Struggling to compose herself, Penny sniffed, fidgeted, spoke in a small, apologetic tone. "With all those bandages, for a minute I didn't know which of you was which."

"We look a whole lot worse than we feel," I said. Even allowing for our grimy hair and massive dressings, I didn't see how Penny had failed to recognize us. Penny was so shaky, so frightened, that both of us felt sicker when she left.

Despite a bout of nausea during the night from swallowing blood, I left the hospital the next morning bruised but not in pain. Marilyn felt even better. We had walked through the fire; we had emerged unscathed. If Marilyn's new look also called attention to her heavy jaw and mine to my slightly protuberant eyes, neither of us noticed. After the bandages came off, we loved our noses absolutely.

After weeks of black eyes and swelling, when our faces returned to normal (except that our noses were still numb, and would be for a year), Marilyn and I decided it was time to show the finished product to Essie Berman. Essie examined us from every angle, nodded gravely, lit a cigarette. "You're pretty girls," she pronounced. "Enjoy it in good health. Use it while you can. The looks won't last. Nothing does. It's all on loan."

Coming from anyone else, we would have suspected jealousy, especially from someone whose nose was as gargantuan as Essie's, whose hair was unkempt, whose sense of style rivaled that of Golda Meir. But if Essie said it, it must be true. I'd cherished the word, *pretty,* but from that time on never forgot it was only on loan.

And like Marilyn, I'd counted on that loan lasting as long as I needed it, using my looks as a crutch well into middle age, even crediting them with bringing me Jon. An image of Jon's face rose up before me, seamed and distraught as it had been these past weeks every time we spoke of Robin's divorce and miscarriage. I shivered. Was he really as solicitous and fatherly as he seemed? And if he was, why did it bother me so? Now it struck me that Robin looked much as I once had — but fresher, earthier, more natural, with my original nose.

Maybe Jon was seeing in Robin the younger version of her mother. The younger woman he'd rather have.

No!

How could I be jealous of my own daughter?

The thought filled me with disgust.

But it also made me understand why, even in the grip of cancer, Marilyn was having a face-lift. Why she had chosen it even after four surgeries, including the painful tummy tuck she swore took two years to recover from. I understood as Bernie didn't why someone would opt for that in spite of what she'd been through and what might still be to come. We hadn't bought beauty when we'd had our noses done at sixteen, but we had borrowed it. And our youthful transformation had provided us with a spark and a confidence that had allowed us to face the world in all the years since. Now, approaching sixty, paying back the loan wrinkle by wrinkle, we knew that if we borrowed again — borrowed youth, borrowed beauty — the results would be superficial, the risk would be great, the price would be pain. What kind of pathetic women would even consider it? Yet what were the choices? And what difference did it make? If it took a face-lift to rekindle the light in a world suddenly stalked by darkness, how could Marilyn settle for anything less?

CHAPTER 4

Riggs Park

"Thought you'd be out of here before I got up, didn't you?" Marilyn bellowed, jolting me out of my reverie. Striding into the kitchen in baggy pajamas, hair tousled and dark circles under her eyes, she looked more hungover than her voice suggested. "I know where you're going," she accused. "Not that I mind. But to be too cowardly to tell me —"

"What are you talking about?" Bernie asked.

"She's going to the cemetery."

"So? I always go to the cemetery. My parents are buried there. Is that a crime?"

"She didn't want to say the word in front of me," Marilyn told Bernie. She shot us an evil smile. "*Cemetery.* She was going to sneak out."

"I wasn't sneaking."

"Go to the cemetery later," Marilyn said. "I have a little outing planned for us this morning."

"An outing where?"

"Riggs Park."

"Riggs Park! *Why?*" Since the mid-sixties, after the phenomenon of white flight had swept all our families into the suburbs, the neighborhood had been almost entirely black.

"I don't know. Just to see it. Out of curiosity."

"After all this time?"

"Well, why not?"

In all the years I'd been coming to visit her, Marilyn had never suggested a sentimental journey to the old neighborhood. The only reason she'd be doing it now was because she thought she wouldn't get another chance.

"Sure. Okay. Why not? Bernie, you come, too," I pleaded, looking for an ally. "You probably haven't been there in ages, either."

Marilyn didn't give him time to answer. "On Sunday morning? Are you kidding? He'd miss every news show on TV."

Bernie and I exchanged helpless glances. Marilyn strode toward her bedroom to dress.

"I'll drive," I said when Marilyn reappeared, looking like she ought to go back to bed.

It was a quintessential October morning:

75

sunny, dry, a bit of a breeze. Our dispositions gradually improved. As we drove down New Hampshire Avenue toward the District Line, my headache notwithstanding, I marveled in the glory of gold and russet trees and gentle hills, all of which I urgently yearned for this particular fall.

At the District Line, the sight of the bus stop on Eastern Avenue made me forget my throbbing temples for a moment as I entertained a nostalgic vision of days past: the rich tapestry of city life when Washington, D.C., was not the crime capital of the nation but a small, manageable, southern city that was also, as far as we'd understood, entirely safe.

"We rode those buses alone from the time we were — what? Ten? Eleven?" I asked.

"Maybe even younger," Marilyn said. We'd traveled unchaperoned to ballet and tap lessons, to sessions in the warm indoor pool at the Jewish Community Center on Sixteenth Street, to the Capitol Theatre downtown. We'd swayed on streetcars down Georgia Avenue to see ball games at Griffith Stadium (not that we'd cared about baseball, but the boys had); we'd executed complicated transfers to buses that had taken us to "the other side of town," a term that had meant, very specifically to Washingtonians of that day, "the other side of Rock Creek Park." Our horizons had seemed boundless, unlimited, compared to the complicated, menacing world of our children.

"Oh, look at the trees!" Marilyn exclaimed as I turned onto Oneida Street, our old block, and drove down the steep hill that pitched precipitously from New Hampshire Avenue, past Third Street, into Sixth Street at the bottom. In the early days, the trees had been nothing but tender stalks springing from patches of ground along the sidewalk (required, we'd been told, by the FHA), and later healthy adolescents with lanky trunks. Now they were mature, huge, casting the block into shadow while the street of our childhood had been relentlessly sunny.

"Yes, but the houses —" They looked amazingly as they had half a century before, yet shrunken, too, as the dwellings of childhood always are: long rows of two-story brick duplexes we'd always referred to as "semidetached," with ugly, chipping concrete patios we'd proudly referred to as "front porches," and closet-sized patches of lawn.

"So tiny," Marilyn whispered. "I'd forgotten." Oneida Street had been among the first streets in Riggs Park to be developed, to sprout postwar homes for growing families who (we were too young to know then) would never be rich. But Marilyn and I had been small, too, and the rooms had seemed enormous; and after all this time it was a shock to our older, knowing eyes to see the truth.

"Functional, unimaginative boxes," I said. It was the best our hardworking parents, children of the Depression, survivors of the war, could afford.

"Not exactly North Portal," Marilyn agreed, naming the stylish neighborhood where, in high school, our richest friends and sorority sisters had lived.

In our teen years, Oneida Street had always seemed too narrow for two-way traffic and parked cars, too, and spaces had always been at a premium. But there was plenty of parking today. "Sunday morning," I mused as I pulled into a spot just above the alley. "People must be at church."

"Yeah, or in jail." Marilyn pointed to a sporty black Mustang, its tires held in place by a bright orange boot. "You can't move your car if you're incarcerated."

Ignoring her, I unlocked the doors. "Does this mean you're afraid to get out?"

"Certainly not. I've already been slashed and poisoned —" Marilyn's favorite terms for surgery and chemo. "What's a little assault and gunfire?"

"Stop it, Marilyn. It looks perfectly safe."

Outside, the sidewalk was dappled with light and shadow under the bright, blowing trees, but except for a woman in an exquisite red suit getting into a car, the street was deserted. I imagined spectators peering at us from behind drawn curtains, wondering why two white women were wandering their block on a Sunday morning.

Marilyn and I had lived two doors apart, in houses with identical floor plans: living room/dining room/kitchen, three bedrooms upstairs, an unfinished basement. Both houses were still intact, and in roughly the same state of disrepair — wrought-iron porch railings rusted and aslant from fifty years of being leaned against.

Back in the forties, our parents had saved for awnings to shelter the front porches. The women had moved their canasta games outdoors on summer afternoons, savored the shade, and had hoped that even in Washington's notorious swamp heat, there might be a hint of a breeze. Marilyn's house still sported what might have been the "permanent" awning her parents had installed, some of its green-and-white plastic slats warped and discolored. But at my house, where the original canvas awning had been torn from its frame by Hurricane Hazel in 1956, there was still no replacement. In front of the house, the FHA tree had been cut down, leaving a slash of reddish soil beside the sidewalk and nothing to soften the sunshine or the view.

"They have a word for this," I said. "Slum."

"Don't say that," Marilyn whispered, though clearly it was. All up and down the block, for every freshly painted slab of woodwork, two were rotting. For every patch of tended yard, two were overgrown with ancient shrubs. For every set of shutters that hung securely at a window, another was falling off. At the house that shared a wall with Marilyn's, a window air conditioner hung precariously from the master bedroom, looking as if it would come unhinged in the next brisk breeze. Someone had tried to paint the trim but had obviously given up — out of money? Paint? Time? Only the old red brick had held up well.

"Hardly the Historic District," Marilyn noted. She crossed her arms in front of her, hugged herself into her sweater. "Were we ever this poor?"

"The houses were new then. We were upwardly mobile." I tugged at her arm. "Come on. Let's check out the alley. Remember Mrs. Warner?"

At the mention of the name, Marilyn revived. "The one who slept in the buff?"

"She didn't think anyone could see her."

"I don't believe it. She was an exhibitionist. She knew."

We turned into the alley, once the early morning domain of milkmen and garbage trucks, but a sheltered haven nevertheless, where in the neat rectangles of yard my father had erected a swing set and Marilyn's mother had planted, against the ugly metal sheathing of the window well, lily of the valley that bloomed white and fragile every spring. In autumn, the Malkins next door built a *succah* hung with fruit and gourds, where everyone was invited to eat honey cake while looking up through the greenery to the harvest sky.

Now the alley was full of potholes, the

chain-link fences that had enclosed our yards were falling down, and most of the lawns had been partially paved to make room for cars people must not have wanted to leave out front.

"Look." I pointed across a sea of trash cans to the window of the room where the Warners had slept, directly across the alley from my childhood bedroom.

"She was such a hussy!" Marilyn laughed.

Younger than our own mothers, more carefree and daring, Jessie Warner had often left the light on while she undressed, and had never closed the shades. The spring we were ten, Marilyn and Penny spent the night at my house as often as they were allowed, where the three of us crowded in front of my darkened bedroom window and spied.

"She's so *flat*," Penny whispered as we examined Jessie Warner's nude form, her narrow torso rising toward small, perky breasts.

"I bet she was a ballet dancer," Marilyn observed. But though her body was more graceful than those of our own curvaceous mothers, we decided it was less interesting, too — a fact that made us feel superior and secure, suspecting as we did that we ourselves would probably grow into versions of our mother's bodies and not Jessie Warner's.

A week or two before school let out, we were regaled by the sight of Mrs. Warner's husband entering the room during our Saturday-night spy session, where he shed his clothes and took his wife in his arms. It was the first time we had ever seen a naked man with an erection. We screamed, then clapped hands over each other's mouths so my mother wouldn't hear us, and whispered for hours afterward with horror and delight.

"I never thought Jessie Warner was a hussy," I told Marilyn now. "I always thought it was because she wasn't Jewish."

"The way she looked, or getting undressed in front of the window? Or giving her husband a woody?"

"All of the above."

Marilyn snorted, but I had actually believed this. Since my family didn't keep kosher or go to services, for me Jewishness was essentially a social matter like belonging to a club. Almost everyone in Riggs Park was Jewish. We followed a certain code of behavior. Jessie Warner didn't. Though I'd been glad for the few Christians who'd decorated their houses in the dark of December, who'd opened their curtains so everyone could view their spangled trees from afar, I'd seen them as exotics with strange and unusual customs. Like Jessie Warner, they might all believe not only in Christmas trees but in leaving the blinds open while they undressed.

Marilyn nudged me and pointed toward a yard farther down the alley. A white dog with a black patch around one eye was jumping against the fence, trying to get our attention. It was the first animal we'd seen.

"A pit bull," Marilyn announced as she marched over and stuck her hand through the chain-link fence to pet it.

"A pit bull! Leave it alone!" I jumped back even though the beast was only slavering on Marilyn's hand.

"Oh, Barbara, relax. It's harmless." Marilyn had always been the expert about dogs. Sometimes she'd owned three at a time when her boys were small, to make up for her parents never allowing her more than a parakeet. "Feel it," she ordered. "Pit bulls feel tough, like a pig."

Gingerly, I extended my hand. Sure enough, the hide was steely, as if strung over one long muscle. The dog wagged its whole hind end with happiness.

"I guess it's supposed to be fierce and

bark at us, but it's just a puppy. Fine watchdog you are," she crooned as she leaned over to let it lick her face. Marilyn's last dog, a black Lab, had died just after her first diagnosis of cancer.

"If you like dogs so much, why don't you get another one?"

"Bernie and I are both at work so much. It would be alone."

"That never bothered you before."

"You're not the one who has to walk it. Who feels guilty." Marilyn wiped her slobbery hands on her slacks as we headed back to the street.

"You have a fenced yard," I persisted. "It might be nice."

Marilyn tossed her head, annoyed, but then we were diverted by the sight of a young woman wrestling a toddler toward a house down the hill and across the street. The little boy wriggled and fidgeted until she put him down. Not much more than twenty, the mother was solid-looking and stylish, in jeans and an imitation leather jacket, hair pulled back into cornrows around her head, then hanging down her back in dozens of braids.

"The people around here look better than the houses do," Marilyn whispered as I unlocked my car.

"Maybe that's because the people are younger than the houses."

Glancing in our direction, the black woman regarded us suspiciously. She minced her steps to let the toddler keep up with her — a tiny boy wearing new red basketball shoes of the smallest possible size.

Finally she swept the toddler into her arms and opened the gate of a chain-link fence that had been erected, hideously, around one of the minuscule front yards. It wasn't until she disappeared inside that Marilyn and I realized, at the same moment, that the transformed, gated house was where Penny's family had once lived.

"My God," Marilyn gasped — whether because she hadn't recognized the house at first or because it looked so awful, I wasn't sure.

"I think aesthetics went out when the gate went up," I said.

But Marilyn slid into the car and clutched her hand to her throat more dramatically than seemed necessary.

"Is this why we came here?" I asked. "To see Penny's house? As a sort of lead-in to Penny's big secret?" I turned on the ignition and gunned the gas as I pulled away from the curb.

Marilyn ignored me. "Imagine having four daughters and only one bathroom," she said.

"Everyone was short of bathrooms," I snipped, annoyed at her dodging my question. "We didn't think about it. Anyway, I think the Weinbergs had a second bath down in one of the basements." But when I tried to remember where Penny had showered, where she'd put on her makeup, I drew a blank.

I drove back up the hill, made a left onto Third Street and then another onto Oglethorpe, the next block. I'd do a quick tour and get us out of there. "Remember that snowstorm when Penny bashed her head over here?" Marilyn asked. "How Helen Weinberg didn't even notice?" Whatever this was leading up to, I decided to let Marilyn get to it in her own time. Of course I remembered Penny's accident. It was one of two youthful snow mishaps we weren't likely to forget. We'd been sledding on Oglethorpe Street, feeling daring because it was even steeper than Oneida. Unable to slow down, Penny had plowed her sled into the tire of a parked car and given herself a good concussion. "Don't tell my mother," she made us promise as we helped her up. We didn't think we'd need to. Penny's face had already turned the color of Elmer's glue. We walked her home, me supporting her and Marilyn carrying her sled. She made it as far as the living-room sofa and slumped down, still in her outdoor clothes. A minute later, Helen Weinberg came in from the kitchen, clad in old slacks and rubber gloves, and said, "I thought I told you to stay out until supper. I'm waxing the floors." She looked with distaste from one of us to another. "Why are you in the living room still wearing your boots?"

Chastened, we escorted Penny to Marilyn's and put her to bed for the afternoon. We didn't know concussion victims aren't supposed to sleep, but somehow she survived her nap and by supper time felt steady enough to go home. She wasn't well — not really — for a week. Her sister, Diane, took care of her. Helen Weinberg had never known.

"That's the thing of it, isn't it?" Marilyn asked. "The whole — motherhood thing."

I'd lost her. Puzzled, I opened my mouth to ask what she meant. Then, in the middle of the block, I caught sight of the Wishners' old house, hunkering onto its lot with even more of a hangdog air than the houses on Oneida Street. For some reason, my first thought was of Pauline Wishner, the kind of housekeeper my mother used to call a *balabusta*, and who would have been horrified at the sorry state of her old home. But it wasn't Pauline I'd ever cared about, not really. It was always her son. "Wish," I whispered, and realized I hadn't uttered that hopeful-sounding nickname for years.

Wish, who would change everything.

For a moment I could hardly breathe, hardly see.

"The name still gets to you, doesn't it?" Marilyn asked, alert.

"I think what gets to me is this neighborhood looking so ratty." Light-headed, I drew a breath, concentrated on steering, headed for the other side of Riggs Road, where the memories were less charged but the neighborhood was no less shabby. Lasalle Elementary School still stood at the edge of the old playground, always a pastel-green monstrosity but now considerably worsened by age. Adjacent to the school grounds, on Madison Street, a wrecked car sat in the middle of a front yard. At the curb, another car was booted. The houses and yards were tumbledown; a surly-looking boy leaned on a mailbox and regarded us with such hostility that all the bones in his face looked frozen.

I stepped on the gas, turned back onto Riggs Road, drove quickly past the building that used to be the neighborhood shul, Shaare Tefila. I wanted to get this visit over with.

"I have to eat something," Marilyn said suddenly. "My head hurts and my stomach hurts and if I don't get this off my chest about Penny I'm going to explode."

"It's about time," I told her.

She pointed toward a combined Kentucky Fried Chicken/Taco Bell coming up on our right. Her expression stayed humorless. "Stop there," she said.

CHAPTER 5

Taco Bell

It was hardly the restaurant I would have chosen, a fast-food emporium sitting where our favorite miniature golf course had once been and just across Third Street from the shopping center where we'd spent half our adolescence trying to attract significant boys. Not a single other white person was in sight. I said to Marilyn, "I saw a bunch of places just across the District Line" — a lie. "It'll take exactly two minutes to get there." She said, "No. Stop."

Both the customers and the help kept their eyes on us as we got our food. I picked a booth by a window and slammed down my tray. "All right, tell me about Penny."

Marilyn unwrapped her straw and inched it into her Diet Coke. She plucked a veggie fajita from its waxed paper wrapper and began splitting open packets of taco sauce. "Well, Steve said something weird on the phone the other day. Not that he doesn't always say something weird —"

"Still jealous of your brother's wealth and fame, I see."

"Yes. All that unresolved sibling rivalry." The strength of Marilyn's relationship with her brother was that there had been no rivalry. She was always the boss. "It was the day I called to tell him about the cancer coming back. We probably talked for an hour. You know, the old, 'whole life flashing before your eyes' routine. Not something we do a lot." Although Steve the superstar now lived in a magnificent house in Pacific Palisades outside Los Angeles, he still spent several months a year on the road singing and was exhaustingly in demand the rest of the time.

"He said —" Marilyn unfolded the fajita and doused it with a packet of sauce. "Remember the time Penny went to see him at college? That last time she saw him?"

"Marilyn, the whole country remembers." It was the subject of the song "Bus Ride" that had made Steve famous. Penny had taken a bus from Maryland to West Virginia where Steve had gone to school. They'd spent the weekend together, and then Penny had travelled back to Washington and dropped out of sight.

"Well, we went over the whole business again, about what happened to Penny after that. Between the last time he saw her at school and before she went off the deep end. Steve said she definitely had a baby."

"Oh, for God's sake." I heard the shrillness in my tone. We'd been analyzing this subject for thirty-odd years. We'd batted it around ad nauseam, and a baby was the one possibility we'd ruled out years ago, conclusively and finally. "Penny was careful about birth control. Obsessive about it. Determined not to bring more children into the world. If there was one thing she was responsible about, that was it. Don't tell me you don't remember. She wouldn't have let herself get pregnant."

Marilyn leaned across her food conspiratorially. "All I can say is, Steve says he knows it for a fact."

"For a *fact?* How? I thought he never talked to Penny again."

"He didn't." Marilyn took a long sip of Diet Coke. Fifty years ago it would have been vanilla Coke from the fountain across the street in People's Drug Store, and she would have been drinking just as slowly. I felt as if I'd fallen through a time warp.

"Barbara, listen to me." Marilyn's voice was crisp. "Remember how Steve always said he kept trying to call Penny all the next summer? While he was on that trip with his band? And how nobody would tell him where she was?"

"Sure," I said. "Her sisters clammed up because either —" I held up a finger "— one, they didn't know, or two, she was in a mental institution and they were embarrassed."

"Barbara, don't."

"*Don't?* Then if Penny was pregnant and she didn't tell Steve, tell me who did."

"I'm getting to that."

"Well, I think it's bullshit," I said. "She always told Steve everything."

"She probably worried the baby was the other guy's. The one from the 'Bus Ride' song," Marilyn reminded me.

"Not even a possibility. If she actually got pregnant that weekend — which I don't believe — the father could have been either one of them. And no matter who the father was, she still would have told Steve. Penny knew he loved her. She knew he'd forgive her."

Marilyn poured another packet of sauce on the fajita. She didn't look up.

"Or she could have done something else," I continued. "In the unlikely event — the *very* unlikely event — she was pregnant and not sure whose it was, she could have had an abortion and decided not to talk about it. So she stayed out of touch."

Marilyn shook her head. "An abortion wouldn't have been like Penny."

I had to agree. Horrified as Penny was at the thought of a pregnancy, it was even more impossible to imagine her destroying a life. And "destroying" was exactly how Penny would have seen it — even though the trauma of having an abortion might almost explain what happened to her later. The hideous, almost unthinkable events that, even now, I quickly censored from my thoughts.

"So who told Steve about this theoretical baby?" I asked. "One of her sisters? Who else would know?"

"Essie Berman."

"Essie! When?"

"After," Marilyn said. "About a year after."

"Oh, good lord." I felt as if the air had been knocked out of me. When I could breathe again I said, "Then why didn't Steve ever tell *us*?"

"Never underestimate the power of guilt." Marilyn doused the fajita with one more packet of taco sauce, rendering it completely inedible. "He's always hated 'Bus Ride' being his first big hit. He's always felt rotten about benefiting from

Penny's problems. You know how he is." Marilyn took a deep breath. "He always felt responsible for her. I think he always loved her, but —"

"Was also glad to be rid of her," I finished. There'd been times when we'd all been glad to be rid of Penny.

Marilyn nodded. "So it was easy for Steve to put her out of his mind. Just like it's easy for us. But then when Essie told him Penny had a child —"

"*Why* did Essie tell him? That's what I want to know."

"Because he bugged her for information for a whole year. You know what a pest he could be. So finally Essie said she'd tell him what she knew if he promised never to ask another question. Never to take it further. To do nothing."

"And he promised? Even though she might have been telling him about his own child?"

"Or somebody else's child," Marilyn said. "Anyway, I think he was pretty surprised to hear there was a child."

"What else did Essie tell him?"

"Nothing. Not even if it was a boy or a girl."

"So he's known all these years. While we were still trying to figure it out."

96

Marilyn shrugged. "Essie told him not to. But now — I think he's curious. I think that's why he mentioned it."

"Either that or he made it up to take your mind off your troubles." All his life, Steve had been nothing if not creative.

"He wouldn't insult me like that." Refusing to look at me, she stared out the window to the shopping center across the street, where the old Giant had become Tiger Foods and the People's Drug Store was a CVS Pharmacy, and the parking lot was badly in need of resurfacing. Then she inhaled deeply, set her elbows on the table, and dropped her head into her palms, rubbing her eyes with the heels of her hands. When she looked up, her eyes were bloodshot and puffy. "What if the baby *was* Steve's?" she asked.

"What if it was?"

"Don't you think he'd want to know?"

"Absolutely not."

She cocked her head in surprise.

"What would Kimberly think?" I asked. "What about the boys? It would be awful." Steve had married late, in his forties, after he had been famous long enough to get used to his celebrity and grown confident enough to confess on national TV what he thought was a momentous personal secret.

97

His marriage had always been rock solid. After his wife had a couple of miscarriages, they had adopted four learning-disabled sons, all now well-adjusted young men.

Scratching her eyelid with a knuckle, Marilyn smeared mascara across her cheek. "I thought even with all those kids he might still be hoping he had one that was his own flesh and blood."

"Listen. Even assuming there's this long-lost child, it would be an adult, older than Mike and Robin, living some kind of life we don't have a clue about. What happens when all of a sudden it finds out it has a famous father? You'd only be opening Pandora's box."

"We wouldn't have to tell the *child.*"

"Marilyn, it wouldn't be a child. That's just my point."

"The offspring, then. And you could help. You're the one who does research for a living." She fixed me with a mournful, lambent gaze.

"Oh, no. You're not guilt-tripping me into this. I do term papers. The influence of Sir Thomas Mallory on the modern novel. Nothing real. If Steve wanted to, he could hire a hundred researchers more qualified than I am. The fact that he hasn't ought to tell you something."

Dramatically, Marilyn said nothing.

"Besides," I said. "If Penny really had a baby, why didn't she come out of hiding after it was born and she made her arrangements for it? Why wait another six months to surface again? What was she doing, trying to regain her girlish figure?" Penny had always been slim.

"That's really lame," Marilyn said.

It was, and the fact of that made me angry. I pushed my tray away from me so hard it clunked into hers. "I hate Mexican food," I yelled. "I don't know why I let you bring me here."

A woman dressed like a desert nomad shot us a withering glance from the next booth. Marilyn raised her eyebrows at me as if to say, "Oh, you've really done it now, Barbara," and stood up. "You could have had fried chicken," she told me. She gathered the remains of our uneaten lunch and carried them to the trash.

I slid out of the booth, followed her, handed her her purse. In our rush toward the glass door to the parking lot, we nearly collided with two huge teenagers, each looking like a linebacker for his football team. Marilyn gave them a brilliant smile. One of them held the door for us. Outside, Marilyn dropped the smile. "I bet she's

99

still alive," she said.

"Who?"

"Essie Berman."

"Essie! That's crazy. She was old even when we were kids. She's probably been dead for years."

"Not necessarily. Kids think everyone is old. She came to my mother's funeral."

"That was ten years ago!" Marilyn's mother had died unexpectedly, and I had missed the funeral because I was on vacation and Marilyn hadn't wanted to interrupt my trip to tell me. I snatched my keys from my purse and unlocked the car.

"At the funeral Essie looked like she'd still be around in another ten years," Marilyn said. "Maybe another twenty."

"She'd be at least in her nineties. Probably senile."

"She never struck me as the type who'd get senile. Even in her nineties." We'd always thought Essie older than our parents because of her salt-and-pepper hair — but as Marilyn said, maybe not. It doesn't occur to a six-year-old that some people simply gray early.

"I don't care," I said. "I'm not interested."

Unfazed, Marilyn got into the car. "I even tried finding her in the phone book," she persisted.

An unbidden bubble of laughter gurgled up through my irritation. "Had a slow week, did you? Didn't have enough to do between selecting medical treatments and scheduling cosmetic surgery? How many Esther Bermans are there in the phone book, anyway?"

"There was no listing," Marilyn huffed. "I tried the retirement places and the nursing homes, too. But I think she's still around."

"Don't be delusional. Did you try Maryland or just D.C.?"

"I only look dumb."

During our years in Riggs Park, Essie's single status had been an oddity, and her family, if she had any, wasn't in Washington. If Essie were still alive, no telling where she might be, or with whom. It was true Penny might have confided to her even a dark secret like a pregnancy — though it was hard for me to believe in a pregnancy even if Steve had said so. Despite all the confusion in Penny's life, on this one issue she'd been firm, even before she was old enough to worry about it. She had not been wanted. She would not inflict that pain on anyone else. End of story. Steve's account was odd enough, but Marilyn setting out on a wild-goose chase for

Essie was odder. As children, Penny and I had looked to Marilyn as the gold standard of sanity. It hadn't occurred to me, until I'd heard the story of how the body could heal itself at the expense of the mind, that that could ever change.

"I know what you're thinking, Marilyn," I bellowed as I pulled out of the parking lot, counting on volume to shake her back to her senses. "You think you'll be in there having your surgery tomorrow and out of guilt and sympathy good old Barbara will be out chasing down Steve's nonexistent long-lost child. Let me tell you right now, that's not going to happen. Bernie and I will both be sitting in the waiting room with our blood pressure off the charts while we twiddle our thumbs. If you want to spare us that, learn to live with your wrinkles."

"Bernie won't be sitting in the waiting room," Marilyn said. "He never sits in the waiting room. I don't want you to, either."

"That's ridiculous." We thudded over a huge pothole that jolted the whole car. "What does Bernie think of this whole 'baby' thing?" I demanded.

"I haven't told him."

"Because you know he'd think it's as crazy as I do."

102

"Steve wouldn't lie to me, Barbara." A mask of exhaustion dropped over her face, and we drove past the District Line in silence.

When her voice came again, it was just a thread. "You remember my baby that died?"

"Of course. Did you think I'd forget?" Marilyn's second child, a girl, arrived two years after Mike. She was so blue that she never left the delivery room before doctors diagnosed the hole in her heart, something that even today might not have been a routine repair. In the confused moments before they rushed her to Children's Hospital for surgery, Marilyn chose not to see the baby. "If she's all right, then I'll have plenty of time to get to know her," she'd said, struggling to keep her voice from cracking. "Better to not get attached yet — just in case." She'd named the baby Carolyn.

The infant lived forty-eight hours after surgery. Steve flew in for the burial, but Marilyn couldn't bring herself to go. The two of us sat together in her living room, entertaining the toddler Mike, while Bernie and Steve accompanied the tiny coffin to the cemetery.

Now Marilyn reached over and touched

my wrist with cold, trembling fingers. "If I had it to do over again," she whispered, "I wouldn't have sent the baby off to Children's Hospital without taking a look at her."

She leaned back against the seat and closed her eyes. Two perfectly shaped tears squeezed out from beneath her lashes. "If I had it to do over again," she said, "I would have held her."

CHAPTER 6

Southern Maryland, 1953

The summer Marilyn and Penny and I were eleven and a half and Penny was about to turn twelve, our parents had decided to send us for the month of July to Camp Chesapeake, a Jewish overnight camp in southern Maryland on the shores of the Chesapeake Bay. Some of our Riggs Park friends had been going for years — notably Wish Wishner, whose charms had not yet captured me, and Seth Opak and his sister. Although we were old to be first-time campers, we were lured by the promise that Marilyn and Penny and I would be in the same cabin. Marilyn's brother Steve was going, too. It would be fine.

Penny didn't think so. She said wild horses couldn't drag her there, or to any other summer camp. "Wild horses!" her mother laughed. "Let's hope that won't be necessary." Waiting in front of the Jewish Community Center for the bus to camp, Penny sat on the steps and picked at a scab on her knee, sulking.

"You're not the only one being abandoned," I pointed out. "My mother's on tour with the National Symphony. She doesn't want me around the house making trouble." She had been offered the job, a plum, because the orchestra's second clarinetist was unable to travel. My sister, Trudi, had been shipped off to cousins in New York.

"Our parents are going on vacation," Marilyn and Steve assured her.

"Leave me alone," Penny said.

The eleven-year-old girls were assigned to Darlene, a counselor with Asian-looking hair and nails the color of cinnamon, who herded us into the bus. The windows were open, but it was stifling. When we finally started to move, a hot wind blew in and ratted Penny's hair into a wild red tangle. Penny didn't seem to notice.

Steve brought out his guitar and began strumming "Ninety-nine Bottles of Beer on the Wall." The campers sang along. By sixty bottles of beer we were traveling through wooded countryside and the singing was so loud that Steve's playing was inaudible. He put the guitar away.

Walking down the aisle to check her charges, Darlene noted Penny's dour expression and smiled at her as if she were some unusual pet. "Are you okay?"

"I have a headache." Penny closed her eyes.

"The singing keeps them under control," a nice-looking male counselor yelled to Darlene when we got to fifty bottles.

"So I see," Darlene said.

"I'm Danny," the other counselor told her. He had high cheekbones, an aristocratic nose, a dark tan.

"Isn't that cute," Marilyn giggled. "Darlene and Danny."

Penny opened her eyes and studied the counselors. "I envy Danny his tan," she said. She'd told her mother redheads didn't belong at a camp where they were in the sun all day. "Twenty years from now I'll have skin cancer just like Aunt Selma." Skin cancer and sun hadn't been linked yet in the official medical literature, but Penny's family offered several redheaded case histories.

"Use lotion," Helen had said. "Wear a T-shirt." While Penny was away, Helen would be painting their house. Penny had spent two weeks destroying diaries, letters, anything her mother might find in her room and construe as evidence of a private existence.

Camp Chesapeake sat on a bluff overlooking the Chesapeake Bay. Two hours after we'd arrived, we were shoving foot-lockers under our cots and getting ready for the first swim of the day. Eli, the camp's manager, believed frequent swims would keep us from heatstroke, given that all the other activities took place in relent-less sun. Even our cabins offered little re-spite — hot wooden boxes with no insulation or air-conditioning. The win-dows were small, the walls unfinished. Wires snaked up bare plywood to un-shaded ceiling bulbs; daddy longlegs lived in the wooden toilet stalls.

In the cabin, our cots were lined up be-neath two rows of windows. Darlene the counselor got to sleep behind a wooden barrier at the front. We campers eyed each other as we changed into bathing suits, lin-gering on the chest of a girl named Abigail, who wore a C-cup bra while most of us were still in undershirts. Abigail undressed facing the wall. Penny, whose chest was still utterly flat, retreated to the toilet to change.

The beach was a narrow strip at the bottom of the bluff, looking out to the brown, slow-moving bay. The net designed to keep jellyfish out of the swimming area was torn. Most of us waded in tentatively.

One girl bravely walked out on the dock and jumped into the water. Seconds later she came up festooned with jellyfish — draped across her shoulders, her bathing suit, her arms.

"Aaaiieee!" the girl screamed.

Bruno, the swim director, blew his whistle. "Everyone out of the water!"

We watched in horror as the girl pulled jellyfish from her body, flung them into the water, retreated to the beach. Bruno scooped more jellyfish from the swimming area with a net on a long pole. He deposited them on the sand, where veteran campers found sticks to poke into their melting, gelatinous tentacles.

"Okay, everyone back in," Bruno yelled. No one moved.

"All right, girls," Darlene said. The polished, well-groomed fingers with which she gestured toward the water were long, delicate, without authority. We stood our ground.

"Rebellion on your hands?" asked Danny, who'd come down with his group of boys.

"Mutiny on the first day," Darlene said. Wish and Seth, two of Danny's charges, sprinted into the water and raced in a strong freestyle out to the net. The jellyfish seemed not to bother them.

"Swim team," Danny told Darlene.

She'd fluffed her hair and smiled.

Four days later, Penny's skin had been burned raw. "On visiting day you'll recognize me as the bright scarlet one," she wrote her mother. "I'm the only one who wears a man's undershirt over her bathing suit." Penny had brought along a whole stack of her father's undershirts for protection. She shed the current one reluctantly — a hundred percent cotton, kind to the skin — and dressed in scratchy shorts and T-shirt for Friday supper. As was required on Friday evenings, all of us were outfitted entirely in white. Darlene zipped herself into a tight white jumpsuit and ducked behind her wooden barrier to curl her hair.

Penny combed her carrot bangs over a magenta forehead. She'd been slightly feverish from sunburn all day, taking aspirin and rubbing moisturizer on her skin. Several times each day, she tiptoed away from the scheduled outdoor activity and retreated to the bunk, where she practiced playing jacks. Invariably, Darlene found her and made her go back outside.

In the dining hall, the smell of greasy

chicken mingled with the odor of pine from the unfinished walls. "Oh, God, I don't think I can eat," Penny wailed. Nausea, she had informed us, was a primary symptom of sun-poisoning.

Marilyn and I sat on either side of her at the long table. Waiters appeared with platters of chicken and mashed potatoes. Penny looked at the food and turned the color of the camp's infamous lime mousse.

"I've got to go back to the bunk," she whispered urgently.

"Try to eat something first," Darlene said.

"I need to get out of here. *Now.*"

"We'll take her," I offered. "She's too sunburned to eat."

Back at the bunk, we made Penny lie down. She could only lie on her stomach because her back was too sore. The cabin was airless, a purgatory of humid heat that coated us like glue. After what seemed an eternity, Marilyn said, "We ought to go down to the rec hall, it'll be better than lying in bed. All you have to do is sit." Penny looked skeptical, but she came with us.

The rec hall was a huge wooden rectangle with vaulted ceilings and window openings with no glass or screens, just plywood shutters that could be closed in case of a storm. After supper on Fridays, there was a short service in the rec hall, followed by a movie for the whole camp. The opening credits of *National Velvet* were already rolling by the time we crept in and took our seats.

In front of us, Danny and Darlene sat side by side, their shoulders touching. They were surrounded by campers. Across the aisle were the older boys. Steve Ginsburg sat on the end, directly across from Penny.

"I've seen this already," he said, leaning in her direction.

"Me, too."

"What a sunburn. Bet it hurts."

"It does." Without further preamble, Penny burst into tears.

We led her outside. Steve followed. "Hey, I'm sorry. I didn't know it was that bad."

Penny pulled up her sleeve to reveal the water blisters on her shoulder.

"After it peels your skin will get some color," Steve assured her.

"Not me. I never get tan. I just get freckles."

"Freckles are okay. Freckles are angel dust."

Penny smiled. I think Steve was in love with her even then.

A week later, the three of us sat on Darlene's cot, hidden from our bunk mates by her wooden barrier, composing a letter to Penny's mother. It was Darlene's night off and she'd gone out with Danny. Becky, the counselor-in-training who was supposed to fill in for her, had slipped out after curfew, the minute Taps ended and the lights went out. We'd filched a few pages of Darlene's fancy stationery and were working by flashlight.

"Tell your mother you've been running a fever of 102 all week," I suggested.

"Tell her all they give you is aspirin," Marilyn offered. Penny wrote it down.

On the campers' side of the wooden barrier, the girl with the C-cup bra, Abigail, got up and rummaged in her footlocker, then walked to the bathroom with a heavy step. Abigail had her period. Marilyn and Penny and I hadn't had this experience yet, so we were fascinated — though Penny, with three older sisters, was less so. Abigail changed sanitary pads at least ten times a day. She was terrified that otherwise the blood might leak through her clothes. When Abigail returned to her cot, she started sobbing softly.

"Come on outside," Marilyn whispered, sensitive to Abigail's plight.

We tiptoed out the door. The sky was gray-black, hazed over, no stars. Marilyn sat on the top step of the little porch and Penny and I sat below, our legs sticking out of pale shorty pajamas.

"Abigail's just homesick," Marilyn said.

"Me, too," Penny told her. "I hate it here."

Marilyn scratched a mosquito bite on her arm. "Hate's a strong word."

"I hate swimming. I hate that I'm the only one here so allergic to jellyfish that I get so swollen from them. I hate the sun. I hate everything but playing jacks." Between scheduled activities, all the girls played jacks. Penny's delicate fingers seemed able to pick up any combination of them, no matter how scattered. It was a matter of pride that she was as good as she was. It was the first thing, maybe the only thing, she'd ever really been good at.

With a crunch of dry leaves, someone walked by in the woods adjacent to our cabin.

"We better go in," Marilyn said.

Penny ignored her. "I couldn't sleep the whole time I was sunburned. Now my shoulders itch and I can't sleep because of the itching." Penny's water bubbles were bursting. A bright red wounded skin was emerging underneath, which had to be covered with her father's undershirts. "I feel rotten when it's this hot. Truly, genuinely rotten."

"It's even hotter at home."

"At home I sleep in the basement." In the subterranean warren of rooms in Penny's house, it was always chilly.

"When we have the overnighter at Locust Point, we get to sleep right on the beach. They say there's always a breeze," Marilyn said.

"We'll like the overnighter," I said.

"What I'd really like," Penny told me, "is to go home."

Danny had been kissing Darlene for a long time outside the rec hall while the three of us had spied on them. Now and then Eli walked around the building to check who was there. Danny let go of her then and they talked. Another week had passed. Darlene had been meeting Danny every chance she could. It was a true romance. Inside, the Friday-night movie was *Ma and Pa Kettle Go to Town*.

Danny pressed Darlene against the side

of the building and kissed her again. We put our hands over our mouths to stifle giggles. It was a testimony to their absorption that they didn't hear us. We were only four feet away.

Danny's hand wandered to Darlene's breast. This had happened several times before and she'd pushed it away, but this time she let it linger on her white T-shirt. He squeezed exactly the way my mother sometimes squeezed a grapefruit to see if it was ripe. Danny groaned with pleasure.

"Gross," Marilyn whispered. We were thrilled.

Out of nowhere, a heavy hand dropped onto my shoulder. Penny gasped. Danny and Darlene flew apart as if shocked by a cattle prod.

"You're supposed to be watching the movie," Eli said.

The next day a rumor circulated that Darlene and Danny were being fired. They would finish working through this session of camp and then be sent home. For the month of August, the twelve-year-old and eleven-year-old bunks would be combined.

On Sunday, visiting day, my father had ridden down with the Ginsburgs since my mother had still been on tour. The

Ginsburgs had cut their vacation short so they could be here. Steve and Marilyn and I stood with our parents around the refreshment table in the dining hall, sipping lemonade that had been set out for the social hour. Penny kept going outside to look for her own family, who were late.

"Are your sisters coming, or just your folks?" my father asked politely.

"I'm not sure. Maybe just my parents or maybe my parents and Diane. Either way there will be room in the car. I'm going to make them take me home."

Just as the campers were about to escort their parents through a demonstration of the daily schedule, Helen and Sid Weinberg finally sauntered in. Helen wore a pair of baggy slacks. She made a great show of kissing Penny without touching her formerly sunburned shoulders.

"So how is it?" Helen asked. "Not as bad as you thought, is it? You don't look nearly as fried as you told me."

"Those pants make you look fat, mother," Penny said.

"What?" Helen put her hands to her hips.

"Now, Penny —" Sid began, but no one paid any attention. Sid was a pale and ineffectual presence in his daughters' lives.

Playing trumpet in the navy band meant he was gone nearly half the year.

The Weinbergs joined us at the activities demonstration. We went to arts and crafts, and then down to the beach. The only people who actually swam that day were the boys on the swim team, headed by Wish and Seth, who demonstrated each of the skills the campers had learned.

"I guess we'll take off," Penny's mother said as we climbed the stairs from the beach to the top of the bluff.

"What about seeing drama club? What about the basketball game?" Penny asked.

"I think we have the general idea," Helen said. "We want to stop for crabs on the way back."

"I'm coming with you," Penny announced.

"You'll be home in two weeks." Helen laughed and turned to her husband.

Sid offered a lame smile. Penny crossed her arms over her chest. "Excuse us," Helen said, planting both hands on Penny's shoulders and guiding her away. My family and Marilyn's proceeded to drama club. We didn't see Penny again until visiting hours were over.

Penny was sitting on her cot. Her face

was swollen from crying, but she was not crying now. "They couldn't even be bothered to stay for the whole show," she said bitterly. "They had to *get crabs.*"

"Think of it this way: camp's half over," Marilyn told her.

"Think of it this way. Don't have kids if you don't have time for them. Don't have kids if you've got better things to do." An imperturbable calm descended over her face such as I had seen only after she had thrown a hand of jacks and was studying how they had landed. "I'm never going to have children," she said. "I wouldn't do that to anyone."

"It's not like you have to make that decision *this minute,*" I told her, hoping to lighten the mood.

"I'll never have children," she repeated somberly. She fixed her gaze first on me and then on Marilyn, as if to reinforce her point. This was not the helpless, falling-apart Penny we knew. It was a determined, confident one we hadn't heard before, full of steely resolve. In her tone was something absolute and scary. Something unstoppable. And that was why, more than forty years later, I still did not believe that Penny had had either an "accident" or a baby.

Locust Point was actually only a post office and a gas station next to the bay — no houses. Our cabin had hiked forty minutes up the beach from camp after dinner, singing "Ninety-nine Bottles of Beer." The stretch of sand along the bay was wide, with stands of trees almost down to the water. Our sleeping bags arrived in Eli's pickup truck, driven by one of the boys' counselors. There was also a picnic basket full of marshmallows, graham crackers, and Hershey's bars for s'mores. In the morning, the truck would come for the sleeping bags, while the girls hiked back to camp for breakfast.

Except for Penny, all of us spread into the trees to gather firewood. Penny hung back and rubbed her right leg, which was more red and swollen than usual from jellyfish stings. The walk up the beach had aggravated it.

"Come on, the stings'll clear up soon, they always do," Darlene said, motioning for her to gather kindling. Darlene brushed sand from her bright red shorts. She had painted her nails to match and curled her hair. We figured Danny would show up sooner or later.

We lit the fire, which made the beach

seem darker than before, the wind louder in the trees, the lapping of the bay more ominous. "Let's tell ghost stories," one of the girls said when the s'mores were gone. "Darlene first."

Darlene positioned herself so her hair wouldn't blow. "Did you ever hear the one about the ghost with the bloody finger?" We shook our heads. She had just opened her mouth to speak when a moaning came from the trees. An eerie light appeared in the upper branches.

Everyone screamed.

"It's nothing," Marilyn said. "It's a flashlight shining through the leaves."

We hugged ourselves, hugged each other, pulled our sleeping bags close.

"I bet it's boys!" someone said.

More moans from the trees. Boys! Giggles.

A dark wind blew across the beach, making the fire flutter. Then the camp was silent.

Minutes passed. We held our breath. Nothing happened.

"I think the boys just wanted to scare us, and now they're on their way back to camp," Darlene said.

We were disappointed. Each of us was poised for something more. But weary from exercise and sugar-dazed from s'mores, instead of keeping a breathless watch we all soon fell asleep. I opened my eyes maybe an hour later, maybe more. The fire on the beach was almost out. Above me the Big Dipper hung in a bowl of black sky. A warm wind made the water lap at the sand. When my eyes adjusted, I spotted Darlene and Danny half-hidden at the edge of the trees. They were lying on a blanket, stretched out against each other, moving in a kind of rhythm that had echoed not the rhythm of the bay but some other cadence I did not yet understand or want to.

In the morning Penny's leg was purple. The rest of us rolled up our sleeping bags, but Penny said she couldn't move.

Marilyn and I touched Penny's calf, which felt hard and slightly hot. Penny sat on the sand, about to cry. Then Eli's pickup truck pulled up to get the sleeping bags. Danny was at the wheel.

"They let *you* drive?" Darlene teased.

"Of course. Their primo counselor. Who else?"

"Maybe someone who wasn't getting fired," Darlene giggled. "Okay, girls, load your gear into the truck."

"I can't," Penny whined.

Marilyn and I rolled Penny's sleeping bag and handed it to Danny. "You're going to have to take Penny back to camp in the truck," Marilyn instructed. "She's not going to be able to hike all the way up that beach."

Darlene pondered this, a cheerful flush creeping across her face. "I better ride back to camp with her," she said. "Becky can be in charge." Becky, the inept counselor-in-training, had come along to help supervise the hike.

"If you really want to do me a favor," Penny told Danny and Darlene after the rest of us marched off down the beach, "don't take me back to camp, take me home."

"Let's take her home," Darlene said. Penny thought she sounded a little giddy.

"Yeah, sure," Danny said.

"Let's. Otherwise they'll put her in the infirmary. She might as well be home."

"If they think she's really sick they'll call her parents."

"They won't. The swelling will go down. It always does. Her parents won't come."

"If we take her home, they'll have to let her stay there." Darlene's eyes were bright and her voice a little crazy. Penny felt hopeful.

"You want them to arrest us for stealing the truck?" Danny asked.

"They won't. We'll call. We'll say she was inconsolable."

"We'll get fired."

"We're *already* fired," Darlene laughed. Penny saw how she was daring him. It was something she would remember. They ended up going down the highway at sixty-five, sleeping bags flopping around in the back, hot wind coming in the windows, rock music blasting from the radio. When Marilyn and I returned from camp two weeks later, Penny came to my house. We'd eaten Popsicles and giggled over her story, and I'd believed all of us were finished with Camp Chesapeake forever, and Penny would never have a baby no matter what.

CHAPTER 7

Seduction

Back at Marilyn's house, I didn't go to the cemetery, didn't call Steve, didn't even indulge in the guilty pleasure of poring over the Style section of the *Washington Post*. The minute Marilyn excused herself for a nap, I collapsed onto my own inviting, rumpled covers and fell into one of those deep, dreamless, black holes of sleep that for me had always been the only cure for tension.

Dragged back into consciousness hours later by Bernie's persistent knocking, I had no idea where I was. Patches of gloomy, twilit sky filled the spaces between the open wooden blinds. Clouds? Dusk? I remembered I was in Maryland. I'd gone to Riggs Park. My head was filled with fog.

"Phone for you," Bernie called from outside the door. I hadn't heard it ring.

"I know it's only been a day, but I already miss you," Jon murmured when I picked up. The hum of background noise almost drowned him out.

"Where are you?"

"The Indianapolis airport. On my way to West Lafayette, a couple of hours' drive. Tomorrow I interview that ex-basketball player who coaches at Purdue. Remember I told you about him? How's Marilyn?"

"Physically, pretty good. Mentally, I'm not so sure. Tomorrow she's going to have a face-lift."

"They're doing face-lifts for breast cancer now?"

"It's a long story." Realizing how urgently I wanted to tell it, in full detail and at leisure, in the style of our old, comfortable companionship, I resented the airport commotion that made it impossible.

"If you need me, say the word," Jon told me. "I can get out of here late tomorrow. I was going to Kansas City, but I don't have to. If you want some company, I'm always a good shoulder to cry on."

"Thanks, but I think I'm way beyond crying. You know me, Jon. Tough." I didn't want to have to ask. I wanted him just to show up.

A loudspeaker blared information about a gate change. "When will you be home?" he shouted. I could picture him holding a hand over his free ear, blocking out the noise.

"Probably Wednesday or Thursday. A few days after Marilyn's surgery. You?"

"About the same." He dropped his voice. "Don't stay away too long. I love you, Barbara."

"I love you, too." It was always so easy to say the words.

Outside, the sky had drained of light, a time of day I'd come to know all too well, when loss and longing seemed to live in the mournful air itself, in the aching, endless length of the hour before dark.

I didn't know why I was so upset.

From downstairs, Marilyn's voice drifted up. Then Bernie's voice. Alto. Tenor. I couldn't hear what they were saying. Quickly, surreptitiously, I dialed Steve's number in California. By the time the answering machine picked up, I had framed a quick, cheery, nonthreatening message to leave, then decided *any* message would alarm him and hung up. I washed my face and went down to the kitchen.

Marilyn stood at the counter chopping vegetables for a stir-fry, cheeks flushed with exertion, looking rested and healthy. She pointed me toward the makings of a salad laid out on the counter.

"I told Bernie about Penny. He thinks you're right. We ought to leave it alone."

"Absolutely," came Bernie's voice from the den.

"So you're going to drop it?"

"Not a chance."

Masking my disappointment, I peeled a clove of garlic and rubbed it around the inside of a wooden salad bowl, not looking at her.

"I know you don't quite believe there was a baby, and I forgive you for thinking I'm so pathetic that Steve would lie to me," she said. "And don't think I didn't take into account your worries about this Pandora's box."

"Well, it's nice to hear you sounding like your annoying logical self."

"You're worried that a baby would have turned out to be someone Steve wouldn't want to know. Some insecure dyslexic who might want to rob him of his fortune." She raised her eyebrows at me.

"Yes." I discarded the garlic and picked up a head of lettuce. I wasn't going to laugh.

"But I still think Steve must be curious. And I think you need to get over thinking everything you did for Steve you really did for yourself, so now you have to protect him."

"That's ridiculous," I said, though it was perfectly true. For the first years of my friendship with Marilyn, I had hardly noticed Steve except as Marilyn's generic, pesky older brother. Then one June day he announced he'd failed third grade, and he suddenly materialized for me like some fascinating alien who'd dropped into the Ginsburg living room from the sky — a goofy boy in plaid shorts, scratching flakes that looked like dandruff off a sunburned, peeling nose — and above all, a boy who could play the guitar almost as well as my mother played clarinet. A boy who, despite his *great musical gift* (the one thing my mother most desired for me) would have to repeat the year.

"If you can't pass school by yourself, then we'll help you," Marilyn told him, gleefully taking charge of her year-older brother. "From now on you'll be in the same class with me and Barbara. Don't worry, we'll get you through."

But although we attacked the task with gusto as soon as school started the next fall, in the first months we seemed doomed to fail.

Then one day Penny said mildly, in a tone that showed she was trying not to offend, "He's never going to learn if you keep writing things down for him. You have to tell him out loud. He's not stupid. He just can't read."

"He can't read?" We were stunned. "How did you know this?"

Penny shrugged. She was always the first to glean our darkest secrets, a kind of perverse and unwanted talent. Having diagnosed Steve's problem, she lost interest and left me and Marilyn to solve it. It was one of the few things the two of us did without her in those years.

We had no idea we could be so righteously devious. We tutored Steve, lied for him, taught him to write gibberish essays in an indecipherable script. "His writing's bad because his hands shake," we informed our teachers. "Didn't you know? There's probably a note of it in his records." We knew because we'd put the letter there ourselves, signed Shirley H. Ginsburg in perfect imitation of his mother's handwriting. Helping Steve was better than psychotherapy. It allowed me to deal with a mother who wanted above all to foster musical skills in a daughter who didn't have a shred of talent. Steve had starred in my childhood as living proof that it was possible to have musical talent and still, in critical ways, not be able to function as well as a neighbor girl with a tin ear.

"The important thing was, you helped

him," Marilyn said now, as I clunked the lettuce on the counter and removed the loosened core. "It doesn't matter what you believe might have been your *motives.*"

"Maybe not," I said. "Maybe I want to protect him from your misguided intentions just because he's my friend."

Marilyn attacked a cabbage with her chopping knife. A slow smile crept across her face. "We had fun, didn't we?"

"We did." We'd worked out a system for Steve to copy multiple-choice tests without getting caught. We encouraged him to endear himself to the teachers. If the class read a poem, he would recite it back from memory. If actors were needed for a play, he would be the only boy to volunteer, and all Marilyn and I had to do was read the script aloud to him, and he'd memorize it overnight. Steve was bright. Steve had potential. Teachers knew his shaky hands were an unlikely explanation, given how well he played the guitar. But they'd loved him too much to care.

"Basically, we taught him to be a con artist," Marilyn said now, chopping with a kind of cheerful rhythm.

"Not a con artist!" I tore mounds of lettuce into the wooden bowl. "We just taught him to use his charm."

In junior high he'd begun calling all the females in his life *sweetie,* which might have seemed affected except that he made everyone feel she really *was* his sweetie. Steve had grown into an adolescent with so little sense of style that even when his friends got crew cuts, his hair flopped greasily onto his forehead. He was no threat to either gender. Calling the girls *sweetie* was safe. Every year from eighth grade on he convinced a whole bevy of them to tape textbooks for him, saying to each one, "Oh, sweetie, I like your voice so much," and smiling so coyly they didn't know whether he was serious or joking. He committed each taped book to memory — he could always remember everything he heard — and not one of his helpers ever found out about the others.

By high school Steve was offering to bring his guitar to anyone's party and sing for free if in return they would write him a term paper. On the day of the SATs, he finagled a seat next to Bernie, knowing Bernie was in love with Marilyn and would let him copy. He was determined not just to avoid humiliation, but to shield his parents, who, like many in Riggs Park, had little formal education and valued it above all for their children. He wasn't planning to go to college (although later, briefly, he did), but even then he wanted everyone to think he could get in if he wanted.

In a way, Steve's enforced charm prepared him well for the irony of becoming our best-known classmate, the one nonreader in a class that worshipped scholarship. Marilyn and I were glad that, in the early years, when beneath his charm and comedy, Steve's affliction gave him pain, we lied to his teachers, stayed up all night before exams, dug earthworms out of the garden to teach him biology. We never minded, not really. And certainly had never minded basking in the twinned glow of his talent and gratitude, which he had beamed on us like a benediction ever since.

I'd shredded my entire lettuce by the time Marilyn suddenly stopped chopping and put down her knife. "You know the only one Steve never called *sweetie* was Penny. And you know why? Because even then she wasn't his *sweetie*. She was his love."

The welcome, light mood vanished. Dejected, Marilyn dumped her pile of chopped veggies into a bowl. "You know, sometimes I wish we could go back to being in love with Eddie Fisher. Before everything fell apart." A determined don't-dare-make-fun-of-me expression settled on her face. "While we all still thought Eddie Fisher was great."

"Eddie Fisher! I haven't thought about him for forty years."

"See? Our first true love, and you repressed it."

But I remembered now. Penny and Marilyn and I had fallen in love with him right after we'd returned from Camp Chesapeake, a curly-haired teen idol we'd thought was the handsomest man alive. A man who sang with the tongue of an angel! And *Jewish!* We could marry him and our mothers would have to approve! We arranged our schedules so we could watch his fifteen-minute TV show, *Coke Time,* in the privacy of Marilyn's basement. We sighed collectively as he crooned the words to "Oh, My Papa." Unless Marilyn's mother was close by, we screamed as Eddie held out his beckoning arms. We took turns kissing his face on the little black-and-white screen. Each of us hung autographed photos of him on our bedroom walls.

One day, Marilyn read aloud from an article about Eddie Fisher in a movie magazine. "Although it isn't generally known,

134

Eddie Fisher shares a problem well-known to many of his fans." Her voice grew low and dramatic. "Eddie Fisher suffers from acne. The scars and eruptions are invisible on TV only because he wears heavy makeup."

"Eruptions!" Penny was horrified. "Makeup!"

From that moment, the romance was ruined. Penny was too appalled to let it continue. Pimples! How disgusting! We'd been duped! Penny wept bitter, genuine tears.

So for Penny's sake, we ended the relationship with Eddie, with *Coke Time*, with the kissable face of Marilyn's TV. Anxious to placate, Marilyn and I vowed the three of us would fall in love only with *real* boys from then on. It turned out to be a difficult promise. We weren't ready for real boys yet. We were happy loving Eddie. I wondered now — and was sure Marilyn was wondering, too — if that hadn't been the first moment, just for a second, we'd resented giving in to Penny's needs.

But by then we had started seventh grade, our first year at Paul Junior High, and we felt so sorry for Penny that it would have been wrong to resent her, wrong not to try to help. She became a worse student than Steve, getting Fs on three English tests in a row before she discovered she was failing because she couldn't see the board. Her mother took her to an eye doctor who prescribed glasses. They were thick, with tortoiseshell frames that were supposed to complement her red hair. Penny hated them. She had worn them only because she'd hated her nearsightedness more.

We were still lost in memory when Bernie came into the kitchen and plucked a handful of vegetables from Marilyn's bowl. "All talked out already?" He looked quizzically from one of us to the other. "You two are mighty quiet."

"Thinking about Penny," Marilyn said.

"Ah." Bernie popped a slice of celery into his mouth. "Don't get too morose. You had some good years with her when you were younger."

"Younger!" Marilyn savaged an onion with her knife. "She wasn't even fourteen when her childhood was wiped out. Fourteen! All the good stuff gone in the course of a single afternoon!"

"You don't know —" Bernie started to say something and then stopped. "Didn't they say she was only — Only —"

"*Only* molested. Not raped?" Marilyn slapped away the hand Bernie dipped back into the vegetables. "Don't you think mo-lested would have been bad enough?"

"I didn't mean —" Bernie was clearly at a loss. Looking at first surprised, then ad-monished, he wandered out of the room.

Penny had had a dentist appointment the day it had happened. Afterward she'd walked over to Wishner's Upholstery Shop, where her sister Diane worked summers as a receptionist. Diane was to drive her home.

When Penny arrived at the shop, it was deserted. Diane had been sent to run an errand. Wish was at Camp Chesapeake where he still went in the summer, al-though now as a counselor-in-training. Wish's father, Murray, was out giving an estimate. The others were delivering a living-room couch. No one was around ex-cept a laborer who worked on the furni-ture. The man came into the receptionist's area and asked Penny if she needed help. She said she was waiting for Diane. He closed the door behind them. He did things Penny never confided. Later, we were told that Murray arrived just in time to stop whatever was happening, but he could not stop Penny's screaming. Nor did Penny calm down when her sister Diane returned and tried to soothe her. Murray and Diane loaded a hysterical Penny into Murray's car and drove her home.

For a week, Penny wouldn't let anyone into her room. Murray fired the offender, but no one pressed charges because Penny would not speak of the event, even to her parents. She wouldn't talk to Marilyn or me at all. She became so withdrawn that finally the family sent her to New York to stay with her grandmother, hoping she would revive.

For nearly a year, Marilyn and I learned nothing more. When Wish returned from camp before school started, we pressed for details his father might have revealed about the incident, but he knew no more than we did. We sent Penny letters, but she didn't answer. Her sister Diane was back at college. Her sister Charlene would say only that Penny was okay. She was going to a school within sight of her grandmother's building. She was fine.

I wasn't reassured. There was a meanness in brick and concrete, I believed. I had seen it the year before when my family had visited New York: the tall buildings that closed off the sky, the stench and sound of traffic, the dearth of trees. Humans were not meant to be confined within the bounds of masonry. I knew

Penny would come back changed.

And she did. When Penny returned to Washington the summer before we started tenth grade at Coolidge High School, she was someone else. She had become beautiful, but it was not only that. Her skinny body had taken on delicate curves; she had developed small, hard breasts. The fullness had fallen away from her face, leaving her with high cheekbones that set off her aquiline nose and accentuated slanted blue eyes framed by long, long eyelashes. No one had noticed her lashes before because they were such a pale red, but now, coated with mascara, they were elegant, lush. Penny still had freckles, but they didn't matter anymore except to Penny herself. And her hair! No longer carroty, it had grown darker and richer, a perfect Crayola auburn. A stylist had tamed its wildness into a shimmering, shoulder-length corona.

At her grandmother's urging, Penny had even been fitted with a pair of contact lenses. These were the first contacts Marilyn and I had seen, hard pieces of plastic that covered her whole eye. When Penny looked to the side, the outline of the lens was visible, signaling to us that such a large foreign object in the eye must be a torture device. Penny said she didn't care; the lenses didn't hurt and even if they did, she'd wear them anyway. She would do anything to be able to see.

Strange, how easily Marilyn and I were dissuaded from asking what had happened at the upholstery shop. "You can tell us," we whispered when she first returned to town. But after Penny's eyes misted with tears and she shook her head because she couldn't speak, we changed the subject. Maybe we were put off by the changes in her. Maybe we really didn't want know — not yet, not then. And later Penny seemed too vulnerable to ask.

It was clear right away that though Penny knew she was pretty, her transformation gave her no confidence. She longed for my blond hair, for Marilyn's upbeat disposition, for everyone else's strengths. She never saw her own tangle-haired, blue-eyed, narrow-waisted beauty except through other people's eyes. The eyes of boys. When Penny returned home two months before her fifteenth birthday, she'd never had a date. She soon made up for that by going out with more than a dozen boys in the weeks before school started — boys who all told their friends she'd let them feel her up, and some who claimed she'd let them go all the way. Knowing how shy she was, Marilyn and I were as mystified as we were stunned.

But as far as Penny was concerned, chastity was not an issue — at least not enough for her to keep her escapades secret. When she phoned me for reassurance late at night, long after my parents were in bed, what frightened her was never boys, never her impending disgrace, never even the memory of what had happened. What frightened her was the dark.

"Talk to me," she'd demand from the clammy depths of her basement bedroom. "It's black as death down here."

"Turn on the light, Penny. Do it right now." I'd wait until I heard the click of the switch. "I tried to call you before. Where were you?"

"I was out with Sam (or Mel or Joey). I had to help him pick out a birthday present for his mother (or take his father's car to the car wash or return a baseball bat to a friend)."

"You fooled around with him, didn't you?" We'd known these boys since grade school — old friends and neighbors that made Penny's behavior seem incestuous.

"Well, why not? He wanted to so badly."

"Oh, sure . . . why not? You could get

pregnant or you could get a disease."

"I'm not stupid," Penny insisted. "I made him use rubbers —" the term we used in those days for condoms "— and besides, I have a diaphragm." I was horrified to think Penny had actually gone to a doctor and been fitted for a birth-control device. Did Penny's mother know? Or care?

Even then I believed the boys wanted her not just for her beauty, but because the only way they could have her was physically. Part of her appeal was her vacantness, her inscrutable mystery, always that. Yet she had been focused enough to insist on not one form of birth control, but several.

I finished shredding the lettuce and started slicing a tomato. "Here's why I can't imagine her having a baby," I told Marilyn. "Not just because she made up her mind way back at summer camp. But also because boys never stayed with her. They wanted her for a plaything, not a mate. She knew that. And it made her just mad enough that she was determined not to get caught. Even with Steve." I threw the sliced tomato onto the salad, grabbed a cucumber, hacked it apart. My salad for three had grown large enough to feed a dozen people. Marilyn's pile of vegetables, too, would make a stir-fry for an army.

We regarded the food with dawning dismay and might have burst into healing laughter if Marilyn's eyes hadn't suddenly grown wide. "Now I remember!" she said, brandishing her knife.

"Remember what?"

"Who would know where to find Essie Berman! Marcellus Johnson!"

"Who?"

"He brought her to my mother's funeral. The hoodlum Essie took up with after we moved. They were still friends."

"Oh, great. Now you're tracking down hoodlums."

"He hasn't been a hoodlum for years."

I put down my knife. "Absolutely not."

"You could work on it tomorrow," she said. "There's no point sitting outside an operating room when someone is under anesthetic. They're not grateful. It's completely unproductive. Even Bernie knows enough to go to work."

"Look at me, Marilyn," I said, and waited until she did. "The answer is no. It was no at lunchtime and it's no now and it will be no tomorrow."

Marilyn squinted a little. Stealthily, but with considerable drama, she picked up an

143

onion. I knew what she was doing: trying to call up tears. And there they were, right on cue, glistening drops in the corners of her eyes. A deliberate parody of the genuine emotions of earlier in the day.

"Marilyn, this is ridiculous." I laughed because she wanted me to, but I felt ineffably sad as she grinned and wiped her eyes. The night before her surgery, she didn't want to fight.

"I know the act doesn't mean you aren't sincere," I said. "But onions? Onions? Who's the con artist now?"

CHAPTER 8

Surgery

During the night, the weather grew dull and chilly, and as the gray dregs of dawn crept into the kitchen, Marilyn looked as if she were having second thoughts about her face-lift.

"Scared?" I asked.

"Always scared, never chicken." Although her surgery wasn't scheduled until after lunch, Marilyn had to be at the clinic early for pre-op tests, and she was dressed in the clothes she'd been advised to wear for the trip home later that evening: sweatpants and a button-down shirt, since she wouldn't be able to pull anything over what would be her sore, swollen face. Her hair was covered by a turban, a relic of the chemo days. She'd been instructed to shampoo before she left home, and not to rinse out the conditioner.

"The idea is that I won't wash my hair again for a couple of days, and by then it'll be all nice and silky."

Instructed not to eat or drink after midnight, Marilyn watched Bernie chew his toast with such concentration that he finally abandoned it on his plate. She insisted he go to work. "Barbara can drop me off, she doesn't have anything to do," she told him. "Then she can run her errands." As if I *had* errands. "The surgery isn't till one, so why should either of you lose your morning? Then I'll be under the knife three or four hours, so you can probably work all day. If I'm out early, I'll call you." As if she were having a tooth filled, or a pesky mole removed.

Of course, Bernie wouldn't really stay at his office. He'd come to the clinic the minute he knew Marilyn had been taken to pre-op and spend the day in the waiting room. I'd be there, too. It was crazy, letting her plot our schedules so it wouldn't seem we were concerned about her, but she'd made such a fuss about it that we agreed.

By the time we left the house, the rush hour had ended and a gray drizzle had started. The plastic surgery clinic was in Rockville, a sprawling modern testimony to the buying power of aging women. The airy reception area had vaulted ceilings, expanses of glass looking out onto dense green foliage, burgundy couches arranged on dove-gray carpets. On the pale walls, a thick, modernistic burgundy stripe had

146

been painted at eye-level, tracing the angle of the ceiling. Several women sat reading magazines, but no one seemed to have touched the pamphlets about laser skin resurfacing.

"Do you have an appointment?" a receptionist asked from behind her glass cage.

"Marilyn Waxman."

The woman consulted a list on her desk and nodded. "Surgery's upstairs." She buzzed us in, pointed us to an elevator.

"There's still time to change your mind," I said.

Lips tight, she shook her head.

The upper floor was a complete surgical suite: operating rooms A, B and C, and yet another glassed-in reception area. With a show of bravado, Marilyn checked herself in and was whisked off for tests and prepping while I was shown to the waiting area. I drank a cup of coffee from the urn on a table. I flipped through the selection of magazines without picking one up. The elevator opened and out walked Bernie, clutching his briefcase as if, after all, he really did plan to work all day.

"Did they take her back?"

"A while ago."

"We should probably have lunch," he said.

I wasn't hungry and could tell he wasn't,

either, but my watch said noon so we followed the signs to the snack bar and got sandwiches. Back in the waiting area, Bernie set his briefcase on an end table, shrugged off his suit jacket, and pulled at the knot in his tie as if in for a long siege.

"We had a meeting with the doctor the other day," he told me. "Marilyn won't be out of surgery until at least four o'clock. Then she goes to recovery, and then 'post-recovery' — whatever the hell *that* is — where we can see her.

"In the meantime there's nothing for us to do. I know you want to go out to the cemetery. I think you should."

"I'd be too worried," I said.

"I'll call if there's any reason to. Do you have a cell phone?"

I didn't.

"Here, take Marilyn's." He reached into his briefcase and drew it out. "She won't be needing it today."

"I can't just *leave*."

"You can. You should. You always procrastinate till the last minute about going to see your parents' graves, and you're never happy until after you go." Bernie took my hand, leaned close, kissed me on the cheek. "Go," he said.

So I did.

I reached the cemetery half an hour later, a hilly expanse of lawn and a few shade trees set behind tall fences in the midst of what had once been rural pastureland but was now suburban sprawl. The bit of woods on one side and tall apartment buildings on the other were far enough in the distance to give me a sense of being in a carefully tended park. Hard as it always was to make myself come there, it was a surprisingly peaceful place.

My parents were in the "new" section, thirty or forty years old, where raised headstones were not allowed, just plaques that lay flush with the ground. The identical bronze markers, engraved with tendrils of vines and flowers, were inscribed in graceful block letters: Harold "Harry" Cohen, Devoted Husband and Father, 1912–1985; Ida Marmelstein Cohen, Musician, Devoted Wife and Mother, 1915–1985.

My father, a pharmacist, hadn't thought his profession important enough to be on the plaque (most people didn't), but he'd put my mother's on hers. At age seventy, she had been killed in an auto accident less than an hour after doing what she liked best: playing her clarinet in an orchestra at the National Gallery of Art. A snowstorm had started halfway through the concert, and the violinist who always drove her home skidded on icy Sixteenth Street and rammed into a telephone pole. He was injured only slightly, but my mother was jettisoned onto the street.

Though I was in my midforties then, I felt too young to lose a parent. Wells and I were divorced. Robin was practically grown. I was alone. At the cemetery, Marilyn and Bernie stood on either side of my father and Robin and me, forming a protective shield. Trudi and her husband huddled next to us. We were all very stoic.

Afterward, as we were getting out of the car back at my parents' apartment, Steve emerged from the building and held out his arms. He had canceled a singing engagement and come straight from the airport. "Oh, sweetie, I'm so sorry I couldn't get here sooner. I'm so sorry."

It was then, clinging to him, that I began to weep — uncontrollably, for nearly half an hour, stopping only because Robin seemed so alarmed. I wasn't sure, later, if my outburst was prompted by grief for my mother or gratitude to Steve for allowing me — years before, while there was still plenty of time — to forgive my mother for what I had once considered her terrible crimes. For making me take piano lessons even before I could read, for wanting her daughters to learn music the way other children in Riggs Park learned Hebrew, for watching with horror (after Trudi threw a temper tantrum and quit piano forever) as I, too, turned out to lack that innate sense of rhythm that might have made music come out my fingers instead of the cacophony that emerged even though I could hear the cadence perfectly well in my head.

I couldn't really read music, either, any more than Steve could read words. "I never heard of anyone who could follow the treble clef but not the bass," my mother said. Her tone was kind — more like "probably we need a therapist for this" than "you stupid fool" — but the words sat against my heart like a red-hot brand. If not for illiterate, talented Steve waiting for my help two doors away, I surely would have been scarred.

Struggling with Steve over his homework day after day, I saw that he had no more power over words than I did over music — and that my mother, like Steve's teachers, was only confused and frustrated and never meant to be cruel. I recalled that even when Trudi and I were tiny, at the hour when other parents were reading bedtime stories, my mother had gone them one better and provided her children with music, too. She'd tucked us in, opened the latest box of reeds that had arrived for her clarinet, and regaled us with the musical themes from all the characters in *Peter and the Wolf*, while testing each reed for tonal quality and strength. Reed number one: the twittery bird; number two: the silly duck; then the sly cat and cheerful Peter, the booming grandfather (in a real concert, she reminded us, he would be played by the bassoon), the menacing wolf whose music really belonged to three French horns. Other times she found a reed of such good quality that she abandoned Peter altogether and played some favorite tune in its entirety: "Morning Mood" from the *Peer Gynt Suite*, the theme from *Swan Lake*, something sweet and haunting, such an ecstasy of sound that our childish crankiness vanished and we were hypnotized, bewitched, asleep. Compared with the uplifting power of music, Trudi and I realized, we were only grubby, earthbound things. How could our mother possibly choose us over *that?* Yet, those enchanted evenings when she sat at our bedside and not in some theater or concert hall, she did. She did!

And later, when other girls hated their mothers because they were becoming women themselves, for me it was just the opposite. It was Steve who finally said, "Sweetie, if piano lessons make you so miserable, the best thing you can do is give them up." And I did. My mother seemed relieved. From that time on, I no longer resented that my mother's eyes shone and a distant joyfulness settled over her features whenever she played (or sometimes merely listened to) music. Now I was transported, too, given over to the same universal language. If I had never been able to reproduce music with my fingers, I understood it very well with my ears, whether I was listening to Chopin or Bill Haley or Steve's increasingly remarkable singing. Oh, I understood! It was the gift she'd passed on to me. I never resented her again.

That was what I thought about, safely cradled against Steve's ample shoulder, the day my mother was laid into her grave.

It was a sad truth, I thought, that people did not always rejoice in the good fortune of friends who prospered. They were jealous, and they did not wish them well. But for Steve, I was always genuinely glad. He'd shown me what I would have learned nowhere else: that all lives are shaped like melody, each with its own theme, its trills, its path. We were all composers, after all.

"Mom, I think you always knew that," I whispered as I set a stone on top of her marker, and another on my father's. He'd died only three months after she had, of what doctors called an embolism, but what Trudi and I knew was a broken heart.

"Well, guys, you've got a nice spot here," I said, pushing my mind beyond the sadness and trying to think only of how devoted they'd been, which always made me smile. The only big blowup they'd ever had was when my mother had been irritated by something and had told my father she wasn't going to be buried in this cemetery at all, but cremated and thrown to the winds. My father, the product of a traditional Jewish upbringing that forbade cremation, had been horrified — which was all the more ridiculous because as an adult he hadn't been religious at all. We went to services on the high holidays only because my mother wanted to hear the bittersweet strains of the "Aveinu Malkeinu" or the haunting melody of the "Kol Nidre." It wasn't that we didn't believe in God, just that we believed in music more. But cremation? Impossible. My father had been so insistent that finally my mother had agreed.

Beyond that, the one Jewish tenet my parents had held dear was also the operative principle of my childhood: *Tikkun Olam.* Repair the world. Religious or not, if you were Jewish, repairing the broken world was the mission God had assigned you. My father was practicing *Tikkun Olam* by dispensing medicine to heal the body, my mother by dispensing sounds to soothe the soul. Trudi and I would find our own paths when we grew up. Our parents took this very seriously.

And for me and Marilyn, *Tikkun Olam* was a handy principle to apply to Penny and Steve. If we had to spend extra time teaching Steve something that seemed obvious, or comforting Penny about imagined slights that shouldn't have upset her in the first place, we'd whisper, *Tikkun Olam* and try to be patient. The dyslexic brother and hypersensitive girlfriend were probably the projects God had in mind for us. Helping them would help repair the world.

Once more I touched the stones I'd set atop each of my parents' graves and blew them a kiss as I turned to walk away. "I'm glad I got to talk to you," I said. "And on such a nice day, too." After the morning rain, a brilliant sun had come out. I was aware of being an aging child speaking to parents who couldn't hear me, but this was what I always did. There was no one within earshot, so I didn't feel foolish.

I wandered aimlessly around the cemetery for a long while. Just as I couldn't bring myself here easily, it was also hard to leave. The grass was the rich green it often was in spring and again in fall before it went dormant; the sunlight was warm but not oppressive. Beyond the fence, brilliant trees burned in the sharply angled light. Autumn afternoons were often like this in Washington, the golden sunbeams so intense and precious they might have been conscious of their own impermanence, keenly aware they were about to fade. When I stopped, I realized my feet must have known all along where they were going. Carolyn Waxman, the headstone read. Beloved Infant Daughter of Marilyn Ginsburg Waxman and Bernard Waxman. Beside it were the two burial plots that would one day shelter her parents.

It struck me that, even as I stood there, Marilyn lay unconscious on an operating table, the skin lifted from her face, the underlying muscles being tugged taut, monitors assuring that her disease-ravaged body was surviving this latest trauma, in the struggle to buy her peace of mind.

How, even for a second, could I have forgotten that?

It took forever to get back to the clinic. A wreck just south of Rockville blocked traffic for nearly an hour. It wasn't until I finally arrived, breathless, that I realized I could have used Marilyn's cell phone to check in with Bernie at any time. What did that say about my state of mind?

"Any word?" I asked. He was alone in the waiting room. The patients from the earlier surgeries must have gone home.

"She's in the recovery room. We can see her pretty soon in 'post-recovery.' So far so good."

I picked up *People* magazine and flipped through the pages, not seeing a single picture. After an eternity, a nurse emerged, wearing green scrub pants and a cheery white smock decorated with smiley faces. She led us across the hall into 'post-recovery,' where a series of cubicles were shielded by aqua curtains.

The minute we stepped inside the one she indicated, I understood why Penny had fled in tears years ago when Marilyn and I had had our noses done. Sitting in what looked like a cross between a recliner and a hospital bed, Marilyn was moonfaced and pale, barely recognizable, a huge pressure bandage covering her entire head except for her face. It seemed clear that she'd made a terrible mistake. The corners of her mouth were pulled back toward her ears; her wrinkles, if she'd ever had any, were hidden beneath the bloated swelling. What threatened to be a nasty bruise had begun to form in the area that had once been her right cheekbone. If there had been jowls . . . well, jowls no longer seemed to be the issue.

Bernie bent over and mimicked kissing Marilyn on the lips without actually touching her. "So?"

"No pain to speak of. I wasn't nauseous when I woke up. Thank God for modern anesthetics. They keep trying to get me to eat a cracker so I can take medicine by mouth and get rid of this IV." She gestured toward the line that ran from the back of her left hand toward a bottle of saline solution. "But I can't. It hurts too much to chew. Nobody told me a face-lift would make your jaw sore."

"Maybe because of the incisions behind your ear," I said, having been treated to a complete clinical description of the surgery the previous night.

Marilyn eyed Bernie suspiciously. "I thought you were going to work."

"I did," he said, and consulted his watch. "It's after five."

Marilyn considered this, accepted it. They chatted a while longer before she shooed him out. "Barbara can drive me home."

Reluctant but obedient, Bernie agreed he'd see her at home later.

"The worst part," Marilyn confessed after he'd gone, "was my heart beating so fast. It scares you."

"Your heart was beating fast?" Mine was, too.

"After I woke up. They said it was all right on the operating table. They gave me something to slow it down. It's a little better now. I'll be fine."

Why hadn't Marilyn mentioned this in front of Bernie? The thought made me slightly woozy. I had never been good in hospitals. Maybe I was only hungry. I'd eaten nothing since that ratty snack-bar sandwich at lunch. Another nurse came in (this one with yellow daisies on her smock), and handed Marilyn a can of Sprite.

"How about a sip for a thirsty friend?" I asked when the nurse disappeared.

"Have at it. I don't want it anyway."

I drank half the can in a giant gulp. Waited for the sugar rush to steady me. Felt better.

"So tell me. What did you do today?" Marilyn asked. "Did you get to the cemetery?"

"I did." I would have told her about the traffic tie-up on the way back, but Marilyn looked too pathetic to care. She raised the hand free of IVs to her neck, found the pulse, pretended she was scratching rather than checking it.

"What's wrong?"

"Nothing."

"Marilyn, tell me."

"I just wish my heart would beat a little slower."

Why weren't they monitoring her more closely? Wooziness replaced by anger, I stood and marched out to find the nurse.

"It's probably from the epinephrine," the nurse said, unsurprised. "It's used during surgery to keep the bleeding down, but it increases the pulse. The maximum reaction comes a couple hours later. The doctor gave her something."

"You need to check her pulse right now," I demanded.

The anesthesiologist showed up next, a

160

George Stephanopoulos look-alike with dark hair hanging in his eyes. "Nothing serious, just scary," he drawled, though he seemed mildly alarmed. "You're full of different kinds of medicine. I guarantee you by tomorrow morning it'll be better." Then he adjusted his stethoscope. "But I'll tell you what. The clinic closes in an hour. It isn't really set up for overnight stays. Considering your history, I bet you'd be more comfortable if we sent you over to the hospital for the night instead of sending you home. It's a good precaution."

Precaution, hell. Who did they think they were fooling? The too-casual attitude. The nonchalant drawl. What the hell was wrong with them? They had messed up.

In the ambulance, I held Marilyn's hand. For once — maybe the first time in her life — Marilyn didn't try to make jokes.

CHAPTER 9

Sisters

Sometimes, when a heart beats too fast or a cell begins dividing too freely, the danger is not from the activity itself but from its continuing too long. At least this was my theory as the ambulance raced toward the hospital. Since my own heart skipped beats and raced and scared me half to death when I lied, it comforted me to think that as long as the unwanted behavior stopped soon enough, it was no problem. The peril was only in the habit.

At the hospital, everything was fast, efficient, cold. Marilyn was whisked off to a room, poked, prodded, EKG'd. A thin balding doctor took charge like a general directing a war, white lab coat flapping as he barked commands. Outside the room, I paced and fidgeted. When Bernie arrived, he looked like he'd run up the stairs. The doctor — Walter DeLoach, his name tag read — finally stepped out, chart in hand, to talk to us.

"I know you're worried, but all the tests are fine so far. If it weren't for her history they probably wouldn't even have sent her. An episode of tachycardia —" he paused and adjusted wire glasses on his sweaty nose as if trying to assess our intelligence "— that's a fancy term for rapid heartbeat — isn't dangerous as long as it doesn't last too long."

My theory confirmed.

"So what caused it?" Bernie asked.

"We'll probably never know for sure. It could be some of the medication or a mild drug allergy. Or — who knows?"

Bernie was so ashen that the doctor added quickly, "She should be out of here tomorrow. Think of this as a wise precaution. One step away from a false alarm."

"Does that make you feel better?" Bernie asked when the doctor left.

"Not even a little bit."

"Me, either."

But Marilyn seemed no worse; in fact, grateful for the institutional security of the hospital with its high-tech equipment. The Waxmans' younger son, Andrew, arrived after work, a young man with Marilyn's face and Bernie's thick body, but taller and bulkier than either of them. He resembled a large, gentle teddy bear. "So tell me, Mom. How is it that you make it home in record time after your cancer surgery, but a face-lift does you in?"

The corners of Marilyn's overstretched mouth turned up. "It's more like a controlled weight-loss program," Marilyn maintained. "If your heart beats fast enough, your metabolism goes through the ceiling."

Andrew soon left, but Bernie and I kept our vigil. By late evening, Marilyn's pulse was down to ninety. "You can go home now," she told us. "I'll be fine."

Bernie's complexion metamorphosed from flushed to beety. "I'll decide when to leave." His tone was gruff. "No more pretending. What if this had been serious? Am I supposed to lose you to something stupid like a face-lift because we're acting like you're only having an ingrown toenail fixed and I ought to be at work? What the hell is the matter with us?"

Marilyn looked to me for support, but I shook my head. "He's right, Marilyn. We're here because we care about you. Why do you keep trying to send us away?"

"When you start that cancer treatment," Bernie added, "don't ask me to pretend it's not happening. Don't behave like it's business as usual. I'm coming with you. If the mood strikes, I'm going to damn well sit there the whole time and hold your hand."

Having made this unaccustomed speech, Bernie settled into the recliner provided for relatives who planned to stay the night, and ten minutes later was sound asleep. When he started snoring, I took Marilyn's hand. "Tell me," I said. "How do you really feel?"

Marilyn settled against her pillow, let her swollen features relax. "You know, when my heart first started racing, they thought I was nervous. They asked if I wanted to hear some music and they gave me this little Walkman with earphones that fit over the bandage."

She mimicked placing earphones gingerly over her ears.

"It was a nice tape. Not one of Steve's, but not bad. But when things inside you aren't going right, you can't concentrate enough to let music calm you down. You get too turned in on yourself to listen. All you can concentrate on is . . . your own internal *stuff*."

She turned to me for confirmation. I nodded.

"Today after my heart calmed down, you know what it made me think about? Penny. Not just because of everything we've talked about the past couple of days, but because —"

She stopped. I waited.

"— because by high school that's how Penny was, wasn't it? Listening to all the bad stuff inside her. She didn't really hear anything else. Don't you think?"

"Even before high school," I agreed. "Penny was turned in on herself right from the beginning."

"So we couldn't really have helped her, could we? I know we made some mistakes, but maybe it wouldn't have made any difference."

Marilyn shifted in the bed, agitated again. What was I supposed to say? Both of us had always felt we could have done better by Penny. I squeezed Marilyn's clammy hand.

"I still wish we'd had the guts not to pledge that sorority," she said.

"Me, too," I told her, and meant it.

It had been the fall of 1956, just after Penny had returned from New York and discovered the joy of boys, just after the three of us had begun tenth grade at Coolidge High School. Clubs like Young Judea served both genders from both sides of town. For boys who preferred the fraternity route, AZA was the religion-oriented choice, while ULPS and Mu Sig were the social ones. For girls, there were two Jewish sororities. Marilyn and I had been planning to pledge for more than a year.

We'd arrived at this decision through what I later saw as convoluted thinking, but at the time believed was perfectly logical. As children of Riggs Park, we'd been taught that the important things were what we carried with us — intelligence, learning, talent, skills. Material things, as the Germans had so skillfully shown during the war, could easily be taken away. On the other hand, our parents had hinted, since the Depression had kept them from developing their own talents fully, we should try to catch up. We must not forget the Germans, but we must forge ahead.

Pledging a sorority, Marilyn and I believed, was the way to do this. At Paul Junior High, where for the first time we were no longer segregated by neighborhood, we met classmates from Sixteenth Street and North Portal Estates whose fathers were doctors, dentists, real-estate moguls; who were, by Riggs Park standards, rich. Their luxurious lifestyle must be what our parents meant by "catching up."

Just look! Our new friend, Rozelle Goodman, lived in a house with not one but two remarkable features: wall-to-wall carpet and central air. Rozelle, we were sure, was the type to pledge sorority in tenth grade.

"Well, it might be very nice for you girls to see what a sorority is like before you make a big commitment like living in a sorority house when you get to college," Marilyn's mother, Shirley, surprised us by saying one day. Marilyn and I eyed each other. We all knew none of us would ever live in a sorority house. We would go to college in D.C. and live at home. There was no money for anything grander. Seeing Shirley so starry-eyed touched us. While my own mother had an independent life as a musician, Shirley had only her hopes for Marilyn. Steve was never going to be a scholar. Shirley had never gone to college. She wanted Marilyn to have all the education and social life she'd missed, beginning with a sorority membership at Coolidge High.

When Marilyn and I posed the idea of pledging to Penny, she was indifferent. "What do I need with a sorority? I don't even know any of the members all that well."

"Of course you do," we told her.

"Well, who?"

I struggled to name a few, but Penny wasn't convinced.

"The truth is, she likes people's approval," Marilyn told me in private. "Why else would she bed down with all those boys?"

After the wild end of summer that had earned Penny her bad reputation, we reasoned that if a whole sorority gave her its blessing, Penny would feel less need to offer up her body.

Besides, by the time school started, she was dating Joel Gordon, the quarterback on Coolidge's football team. As Steve pointed out, this could be an important plus. "Your snazzy sorority buddies won't care what she does with Joel in private as long as she shows him off at their social functions."

"Very nice, Steve. Very delicate," Marilyn sniffed.

"Watch. Somebody'll offer to bring her up. Wait and see." Steve turned out to be right. Joel Gordon was as socially desirable as Penny was questionable. Three upperclass members offered to "bring up" Penny, when she needed only two.

"You owe it to yourself to pledge," Marilyn and I urged when Penny still hesitated. We were convinced of the rightness of this move. Penny was often too dreamy to act in her own best interests. "Think about us, if not yourself," I said. "How will we feel if our best friend won't pledge with us?" Outmaneuvered, Penny finally agreed.

We had been told how annoying pledging could be: carrying gum and mints for the members at all times, carrying a little notebook where demerits could be recorded if we failed to comply. But the activities were more fun than we expected. While the members planned the big Christmas Night Dance at the Sheraton Park Hotel, the pledges manned bake sales, visited an old-age home, helped handicapped children into their coats after class and wheeled them down ramps to waiting buses. On Wednesdays after school, we discussed these charitable efforts at our pledge meetings. Elaine Marshall, the pledge mistress, was as sweet as she was cute. Marilyn and I were elected co-vice-presidents of the pledge class, and Francine Ades, who lived across Riggs Road on Chillum Place, became the treasurer.

On Sunday afternoons, the pledges had to attend regular sorority meetings at various members' houses. Here we sat in a separate room waiting to be "brought down" and questioned. Though the waiting was tense, I believed it made us closer.

Members and pledges alike arrived at the meetings dressed up in skirt-and-sweater sets and heels. We emerged from cars in groups of three and four, smoothing skirts, touching freshly painted nails to just-washed hair. Inside, the scents of our perfumes mingled — a fresh and interesting effect, never sour. Standing among the well-dressed, sweet-smelling girls who would soon be our sisters, Marilyn and Penny and I felt part of something large, secret, different from anything we had known. The perfume tickled our nostrils, the word floated on our tongues. We loved the sound of it: *sorority.*

Members had such power over us that they could discuss anything about a pledge that seemed either outstanding or unbecoming. They could even blackball any girl they didn't think would be an asset, though no one had ever heard of that happening. Marilyn and I felt as all the other pledges did, anxious never to do anything to make the members think we were unworthy. Penny didn't seem to care as much, but mostly she went along.

All through the fall, there were more social events than any of us had ever gone to in a single semester. Mixers, teas, parties. Lacking a regular boyfriend, a pledge had to find a series of boys to escort her. This was never a problem, given the prestige of the sorority, though Marilyn complained it made her ask Bernie out more than she wanted.

"Why not admit it, you're asking him because you like him," I said.

"I'm asking him because he's convenient. It's not that I don't like him. He's okay. He's not the love of my life."

Hearing Marilyn say that, I suddenly knew that he was.

The social season culminated in the formal Christmas Night Dance, with a live band and a memory book that listed everyone and their dates. Penny was the only one I'd ever heard say anything against it. "We can rent the ballroom Christmas night because a Jewish sorority is the only group that wants it," she asserted. "But imagine if you were part of the help. No one wants to work Christmas night."

Penny's comments seemed sour and unfair, a slur against the sorority. But they didn't stop her from bringing Joel Gordon to the dance.

Marilyn came with Bernie, as I knew she would. And I got up the nerve to ask Wish, in that innocent time before I knew I was going to fall in love with him.

That night, Penny and Joel Gordon danced belly-to-belly even when the music didn't call for it. Marilyn and I were both disturbed that she'd do such a thing in front of so many members. Most of the other pledges, wisely, didn't dance close at all.

After the dance, everyone went home to change clothes before the party at the house of the sorority's president. It was such a relief to shed long-line bras and layers of crinolines under semiformal dresses that by the time we reached the party, the mood was giddy. The basement was dim and cool. A few of the senior members, girls who were pinned or even engaged, started making out with their boyfriends. Bernie held Marilyn close during the slow songs on the record player. Marilyn admitted later that, under the spell of the soft music, her stomach had churned in such a pleasant way that she let Bernie press against her as tight as he wanted.

Wish and I danced, too, but we maintained a little distance since it was our first date. We stopped dancing when we spotted Penny sitting on Joel Gordon's lap, kissing him and stroking his neck. Not a single other pledge was making out. Penny looked small and slender in her skirt and sweater, but her hair was disheveled and her face smudged with a serious, desperate expression that I supposed was the look people got when they were ready to have sex. There was something wrong with Penny — with the desperation on her face, with what she was doing, what she would do later. It occurred to me then that this — *this* — was why they called girls *bad*.

Joel Gordon broke up with Penny a few weeks later. To Marilyn and me, this seemed inevitable, though we couldn't have said why. Penny showed no emotion. Instead, she stepped up her social life, going out with one boy after another even on weeknights.

Whenever the three of us were together, I found myself picturing Penny on Joel Gordon's lap at Christmas. It seemed wrong to behave so seriously and desperately about a person if you were not going to set aside even a single weekend to mourn him. For the first time since kindergarten, I didn't feel sorry for Penny and want to protect her; for the first time, I wanted to give her a piece of my mind.

Marilyn felt the same way. We agreed to have a little talk with her.

"I think you're making a mistake," I told

Penny on the appointed day. "I mean, you can't really want to go out with just everybody."

"You ought to find just one or two boys you really like," Marilyn added.

"You think so? Well, I'm looking." Penny's tone was flip, but Marilyn and I knew she felt hurt and bitter. She kept going out with anyone who asked.

Steve was one of the few who didn't take Penny on a date during that time, and who sounded worried every time he mentioned Penny's name. "She better watch it. She's only safe with someone who'll look out for her." If he were Penny's boyfriend, he said, he'd never tell what went on between them. "But most guys don't think like that." He was picking out a new song on the guitar, strumming the same chord over and over. I knew he was writing the song for Penny, who was on his mind all the time. Accustomed to being the smart one, I hated to admit Steve was right about Penny's need for protection.

Yet I heard the truth in what he said. Penny seemed to let boys touch her in some important way that other girls never did, even girls like Francine Ades, who was also known for being easy. It was unthinkable, given the standards that prevailed in those days, to sleep with a boy you weren't married to (or at least engaged). But Francine got away with it because she viewed sex as an act of kindness, no more important than offering a drink of water to someone with a wicked thirst. Afterward, Francine talked to her lovers about algebra, sports, politics — business as usual. She was running for sophomore-class treasurer, and all the boys helped with her campaign. They wanted to pay Francine back because they knew she had done them a favor. With Penny, it seemed the other way around.

During Easter week, just before the pledges were usually let into the sorority, Penny went out three nights in a row with a boy named Allan Kessler. He had been dating Darlene Zimmer, a member who was spending Easter in Florida with her parents. No one liked the idea of Penny moving in on another member's boyfriend. This was more a matter of principle than a vote of sympathy for Darlene, a brusque, authoritarian girl who served as the sorority's parliamentarian.

The pledges never knew what Darlene actually said to the members, because we were sitting upstairs during the Sunday-afternoon meeting while the members met in the basement. But the story got around that when Darlene returned from Florida, Allan told her he'd taken Penny out just to see what he could get, and it turned out to be quite a lot. "He's asked me to take him back," Darlene supposedly said, "but I'm not sure I can after that." Tears reportedly came to Darlene's eyes, which no one would have believed because of her toughness.

She could not bear the thought of belonging to a sorority with a girl who would do something like that, Darlene had sobbed; she could not bear the thought of the entire group being tainted by Penny's reputation. She invoked social rules the way she invoked Robert's Rules, but with considerably more emotion. Something had to be done.

Outside the sun was bright, the tulips blooming, the grass a sudden green. The den where the pledges sat was warm and stuffy. All twenty-two of us believed, secretly, that this was the day we were going to be made members. The initiation ceremony was secret but very beautiful, we had been told. Usually we were brought down in pairs. That day Penny was called first. She was called alone. She was gone for perhaps ten minutes, but to us the time seemed interminable.

When Penny came back upstairs, Elaine the pledge mistress was by her side. They were both silent, with hard grim expressions on their faces. Penny did not return to the den. She walked through the hallway and out the door. She held herself stiffly, as if she wanted to cry but wouldn't give them the satisfaction. Marilyn and I knew we ought to follow her. We knew Penny was waiting for her mother to pick her up. We remembered Penny waiting just like this in elementary school, after the boys called her Red. For a moment, it was as if nothing had changed in all the years since, and the least we could do was go to her. Both of us felt an aching in our chests at the sight of Penny, standing so stiffly in the sun, her bright hair cheerful as ever. But both of us froze. Our legs would not move to carry us out of the den. We kept smelling the perfume the other pledges were wearing, seeing their long, stockinged legs under springtime skirts, and it was as if going out that door would be the end of the large, secret thing we were part of, and neither of us could bear it.

Francine Ades finally whispered to the pledge mistress, "What happened?"

"You'll find out in a minute." Helen

Weinberg's car pulled up to the front of the house, and Penny got in. Then all the pledges were called downstairs at once and lined up against the wall.

"A very serious thing has happened," the president said. She spoke in a low, dramatic tone. "We've had to ask one of you to depledge."

A murmur went through the pledges, though all of us expected this.

"This is something we don't do lightly, girls," the president said. It was done only in a case of utmost seriousness when a girl turned out not to have the qualities — the ethical and moral qualities — that the sorority expected of its members. She hoped this would serve as an example of the sorority's serious commitment to admitting only girls of good character. The basement was cool, lit with recessed lights. The members stared at the pledges without blinking. Darlene Zimmer's mouth was drawn into a tight line. Everyone knew what Allan must have told her about his dates with Penny. I tried to catch Marilyn's eye, but Marilyn was looking at the floor.

Afterward, I went to Marilyn's house because neither of us wanted to be alone. We didn't know quite what to do. Seeing us come in without Penny, Steve demanded to hear the story. He said, "You have no choice but to depledge." His words fell on our ears like stinging shards of glass. Of course, he was right. We had to stand up for Penny. We always had. And especially now. As officers of the pledge class and Penny's good friends, it was our duty.

We were being sucked into a whirlpool. There was no way out. For the rest of the afternoon, we made our plans. We'd ask to be brought down together at next Sunday's meeting. We would make a little speech about fairness and, at the end, depledge. Marilyn, who knew something about politics, said that was the most dramatic, the most effective way.

All week Penny stayed home and isolated, just as she'd done as a child when the boys had called her Red and as an adolescent after the incident at Wishner's Upholstery Shop. Helen Weinberg said Penny had the flu. Marilyn and I called every afternoon, but were told Penny didn't want to come to the phone. When we knocked on Penny's door, Mrs. Weinberg said Penny was sleeping.

On Sunday, Marilyn and I were sick with nerves and shame. Once we depledged, no sorority member would speak to us. We'd been careful not to tell anyone what we were up to. We almost wrote Penny a note about it, but in the end we decided she would find out soon enough.

At the meeting, we asked to be brought down together and the pledge mistress said all right. The pledges started being taken down five at a time, which was odd. When it was our turn, Marilyn and I were blindfolded at the top of the stairs. A pleasant melody reached us as we descended in the dark. We could make out the voices of a choir, the words of a song. At the bottom of the steps, our blindfolds were removed. We stood in cool half darkness, illuminated by halos of yellow flame. The smiling members stood before us, each with a lit candle in her hand. They were singing the initiation song. So before Marilyn and I could depledge, we were members.

As the scent of perfume rose into the candlelit darkness, Marilyn and I didn't think about Penny or about the happiness Marilyn's mother would feel knowing her daughter had been installed after all. We didn't think of any one person or one thing because we were part of something larger. We were warm and complete. At the same moment, in the grip of the same emotion, we whispered to each other, "Sisters."

We went back to Marilyn's house afterward. When we walked into the living room, Penny was sitting on the sofa with Steve. He was playing the song he'd written for her on his guitar. Penny looked beautiful and desperate. The music was sweet, but we were part of a sorority now — we couldn't help it — and knew that Steve and Penny could only cause us shame.

CHAPTER 10

Old Neighbors

In the hospital, still clinging to my hand, Marilyn had fallen into a fitful sleep. Her fingers loosened their grip, then tensed again and held on, while her eyes darted about beneath closed lids. Beside us in the recliner, Bernie snored lightly. After a few minutes, Marilyn jerked awake and said, as if her nap had never interrupted our conversation, "Who am I fooling? Who says high school didn't make any difference? We treated Penny like shit."

"Like *shit?* Don't you think that's a little strong?" I forced a little laugh. "Maybe we were selfish teenage pukes. Maybe we acted accordingly. But treat Penny like *shit?* Come on, Marilyn."

"We avoided her because we had all that sorority stuff to talk about. Snuck around to go shopping without her. To go to the movies without her. Don't say we didn't."

"Only because we didn't want to talk in front of her about things it would be hard for her to hear," I murmured, truly alarmed now. "And Penny never seemed to care. Think about it. She really didn't. She was still our friend. She never got angry or upset."

"Just because she never said anything didn't mean she didn't care!" Marilyn sat up straighter in the hospital bed, already rolled nearly upright because of the drains behind her ears. As if bewildered, she lifted her hand to her face, patted her bandages, looked uncomprehendingly toward the darkened window, then with dawning recognition at Bernie now stirring in the recliner. "Let's get out of here," she said.

In an instant, Bernie was fully awake and on his feet. "Relax, Marilyn. It's just for one night."

"I mean it. I want to go home." Her tone carried a thread of panic.

"What's the point?" Bernie shrugged with great nonchalance. "So you can walk the floors? So you can worry about yourself? Here they're keeping an eye on you."

"I'm not worrying about myself! I'm thinking about Penny." Marilyn threw the covers back and flung her legs over the edge of the bed.

Bernie clasped her wrist, held it tight. "Relax," he said again. "What do you think you can do for Penny in the middle of the night? Remember what Felicia used to say?"

"Who's Felicia?" I asked.

Marilyn grew still for a moment, then turned a worried, swollen face to Bernie, sighed, and leaned back against her pillow.

"Felicia said you wouldn't forget the relaxation exercises. You could revive them anytime you needed."

"It's been three years," Marilyn muttered.

"Who's Felicia?" I asked again.

"Then maybe you should call her," Bernie said. "Get a quick refresher course."

I might not have been in the room.

Five minutes later, Marilyn was propped up in bed doing deep-breathing exercises, and I had been dismissed. A nurse had checked Marilyn's pulse; everything was under control.

"You might as well go back to the house and get some sleep. One of us should." Bernie walked me to the elevator with a firm hand on my shoulder as if he feared I might change my mind. Felicia, he explained, was a holistic healer Marilyn had consulted during her chemo, who had helped calm her down.

"I know how it sounds — 'holistic healer.' I had doubts myself. But she was okay. Marilyn had no hair. Her nerves were shot. Felicia taught her deep breathing, biofeedback. Told her to take vitamins and some herbs I don't think did any harm." He punched the elevator button.

"Some — hippie healer," I said. "I talked to Marilyn every day on the phone and never heard a word about any Felicia."

"Felicia's not a hippie. She's a doctor's wife, fifty years old, who wears designer jeans. Don't feel bad, I think Marilyn was afraid people would think she was a weirdo if she mentioned it. She didn't even tell *me* at first. You can be around somebody all your life and still not know them as well as you think."

"As I'm finding out," I said. It amazed me that Marilyn still felt guilty about high school. That she felt there was no way to make it up. That — at what might be the end of her life — she was hoping Penny had a grown son or daughter she could do better by than she'd done by the mother. This had nothing to do with Steve. Not really.

The elevator door opened, and Bernie patted me on the shoulder as if to ease me inside. "Get some sleep, Barbara," he said. "In the morning we'll all feel better."

I realized that sleeping was not on the agenda.

Tikkun Olam, I thought. The piece of my world that most needed healing was Marilyn. And what Marilyn wanted from me was research. All right: reluctant as I was, I'd try to find Marcellus Johnson and ask him about Essie. It was the least I could do.

Considering that Essie was probably dead, maybe it wouldn't be so bad.

Back at Marilyn's, the house felt loomingly quiet and eerie, and the portable phone on the kitchen counter, illuminated by the fluorescent glow of an automatic night-light, seemed to beckon menacingly. The gloom reminded me that on earlier visits I had usually been greeted by at least one animal, often more. Even the mangy cat that had been the last of Marilyn's menagerie to go would have made the scene more cheerful.

At least I had the benefit of solitude. Thinking things through, I decided Steve's story about the baby was true. As Marilyn had said, he wouldn't have made it up just to distract her. I still wanted to talk to him — partly to ask why he hadn't told Marilyn until now, but mostly just for comfort. Talking to Steve always made me feel better. But I wasn't going to call him. I'd end up telling him Marilyn was in the hospital, and why, and I'd let him make me feel better by upsetting him — selfish Miss Barbara all over again — and there was no reason for that, now that Marilyn's crisis seemed under control. Instead, I'd get straight to the task of finding Marcellus Johnson. I half hoped it would be impossible, that he and Essie Berman had disappeared into the mists of history and thus discharged me of my obligation.

Assuming that if he was around at all, Marcellus would live in Washington or Maryland, not Virginia, I tackled the phone book first. Although the day had seemed interminable, it was not even nine o'clock. I called dozens of numbers, feeling foolish each time I said, "I'm looking for the Marcellus Johnson who used to live in Riggs Park and knew a woman named Essie Berman." An hour later I was hoarse, but no closer to finding him. I'd begun to believe I'd done my honor-bound best and could honestly say I'd failed.

Then it occurred to me that Marcellus could be a middle name.

"Yeah, that's me," he answered three calls later — a J. Marcellus at an address in Adelphi, only a few miles over the District Line into Maryland from his old house in

Riggs Park. "Who's this?"

"My name is Barbara Cohen. Essie was my neighbor when I was growing up in Riggs Park. You and I have never met, but I've heard about you."

"I bet." A smile in his voice, or maybe menace. "So you moved out of Riggs Park thirty-some years ago, and now you looking for Essie?"

"She's alive, then?"

"Yeah, she alive. She old, but she alive. What you want her for?"

"Like I said, I lived near her when I was a kid. Now I live out of town and I'm here for a visit. I just want to see her."

"You want something from her." A flat statement. She didn't deny it. "Don't matter," he conceded. "She probably like to see you anyway."

"Where is she?"

"Same place as always. Where you think?"

"In Riggs Park?"

"She never moved." A weighty pause. "Not like some people."

I ignored that, though the accusation in his voice was unmistakable. "She still lives there by herself?"

"Naw, she too old for that. My daughter stays with her. Sometimes I stay with her myself."

189

Stay. As if a house were always a place of impermanence. He'd probably never *lived* anywhere, only *stayed.*

"You didn't find her because the phone's listed under my daughter now. Taneka Johnson."

When I hung up my mouth was dry as sand. This was far too easy, and not at all what I'd expected. Now I was obligated to see it through.

"Essie's sleeping," Taneka said when I dialed her number after gulping two glasses of water. "It's late. I'm about to go to sleep myself."

I apologized profusely for the hour and repeated the story I'd told her father. I adopted my meekest tone. "I'd really like to see Essie. Your father said she'd probably like to see me, too."

"She's at her best in the morning." She hesitated. I thought she might hang up. Then she said, coolly, "Come tomorrow at ten."

I wanted to suggest afternoon instead, wanted to spend the morning with Marilyn, but Taneka was firm. "Ten o'clock," she repeated.

I set my alarm, tossed my way through the night, and the next day got to the hospital just after eight.

190

"You didn't need to come check up on me," Marilyn scolded, very much back to normal, her face still swollen, but far less pallid than the day before. "They're releasing me as soon as the doc checks me out."

I turned to Bernie, who sat disheveled and bearded in the recliner where he'd slept. He nodded.

"See?" Marilyn said. "You could have lazed around the house till I got home."

"No. I have an appointment. You'll be thrilled to hear it's with Essie Berman."

Marilyn's jaw dropped open just far enough to remind her it was sore. "She's alive." She put her hand to her face. "You found her. I knew you would."

"Get this — she still lives in Riggs Park. With Marcellus's daughter. Taneka."

Marilyn could barely contain her merriment. "Go," she said. "I'll await the full report at home."

Riggs Park looked even less prosperous than it had the other day as I pulled into the space in front of Essie's house. It was drizzling again, everything gray. But I took the patch of golden chrysanthemums blooming in Essie's yard as evidence that this residence, at least, had been cherished.

My heart drummed wildly as I ascended

191

the steps to the porch. Aside from what I might learn about Penny, what if Essie gave me a tongue-lashing for never writing or calling, and then showing up after all this time? Even at ninety, I wouldn't put it past her. Essie had always been known for forthrightness.

I raised my hand to knock, but before my fist touched wood, the door was flung open by a pretty and oddly familiar young woman in a University of Maryland sweatshirt and jeans, smiling so cheerfully, and with such an air of welcome, that I thought we either must have met before or else the girl was putting on an act.

"Taneka?"

The girl laughed, revealing large, perfect, pearly teeth. "You! I saw you on Sunday!"

Of course! This was the young woman we'd seen carrying the toddler into Penny Weinberg's old house. Today her long braids were pinned close to her head, but the most remarkable change was her lack of a scowl, her sunny manner.

"Sunday I thought you were the cops," the girl said. "They hassle you even if you're minding your own business."

"Not cops. Just an old neighbor." Why was the girl worried about police?

"Come on in. Essie's waiting for you."

Taneka literally pulled me into the living room, cluttered with furniture I didn't recognize and cut off from the dining area by a solid wall that hadn't been there before, with a door open just enough to show the dining area had been converted into a sleeping space. Did that mean Essie could no longer climb the stairs to the bedrooms? A familiar, heady scent hit me. Strong coffee. Essie's great weakness.

"So. Barbara Cohen." The voice was raspy instead of booming, but had lost none of its bite. In a wing chair by the window, always her favorite spot, sat an ancient but unmistakable Essie. "I'd get up, but I'm not so sturdy anymore. Come here."

In her younger days Essie's sharp features had made her grotesque enough, but in old age, whatever cushioning had softened her face had fallen away so thoroughly that her beaky nose and jutting cheekbones seemed about to break through the skin. Always thin, she was almost skeletal now, and her once-sallow complexion had grown pale and powdery.

Though I'd expected no better, Essie's appearance was a shock. Measured against the long swath of eternity, the thirty-odd years since we'd seen each other seemed too short a span to have made such a mockery of her: robbed her of flesh, creased her face, bent her spine. I took the old woman's hand, so papery and crushable, that I was afraid to grip it. But Essie squeezed amazingly hard for a woman of ninety — a clear, "I might be old but I'm not finished yet" squeeze, so deliberate that I wanted to laugh.

Then, holding the frail hand with the firm grasp, I realized how shriveled and small Essie had become. My earliest memories were of a giantess, huge and loud, a force to be reckoned with no less than thunder or lightning. Now, even in a sitting position, she seemed several inches shorter, hunched, dwarfed by the high back of the wing chair. More distressing yet, her head seemed smaller despite the prominent nose, which puzzled me until I realized what was missing was Essie's voluminous hair, once a salt-and-pepper pandemonium, now white and sparse, sadly diminished.

"Sit down. Please." Taneka pulled up an extra chair. "I'll get the coffee."

Essie waited for the girl to disappear. "So, what brings you here? Don't tell me nostalgia."

"Not nostalgia. I came to ask you something." There had never been any point lying to Essie.

"Ah. A mission." Essie nodded, leaned back. "Why am I not surprised?"

I reached over, took her hand again. "Are you going to send me on a guilt trip, Essie? For not coming to see you? I don't even live around here anymore. It's a seven-hour drive."

Essie didn't ask where I lived or if I visited D.C. regularly or why I hadn't come to see her before. "Fine, you can tell me about your mission. But first catch me up. My old friends from the neighborhood are either dead or we don't keep up. Mostly dead. Tell me who you still keep in touch with."

"Marilyn and Bernie, mainly. And of course Trudi." Grateful for the distraction, I filled Essie in on my sister's history and a little of my own, and told her about Bernie and Marilyn in a cursory way. Bernie was fine; Marilyn had had a bout of cancer.

"Had one myself," Essie said. "The disease is overrated, if you ask me."

I didn't go into detail. I didn't mention the face-lift. "And Steve is fine. You probably read about him in the papers."

"I do." Essie's smile threw her face into a spider's web of wrinkles. "Steve. Mr. Bigshot."

I leaned closer. "Actually, I'm here because of something Steve told Marilyn. Something she wants to find out about."

"Oh?"

"You told him Penny had a baby?"

Essie's smile vanished. "On the condition he leave it be."

"That was a long time ago," I said.

Essie turned to the window, studied the rain. Long seconds ticked by. I'd forgotten Essie's habit of never responding until she was good and ready, and how infuriating that could be. "What would be the harm?" I pressed.

Essie snorted. She'd always played this game with me. When I was young, she'd let me hang around her house, but made me wait endlessly if I asked a question, sometimes pretending not to hear. She was far more responsive to Steve and Penny — finding them more needy, I supposed — but if her offhand manner meant she found me more self-sufficient than they were, still it annoyed me no end.

Essie didn't offer any more help. She looked toward the doorway, where Taneka was shouldering her way back in through the bedroom that had once been the dining area. She carried a tray of coffee and cookies.

"Good. Caffeine," Essie said. "These days, believe me, I need it."

"At your age you shouldn't drink coffee at all," Taneka admonished. The affection in Taneka's voice reassured me. I began to like her better.

Taneka handed us steaming, clunky mugs. "If you're going to be here a while, how about I just run down to the store? It won't take long."

"Please. Of course."

With the haste of the young released into welcome freedom, Taneka grabbed her purse and let herself out. Essie took a big, unladylike swig of coffee, bit into a cookie. "You're wondering who's taking care of who, that's what you're wondering."

"What?"

"Whether I'm supporting Taneka or she's supporting me."

"No, Essie, I —"

Essie waved her cookie in my direction to stop me. "She goes to school part-time. She needed a place to live. Her mother ran off years ago, and it doesn't hurt her to have an older woman to live with. Marcellus pays her tuition. You think I'd let him off without paying her tuition? His own child?" She gave a shiver of disgust. "I give her room and board. She helps me out. A smart girl. It's a good arrangement."

"She said she thought I was the police."

"Drugs," Essie said. "Not her, but plenty of others. The neighborhood isn't what it used to be." She put down her mug. Although fragile, Essie's hands didn't shake. "She takes care of me," she said. "White people never did."

Deliberately ignoring that, I rushed to change the subject. "What about her little boy?"

"What?" Essie's eyes narrowed, and I realized too late I couldn't pursue the subject of Taneka's child without admitting I'd been there on Sunday.

"Nothing. I was —"

Essie had taken me to mean something else. As glazed and yellowed as her eyes were, the glance she leveled at me was piercing. "So. You thought it was a boy."

"What?" I was lost.

"It wasn't a boy," Essie said. "It was a girl."

"Who was?"

"Penny's baby. That's what Marilyn wanted to know, isn't it? If it was a boy or a girl. The whole story. Right?"

"Right." I felt as if someone had cut off my air.

"Penny stayed with me while she was

198

pregnant. From the time she started showing." Essie's voice was sharp.

"Here?"

"Where else?" Essie lifted the mug again, slurped some coffee, wiped her lips with a hand. Her manners hadn't become more delicate with age. "The neighborhood was completely colored except for me and one or two others. Who was going to see her? I arranged the adoption, too."

"With an agency?"

"A private adoption. Penny wanted to know who the baby would go to. Also, there was money in it. She wanted money for afterward."

"Then — once it was done. Was Penny all right?"

Essie waved a hand as if to shoo away her disgust. "Was she all right? Of course not. Penny was never all right."

"That's not what I meant. I —"

"The adoptive parents were fine. Nice people. The baby grew up and turned out fine, too."

"So you kept in touch with her?"

She reached for another cookie, bit into it, spoke with her mouth full. "What does Marilyn want to know this for?"

"I'm not sure. Maybe because she never had a daughter and would like a niece.

Maybe because she's sick and wants to tie up loose ends."

"So you got railroaded, huh?" She stared at me while she finished off the cookie. "You don't even know what you got dragged into, do you? If Marilyn wanted to find out so bad, why isn't she the one asking?"

"She had some surgery yesterday. I told you, she has cancer."

"She had cancer surgery?"

"No. Just some minor —" I couldn't say it. Helpless, I went on to something else. "So it was a little girl."

"A girl. Yes. Penny named her Vera. You know what that means? It means *truth*." Essie slid yet another cookie off the tray, demolished it in a single bite. There was certainly nothing wrong with her teeth.

"If Steve knew he had a daughter, he could have helped. He could have —"

"Who said she was Steve's?"

"Well, was she?"

Essie shrugged.

"The man in the bus station," I said. "She could have been his." The man in the bus station reportedly looked like Steve. I didn't know what, if anything, they did to prove paternity in the days before DNA testing. Essie said nothing.

"So it was a private adoption." Slowly, I tried to feel my way through the thoughts racing through my head. In those days, adoption papers were sealed. Could a potential father, or a potential aunt, get hold of them? "Who drew up the agreement?" I asked. "Did you have a lawyer?"

"Bring Marilyn with you and we'll talk about it," Essie said.

"But she can't —"

"Never mind, she can't. You waited all these years, you can wait until she's up and around." Essie gulped the last of her coffee and put down her cup, as if to close the subject. "So. Besides Marilyn and Bernie, tell me who else you keep up with. Linda Schecter?"

"I haven't seen her in years. Seriously, Essie, about the baby —"

"Not a baby anymore. Not for a long time." She crossed her arms in front of her, a shield. "What about Wish?" she demanded. "You always liked Wish."

I crossed my own arms, locking her out. How like Essie to veer the conversation exactly where she wanted it to go. "He doesn't call himself Wish anymore," I said. "He hasn't been called Wish for years."

"No? Why not?"

"I guess he outgrew it."

"So what does he call himself now? *Mister* Wishner?"

"Just Jon, Essie."

"And where is he? I used to read his columns. A writer . . . I guess he could live anywhere."

"He's with me, Essie," I whispered. "In North Carolina. We've been together the last couple of years."

CHAPTER 11

Snow

I held my breath as I waited for Essie to respond. The fact of my live-in relationship with Jon seemed a momentous revelation, but for all the reaction I got, I might have confessed to the air. Essie's hands lay limp in her lap. She seemed blanketed by a great stillness. "So. You got together after all."

"Yes."

She turned toward the window, features masked by the unyielding fatigue of old age, eyes almost closed. "That big snow," she said. "Sweet sixteen and never been kissed."

"Kissed once or twice, maybe." I smiled, remembering.

"You gained a boyfriend and Penny lost a tooth."

It seemed an odd thing to say, though true enough. "Penny got a bridge," I reminded her. "Her teeth looked okay. You couldn't tell."

Essie's head bobbed, nodded onto her chest. Her white scalp glowed dully beneath the wispy hair. I leaned over and touched her wrist. "Essie?"

She was sound asleep. She was still snoring when Taneka returned ten minutes later, her halo of braided hair frosted with tiny drops of rain.

"She ate a cookie, didn't she?" She put down a small grocery bag and studied Essie.

"More like three or four."

Taneka glared as if it were all my fault. "She's a little bit diabetic. Anything with sugar, it puts her right out."

"Why didn't you tell me?"

"She'll sleep it off. It happens any time I don't watch her."

"You should have told me."

"She would have been embarrassed. Would have made my life miserable for weeks." Leaning over, Taneka eased Essie up from her chair and half walked, half carried her into the dining-room-turned-bedroom. Through the open door, I watched as she tenderly helped Essie onto the bed, slipped off her shoes, pulled up the cover. But when she returned to the living room, all traces of the tenderness she had lavished on the old woman were gone.

"You better go now," she told me sharply. "She'll still be fuzzy when she wakes up. That's from the sugar, too. You can come another time."

"We were in the middle of a conversation when she fell asleep," I said. "She was just telling me —"

"Another time." Taneka motioned me to get up.

What the hell, I thought. As long as she was throwing good manners out the door with me, I might as well say what was on my mind. "What about the little boy?" I demanded. "The little boy who was with you on Sunday. Is he yours?"

Taneka tilted her head back and gave a mirthful bark. "Yeah, he's mine. Mine to babysit," she said. "How do you think I pay to go to school?"

Back in the car, I was thoroughly shaken, and not just by Taneka's tone. There was no question of asking Marilyn to come here with me. She was perfectly capable of getting out of a sickbed to do it, even if it meant a relapse, and I had no intention of being responsible for *that.* And since Essie was stubborn as concrete, I had no idea how I was going to get her to talk to me without Marilyn coming along.

Nor could I shake the sting of Essie saying I had gained a boyfriend and Penny had lost a tooth, as if the two were of equal significance. It was bad enough that I'd always felt a little guilty about the foolish, selfish Sweet Sixteen Marilyn and I had shared. But for Essie to be rubbing it in after all these years? What could be the point?

Even at the time, Marilyn and I had worried that the party would be awkward. Penny had turned sixteen in October and proclaimed Sweet Sixteens silly, but Marilyn and I wanted one. We both had birthdays in December, an impossible month because of Hanukkah and Christmas Night Dance and vacations. Our nose jobs were coming up at Easter. Terrified of that as we were, it seemed important to celebrate ourselves in some small way while we still could. We scheduled our joint party for January. Penny was our best friend, true enough — but if there was never any telling how she'd react when our sorority sisters were around, was that our problem, or hers?

We decided on a Chinese lunch because no one had done that yet. There had been sleepovers, a tea, an excursion to a downtown show, even a cosmetics makeover at Francine Ades's. But no one had done Chinese. Marilyn's mother would pick up the food, bring it to my house, and help my mother serve. It turned out to be the kind of gray Saturday afternoon when everyone was glad to have somewhere to go. Marilyn and I kept telling each other that plenty of the guests besides Penny would be from outside the sorority. Penny wouldn't be ostracized. Penny would be fine.

We hadn't counted on Rhoda Apple. Chair of the sorority's Midwinter Carnival, Rhoda saw the party as a chance to have a committee meeting. After the chicken and snow peas and rice had been eaten off paper plates in my living room, after the fortune-cookie fortunes had been read and passed around, while Marilyn and I opened our stack of presents, Rhoda herded her three committee members upstairs to the master bedroom. There, where dozens of coats were stacked on my parents' bed, they had their meeting and used the phone to consult Bertie Eiger, who'd stayed home with the flu.

Lying under some of the coats, half asleep in a fetal position, they found Penny.

"Penny, you all right?"

"Just cramps," Penny said. "I'm all right. The aspirin should kick in in a minute."

"Well, what about lying down somewhere else?" Rhoda asked. "We're having a committee meeting. About Midwinter Carnival."

"Well, go ahead."

"It's a sorority function," Rhoda said. "It's — Well, you're not a member. Sorority business is confidential. I don't think you should stay."

"Oh." Cowed, shaken, Penny retreated to the bathroom. Fearing her red and splotchy face would give her away, fearing the others would assume her tears were not from anger ("I should have told Rhoda to go to hell instead of just thinking about it"), but from the humiliation of being forced to depledge the year before, Penny stayed in the bathroom for nearly an hour. She ignored the other girls, full of Coke and Seven-Up and Chinese tea, who knocked on the door and begged to get in. Downstairs, the presents had all been opened. Although my mother and Marilyn's mother tactfully sent the full-bladdered guests to the half-bath in the basement, word of Penny's standoff spread like wildfire. Marilyn and I feared our curious guests would stay all day.

Then, like a mercy, it snowed.

Most of the girls who'd driven to the party had had their licenses less than a year. None of them knew how to handle a car on slick roads. All were in a sudden panic to get home. Within minutes, the house was cleared, and Marilyn and I were able to coax Penny out of her retreat. The three of us spent the next hour filling trash cans with Chinese take-out cartons, used paper plates, cardboard gift boxes, crumpled wrapping paper and yards of ribbon. By the time we were finished, Penny's good mood had returned.

It snowed on and off for more than twenty-four hours. Over a foot accumulated before it stopped on Sunday afternoon. The city was paralyzed. The temperature dropped and stayed below freezing the better part of a week. School was canceled. In the bright, bitter weather, the crust of the snow melted repeatedly in the sunshine, only to freeze again into a slick surface, shiny as icing on a cake and hard enough to walk on.

Snowplows rumbled along New Hampshire Avenue and Eastern Avenue. Occasionally they came across Third Street at the top of our hill and Sixth Street at the bottom. The effect was mainly to pack the frozen surface even more.

With the raw, edgy energy of girls trapped in our houses, Marilyn and Penny and I sledded each morning in the bitter cold, then broke for lunch and came out again. There were never enough sleds for everyone, so when the twelve-year-old boys urged Penny to belly flop on top of them, she did, offering the boys one of the great thrills of their sexual awakening, even though every inch of her body was insulated with layers of cotton and wool. Not seeing the harm, Marilyn and I stretched out atop the younger boys, too, racing with them on sleds so fleet that our world blurred into a collage of black tires at the curb, white snowmen in the yards, scarves and jackets in a pastiche of primary colors. At the alley, we began scraping our feet behind us to slow down and avoid crashing into Sixth Street at the bottom. No car had been by for days, but the snowplows had left frozen ruts and mounds in the cross street, dangerous at full speed.

While the boys pulled the sleds back up the hill, we girls walked unencumbered, sun glittering off the snow and into our eyes, ice crusting on our lashes until the street lost its shape entirely, became nothing but shooting prisms of light, transformed.

By the third morning, the holiday had turned wild. Children dug through the ice for handfuls of pebbles to pack into their snowballs. The sledders careened reck-lessly down the hill, racing each other with gleeful abandon. When the ice melted enough to make slick spots on the walk, no one noticed.

When Wish Wishner and Seth Opak and Bernie Waxman appeared at the top of the hill for the first time in three days, they swaggered down a shoveled thread of walk with their usual pack of friends and watched disdainfully as we flew past them atop the twelve-year-olds. As if at a signal, the older boys plunked their own sled onto the street and piled one on the other like tiers of a huge cake. With exaggerated comic gestures, they fell off one by one as far as the alley.

"You're real champs there," Marilyn taunted as we trudged back up the hill.

"Champs at comic relief," I clarified.

"I sense a twinge of doubt at our racing abilities," Wish said.

"More than a twinge," I replied.

"Then you're in for a treat." Elbowing my twelve-year-old partner out of the way, Wish took my sled in his hands and led me to the top of the hill. Bernie did the same with Marilyn, and Seth was climbing the incline with Penny. The displaced younger boys protested noisily.

It was exciting, being shepherded up the hill like that. Wish was in some of my classes at school, but otherwise I hadn't seen him much since our one date a year before on Christmas night. He swam on a city-wide team that practiced both morning and afternoon and traveled most weekends. During the summer he was gone, working as one of the junior swim instructors at Camp Chesapeake. It was only now, walking by his side, that I realized how much bigger he'd grown — not taller so much as broader-shouldered and more massive, maybe from all that swimming. Situating myself on my sled on top of him, with all the neighborhood watching, for a moment I felt as naked and as awkward as I ever had in my life.

We pushed off and instantly were two lengths in front of Penny and Seth, Marilyn and Bernie. Oh, we were a team! Unable to stop, at the bottom I rolled off into the crusty snow just before Sixth Street, and Wish dove off a split second later, so smoothly our moves might have been synchronized. Walking back up the hill, Wish bowed to his friends on the sidewalk, who whistled and cheered. The attention made me feel important. On subsequent runs, Penny and Seth lagged so far behind us that they were hardly in the competition, and Wish and I beat Marilyn and Bernie seven times in a row.

Once on the way down, caught in the eye by a drop of water and forced to push my head into the collar of Wish's coat, I was certain I felt the warmth of his neck underneath. When we reached the bottom and he pulled me up, his hands, too, seemed warm under his gloves. I could not imagine, as we stood there in that snow, what it felt like to be cold.

On our next trip down the hill, I saw the car. Saw it dreamily at first, through a film of snow in my eyes. Creeping into the intersection where no car had been for three days, it labored its way along Sixth Street, directly in our path. I had neither the time nor the presence of mind to think. I catapulted off the sled and hit the street hard. Behind me, Wish landed on his right shoulder, then instinctively jerked the rope toward him so the sled would not go under the car.

The driver saw us and jammed on his brakes.

Marilyn and Bernie were right behind us, and Penny and Seth a few yards back.

"Watch out!" I yelled. "Car!"

The car's wheels locked, but the ice carried it forward. It skidded in slow-motion over the snowplow ruts.

Marilyn and Bernie lunged off, rolled over and over, a tangle of arms and legs and coats. Seth and Penny did the same.

Shocked and dumb, all six of us sat up where we had landed on the snow. We watched as the skidding car finally came to a halt on the rutted street.

The driver got out, dazed. His eyes slid over me and Wish, Bernie and Marilyn, and settled on Penny. At the sight of her, he muttered, "Oh, my God. Oh, my God." We all turned to look. She must have landed with her mouth open, hit her upper teeth on the ground. Her gashed gum was dripping blood onto the sunshine-white street, and her upper left front tooth hung crazily by a thread.

She hadn't yet been aware of it. Seeing the man's alarm, she removed one of her gloves and lifted a hand to her face to touch the injury. Even before her fingers found the tooth, she noticed her own blood on the snow and started to scream.

Except for Marilyn, who coddled a bruised knee, the rest of us had no idea if we were hurt. There is a moment when you suffer a traumatic injury, when you are numb and still free of pain, a moment of grace. Bernie and I were fine, but we did not know yet — even Wish did not know — that he had broken his shoulder. We did not know that when it healed it would never again be right enough for swimming, which had been half his life. Or if he knew, he understood only in some visceral, unconscious way. Later that was how it seemed: that Wish knew, and that I knew, that in the instant we had flown together off the sled, he had ceased being Wish the swimmer and become Wish who loved Barbara Cohen. And I had become the girl who loved him back.

Then the street was full of people, all noise and color. Penny's mother, Helen Weinberg, coatless, came running down the block like the devoted parent she'd never been. Trudi dragged my mother down from our house. Pauline Wishner appeared, a frilly apron tied around her waist and a jacket flung over her shoulders, hands clawing at her face in disbelief.

Seeing his mother so distraught, Wish finally caught his breath and stood, and in the same motion I stood with him. "I'm all right," he told Pauline. It was to me he whispered, "I think there's something wrong with my shoulder."

Implicit in that confidence made against

the dazzle of brilliant snow and drying blood was that we had found each other and formed the sort of complete and un-yielding bond that offers itself only once in a lifetime, an awesome and permanent thing. Yet we must have known we were too young for it, too; must have felt its strength and feared its power to tear us from our youthful moorings, leave us clutching at air. We were always together after that, yet not together at all. Wish's father wanted him to be a doctor. My sister Trudi was in college, and my parents expected me to follow. That day in the snow, Wish and I had moved apart, knowing we had to wait, be patient, until that moment of consummation, still several years off, that would turn out to be every bit as grand as we had imagined there in that raw January light.

Driving away from Essie's, I wanted desperately to talk to Jon again, hear his voice. We'd spoken last on Sunday, and now it was Tuesday. It seemed forever. His absence was almost like physical pain. If he called again, at least he would help me decide what to tell Marilyn until I could get Essie to talk. We'd be together, even if only on the phone.

With a mounting sense of dread, I dug out Marilyn's cell phone and called Bernie to make sure she'd been released from the hospital. "No complications, for once. We're home. She's taking a nap." That meant she'd soon be awake, waiting for my news. Why had I been stupid enough to let her know I'd found Essie and was going to see her? Why couldn't I have waited?

Killing time, I stopped at McDonald's. The first bite of greasily satisfying cheese-coated beef calmed me. The second brought inspiration. Given the desperation of my circumstances and the likelihood of Marilyn grilling me for information I didn't have, I had no choice. I had to appeal for help from the one person most likely to melt Essie's heart and loosen her tongue: Marcellus Johnson himself. I reached into my purse, extracted the phone once more, and dialed before I lost my nerve.

CHAPTER 12

Truck Ride

Marcellus answered on the first ring. I didn't expect it, thinking he'd probably be at work and I'd get an answering machine. But there he was, bright and lively on the other end, sounding amused to hear from me and not at all surprised. When I told him I'd like to meet with him, he gave me his address in Adelphi. "I got two jobs to check on this afternoon. You got the time, you can come along."

"Fine." Now I'd have to spend hours trapped in a moving vehicle with the man. Nothing I knew about Marcellus made that seem appealing — not the story of how he'd met Essie when he was a teenager and had later moved in with her, even though his own mother lived on the next block, not Essie's proud assertion to former Riggs Park neighbors that as an adult, Marcellus had "gone into business for himself." I'd always assumed "business" in Marcellus's case meant bookmaking and drug deals, the kind of entrepreneurship his young years had promised. I only hoped Essie had brow-beaten him long enough to assure that his current "business" was something legal.

As I followed the directions Marcellus had given me, I wasn't sure if I was actually afraid of him or just curious. All I knew about him were oft-told stories, and I had no idea which of them, if any, were true.

By 1965, the old Riggs Park home-owners had fled into the suburbs in such numbers that what had been a Jewish, working-class neighborhood was almost entirely black. Essie was one of the few who claimed she'd stayed on because she could see no reason not to.

Marilyn's mother, Shirley, probably the most faithful among the women Essie had played canasta with for so many years, was genuinely worried. She called Essie from the Ginsburg's new home in Maryland at least once a month, to warn Essie that the city was no place for a woman alone any-more. Affordable, but certainly not safe.

"Why should I change now just because you did?" Essie snorted. If the white youngsters who'd occupied her time were grown and gone, she claimed, eventually black ones would replace them.

But no such thing happened. When Essie's new neighbors ventured onto their porches, they nodded and exchanged a few words with her, but never really tried to be friends. The woman next door, who chatted with Essie almost daily, invited her in once for coffee and then never again. The children, with whom Essie had always had such rapport, averted their eyes when Essie greeted them and giggled after she turned away. One night in the middle of the summer of 1965, Essie went to bed and dreamed about her husband and son, which she hadn't done for twenty years. She woke up so shaken that she put on a dress and high heels and took the K-4 bus downtown and applied for a job at every store on F Street. By the end of the week, she was clerking in Woodie's men's department, selling shirts and trousers, regular daylight hours except on Thursday, when she stayed until nine.

One Thursday night, the air was so hot and sticky that it seemed to coat the city like a shroud. Essie got off the bus at the District Line and started walking home at a good clip, feeling more unsettled than tired. She never heard the footsteps approach from behind, only felt someone grab the strap of her purse. Instinctively, Essie hung on. She rocked back and forth, having a tug of war with her attacker.

Finally she slung her whole weight at him and, to her surprise, knocked him flat. On the dark sidewalk, she couldn't see him well, so she lugged him to his feet.

"Hey . . . let go of me!" he yelled in a voice newly deep and frightened.

"Not on your life. You're coming with me." She reeled him in and pulled him toward her house.

"What the hell, lady . . ."

"Watch your language," she scolded. To his credit, the boy shut up. Five minutes later, she had him inside her living room. She shoved him onto her sofa.

Her first good look at him stunned her. A pretty kid, but so young. "Good lord," she said. "You can't be more than twelve."

"Fourteen," he told her, growing surly.

"What's your name?"

"What's it to you?"

"Look — you want me to call the cops?"

"You will anyway."

"Not necessarily."

"Boozer," he spat.

"Ten years from now maybe you'll be a Boozer. Let's hope not. What's your real name?"

"Marcellus."

"Marcellus what?"

"Johnson."

"Nothing wrong with the name Marcellus." She still couldn't believe he was fourteen. "A Marcellus could grow up to be somebody. A Boozer can only case the place." Which of course he was, now that she'd let him off the hook about the police: eyeing the stereo and the console TV.

"You bring me here for a lecture, lady?"

"Where do you live, Marcellus?"

He inched up from the sofa, edged toward the door, didn't answer. She grabbed his arm, dug in her fingers.

"I'm talking to you, Marcellus."

"What's wrong with you, anyway?" he asked, trying to shrug her off.

On the second try, she let him go. "Where do you live, Marcellus?" she asked again.

"Quackenbos Street," he whispered.

"I didn't know people were so poor over there that they had to rob little old ladies of their purses."

"You ain't that little," he said.

"A sharp observation, Marcellus." She allowed him to contemplate her size in case he was thinking of escape. He sank back onto the couch and endured her.

"You're at Paul Junior High, right? Eighth grade?" His lip curled and she

222

knew better. "No, seventh. They kept you back and you're still in seventh."

"You don't know nothing about it," he said.

"What don't I know anything about? Hard times? Failing math? I'll get my violin out and play you a little tune."

The boy shifted uncomfortably, looked at the carpet. "What you bring me here for?" he mumbled.

"To get a look at you. You tried to take my purse."

Marcellus took a deep breath, sank deeper into the couch. "Listen, you gonna call the cops or what?"

"Maybe," Essie said.

He stood up again. She pushed him down and all at once knew what his problem was. Too small for his age. Compelled to play tough. She'd seen it before. Morty Landau. Lenny Kirsch. She began working herself up the way she'd done with the white teenagers when circumstances demanded. "Listen," she said, bringing her face close to his. "You plan to snatch purses and smack people around until they catch you, then spend your life serving time?" she shouted. When they were small for their age, they thought being in trouble made them bigger. "I had a kid myself once that got killed, and I never stole anybody's purse to get back. You think I'm sorry I didn't?"

Marcellus looked up, shocked into attention. "You had a kid get killed? What happened?"

"He got chewed up by a coyote," she said.

"Yeah, sure."

"He did." The words rolled off her tongue. Later she told Shirley Ginsburg it was the first time the scene had come back clear to her in twenty years: Her young self with hair black as Marcellus's, pacing the frayed carpet of her living room near San Diego, colicky baby in tow, hot Santa Ana wind blowing in, sweat rolling down her chest. The baby fussed until she carried him outdoors, set him on his blanket under the eucalyptus tree in the yard — a tiny backyard with brown hills behind it, rising dull-edged and dry from the California dust. She dangled a rattle at him and his crying stopped. He liked it out there and couldn't get far, only seven months old. She left him and went inside to clean as she often did, watching through the sliding door. She turned on the vacuum, a big loud Hoover. When she turned off the machine, she looked to the yard to check on her son, but saw the coyote first. It was tearing away at something, a dead thing; she did not see what — did not understand what — for the first moment. Later, she went screaming into the brown-and-blood-colored yard, facing down the beast that had come from the hills because it had nothing left to hunt. It heard her and fled — eyes angry, deprived of its meal, but too frightened to stay. She turned to what a moment before had been her son, screaming. But he wasn't a baby anymore, only a dead thing, pieces missing, smeared.

Essie said all this, in a straightforward way, to the boy.

"Christ," he said. His eyes had grown wide, not defiant.

She'd looked at the body for a long time. The skin white against darkening blood. The face set, grotesque. She'd understood at once: that she was responsible for her son's death, a murderess. That simple. And months later, when she'd stopped screaming and her husband had given her enough money to go East and live the rest of her life, if she would just stay away from him forever, she'd understood she was responsible for all sons.

"Christ, lady," Marcellus said again.

225

"After that, I decided I was never going to let any wild animal take anything that belonged to me again," she said. "That includes you."

"I'm no animal," he said.

"No?" She moved to the door and opened it. "If anything happens to this house, Marcellus, I'll know who did it. I wouldn't let anybody else mess around here, either, because it would still be Marcellus on Quackenbos Street who got blamed."

"You telling me I have to guard your house?"

"If you're not too gutless." She knew what that word did to them: gutless. She pointed out the door toward the night.

The boy got up slowly, stiff-legged. He paused at the edge of the porch. "I'll see you," he muttered uncertainly.

"If you have the guts," she said. And by the way he'd moved off, in no hurry now, she'd thought maybe he did.

Now, thirty-five years later, I found the grown Marcellus in a cluttered office that had once been the garage of his house. His front yard had been turned into a parking lot. I wasn't sure exactly what I'd pictured when I tried to imagine him, but this wasn't it. Marcellus Johnson was short and wide and powerful-looking except for a round and very tame-looking potbelly that ballooned beneath his shirt. His weight lifter's shoulders were massive, and he had a thick, muscular neck, but his face was a narrow surprise, high-cheekboned and intelligent, with an aquiline nose and large, slanted eyes that showed where Taneka had gotten her good looks. Though he was not yet fifty, his tight-cropped hair was salted with white, and he wore a thin black mustache that by contrast looked dyed and artificial. It rather disappointed me that he looked no more like a hood than a movie star. Not that I was any expert on what a hood ought to look like.

"I'm Barbara Cohen," I said offering my hand.

He nodded but didn't take it. "The ex-neighbor," he said.

"Yes." I stuffed my hand into my pocket.

"Looking for help with Essie," Marcellus said. "Found her more trouble than you expected."

"Yes."

He uttered a dry, humorless chuckle. "Like I said on the phone, I got jobs to check on." He gestured toward the door. "You coming?"

Two minutes later, we were bouncing along in an old Ford pickup, a well-worn relic with shocks that had known better days. Instead of discussing Essie, Marcellus was making and receiving one call after the other on the cell phone that sat between us.

Johnson's Enterprises, I soon learned from these conversations, included a rug-cleaning outfit ("Tell her you'll spot it but there's no guarantee"); a handyman service ("Sure we can stain instead of paint, but it's extra"); and, remarkably, a company that installed and sanded hardwood floors.

"A lawn-mowing service in summer, too," Marcellus informed me between calls, sure of my captive attention.

We went to three different jobs. I would have waited in the truck, but Marcellus beckoned me out, seemed to want me to observe him at work. His employees greeted him with deference. He responded to one in street talk that sounded straight off a rap record; the others he greeted in slightly black-accented lingo; and for the white homeowner having his yard cleaned up, he adopted such formal, standard grammar that I waited for him to break out in an English accent. I found it so remarkable that Marcellus was perfectly trilingual that I almost forgot my mission. We didn't get back to the subject of Essie until the return trip to his office.

"So, you saw her," he said. "Whatever it was you wanted, Essie didn't give it to you, otherwise you wouldn't be coming to see me."

"I guess not," I agreed.

"You ain't seen her for what? Thirty, forty years?" He slid into the second of his three languages, nongrammatical but clean, and wrestled the truck out of first gear.

"Essie looked different, but she seems sharp as ever," I said. "I was surprised."

The phone rang, but instead of answering, Marcellus turned it off. "So what you want from me?" he asked bluntly.

Given the opening, I tried to give my story the best possible slant. Steve had told his sister about Penny's baby. Marilyn wanted to find the now-grown child, but Essie balked at giving more information unless Marilyn was there to hear it. The catch was, Marilyn was just out of surgery (I did not say "face-lift") and couldn't travel. It was important to Marilyn, given her illness, to find her niece. As Marcellus could surely imagine.

We bounced over a railroad track and onto a road so full of potholes that my bottom promised to be sore for days. "Did Essie ever talk about Penny to you?" I asked. "Do you know what happened?"

"I know the name." Cautious now, reluctant to give me anything I didn't work for. "It was before my time."

"Not really. Not much. I'm not asking this for myself," I said. "I'm asking you to help me help a friend."

"I see. To be a friend to you, to 'help you help a friend,'" he mimicked. "For old times' sake, right? Inasmuch as we lived in the same neighborhood once."

"I didn't say that."

"Yeah, but let's be clear. We lived in the same neighborhood at different times. We never met each other until right now. You and Marilyn might be friends, but not you and me. Don't make like I owe you."

Marcellus actually smiled. I drew a breath. "You like jerking me around, go ahead," I told him. "All I asked for was a simple favor. Big mistake."

Turning on his blinker, Marcellus swung onto East-West Highway near his office. "Essie's old, but she's her own woman," he said. "Even if I know something, if she don't want me to tell you, I won't."

The truck sputtered, but as if on signal Marcellus's parking lot appeared just in front of us, and the motor didn't die until he'd pulled into a space. "Listen," he said as I undid my seat belt. "What if there's more to the story than you think? What if it's more involved? You still want to hear it?"

"Of course I want to hear it!" What did he take me for? How complicated could it be? Either Penny's baby was Steve's or it wasn't.

"All I'm saying is, think what you're getting yourself into." I let myself out of the truck onto the pavement. By the time I'd closed the door, he'd come around and was standing next to me.

"I'd go over to Essie's with you, if I thought it would make any difference," he said. A victorious jolt of adrenaline shot through me, but Marcellus held up a hand as if to fend me off. "But you know what I think?"

"What?"

"There ain't no way she's gonna tell you anything unless your friend goes with you. No matter what I do. Essie's no different than she ever was. Does what she damn well pleases." He laughed dryly. "She not gonna tell you a damn thing she don't want to. There ain't no way."

My high spirits drained in a single whoosh. Well, what did I expect? I felt like a fool. He'd probably known what I was going to ask him and known he was going to say no. And I'd let him take me — literally — for a ride.

On the way home, I drove aimlessly for a while, leaden from realizing that Marcellus was right. I wasn't going to be able to tell Marilyn anything that would give her peace of mind. How could I face her without having more to offer? Without having at least *something*.

By the time I pulled into the driveway, I was exhausted. But Marilyn, when she called me groggily to her room, looked more exhausted by half. The bedcovers were loosely thrown over her as she leaned against her pillow, but she was still clad in the sweats and loose blouse she'd worn home from the hospital, a chin strap circling her swollen face instead of the pressure bandage, her conditioned hair slicked flat and dull against her head. This morning she'd looked odd but sounded almost normal. Now, she still looked odd and sounded like she needed at least a week to sleep.

"Don't look so terrified," she told me.

"The first day home from the hospital is always a doozy. Sit down." She patted a spot on the king-size bed.

I dropped down beside her. "What about your heart rate? Do they still have you on medicine?"

"No. I'm fine. Danger averted."

I squeezed her hand.

She sat up straighter in the bed. "So. Did you see Essie? What did she say?"

"Not half as much as I thought she would." I decided not even to mention that the baby was a girl. "Essie looks like a skeleton. She's half the size she used to be, and she has diabetes. I'm not sure her mind's what it used to be, either." Silently, I asked Essie's forgiveness for this lie. "We no sooner sat down than she fell asleep on me. I couldn't wake her up. Taneka put her in bed and then kicked me out."

Marilyn sighed as if she'd been holding her breath. "So she didn't tell you anything." It was a statement rather than a question. I didn't elaborate.

"Are you going back?" she asked suddenly.

"If Taneka lets me."

"Before you go back to North Carolina?"

"Well . . . sure."

"Promise?" Her tone had grown urgent.

"Promise." I squeezed her hand again. "I won't leave before I go back and find out everything you want to know. Even if it means depriving myself of Jon."

She tried to smile.

"Go back to sleep." I leaned over to kiss her swollen cheek. Where my next bright idea would come from, I had no inkling.

Out in the hallway, I heard voices coming from the kitchen. Visitors, already. What was the matter with people? I descended the stairs toward the conversation. The voices grew louder. My breath caught in my throat.

In the entryway to the kitchen, arms held out in welcome, stood the answer to my dilemma.

"Steve!" I exclaimed, and let him fold me into his arms.

CHAPTER 13

Star

When he released me from his embrace, Steve held me at arm's length and looked me up and down, a loopy, comic expression on his face. "Well, sweetie, aging very well, I see. Still the towhead. Do you bleach it now? Wash out the gray? Tell Uncle Stevie."

"Never!"

"Me, either," Steve admitted.

"What's to bleach?" I laughed. Steve's baldness was legend. "Oh, Steve, I'm so glad to see you!" I reached up to pat the shiny top of his head.

"An effect he achieved even without chemical intervention," said Marilyn, who startled me by appearing suddenly behind us. During Marilyn's chemotherapy, Steve had insisted that his ability to shed hair without drugs proved once again, as ever, that he was the superior sibling, and the silly joke was one of the few things that had cheered Marilyn in those days. Now, regarding us like a moonfaced specter, Marilyn said, "He came because he thought my heart would beat me to death."

"How did you know?" I felt foolish for having been afraid to call him.

"Bernie and I have an agreement that I'm to be informed about all medical developments in my beloved sister's case. Including cosmetic ones." He winked. "I came because I have to be in New York tomorrow night, and when I heard about the little complication I thought I'd drop in on the way."

"Liar," Marilyn sniffed. "He was paralyzed with worry."

Bernie came over and took Marilyn's arm. "Now I'll escort you back up to bed."

"Later." She shrugged him off.

"You're in luck," Steve told her. "I brought you a bunch of new movies you can only get if you're a big Hollywood pooh-bah like myself. You can spend the next week watching them. Starting right this minute."

"I'll watch every one. Two or three times. But not right this minute."

"You ought to rest," Bernie said.

"I tossed and turned in that bed all afternoon. How often do I see my brother? I'll go to bed early. I'll be fine. Right now I'm too antsy to sleep."

I understood. Monster that it was, fa-

236

tigue could wait. After surgery, after the breakup of a romance, after many kinds of trauma, the objective was not to rest, but simply to get back to normal — to walk, to talk, to *function;* to come back from what might have been (but could not be allowed to be) the dark.

Bernie decided we might as well have dinner, so he set out cold cuts and bread and warmed up some vegetable soup that one of Marilyn's face-lift veteran friends had brought, knowing her jaw would still be too sore for chewing. I found myself casting worried glances across the table because without the pillows and bedcovers marking her as an invalid on her way to recovery, Marilyn looked truly awful — the chin strap like an Ace bandage holding her misshapen face in check, the mouth so pulled back that it would surely never return to normal, the cheekbones slightly purpled, masking an underlying pallor. But Marilyn had cheered up at the sight of her brother and swore that, after fasting all day yesterday and having practically nothing for lunch, she was starving.

Surreptitiously, despite my concern, I was busy making a few calculations. Steve had been one of Essie's favorites, and since he was the possible father of Penny's baby, the old woman would not refuse to talk to him. I would bring him to her house in place of Marilyn, and Essie would tell us what we wanted to know. If Steve had to be in New York tomorrow night, there was no time to waste. I'd have to take him to Essie's in the morning.

Over coffee, Marilyn exclaimed over the snapshots of Steve's children, who had grown into handsome young men, three of them in college, one on the road with his band ("Oh, no," Marilyn groaned. "Another *musician*."). Then Bernie turned the conversation to Steve's own music business and Steve responded with an enthusiasm I didn't expect. He was on his way to New York to recruit an up-and-coming singer to record one of his songs. "A love song. I'm too old to do it."

"Too old! Oh, Steve!" Marilyn chided.

Steve patted a hint of belly under his shirt and grimaced. "Too paunchy for the video. Even my personal trainer has given up on me."

Marilyn snorted. Although I feared the conversation might go on all night and give me no chance to speak to Steve privately, all the same I was enjoying myself, filled anew with admiration for Steve's lack of ego after so many years in the heady air of

Hollywood. Without writing drug songs or war protest songs, without being seduced by hard rock or rockabilly or rap, Steve had put his own brand of folksy, not-quite-country, not-quite-rock songs on the charts almost every year since the meteoric rise of "Bus Ride" in the seventies. He had even handled his baldness with grace, during the hairy hippie era after his manager had insisted he wear a toupee when he was performing. The "rug," as he called it, was hot and didn't look natural. Steve hated it. And finally, one night in confident defiance, he snatched the hairpiece off in midconcert and tossed it to the audience, which reacted with wild delight. Later, when I asked him how he'd gotten the nerve, he said he'd already taken the stage name Steven Simple because he'd always been so stupid, and figured if people could stand the new name, they could put up with his cue-ball head, too.

"You were never stupid!" I protested.

"I didn't know that then," Steve had said flatly, and I'd realized that was true.

It still made me proud to think that Steve was the only star regularly described by columnists and talk-show hosts as a "man of integrity" — a man actually reputed to be fair to his employees and faithful to his wife. The feeling that swelled up in me now reminded me how thoroughly he'd been like a brother to me, and how much I'd always missed him after he went away — how much I still did. As the only male I'd been close to where sex was not an issue, he'd allowed me a kind of selfless pride in him I could have had for no other man, even Jon.

"These days I farm out almost all the new songs," Steve told Bernie now. "I almost prefer it. I record just enough to keep my name out there."

We all nodded. For the past ten years, Steve had been known as much as a songwriter as a singer.

"So why go to New York? Why not send somebody? Or talk on the phone?" Bernie asked. "Some up-and-comer, you'd think they'd be grateful to have a chance to record a Steven Simple song."

Steve turned to Marilyn and winked. "I know you think I actually came East just to witness your medical crisis, but don't flatter yourself. I always like to give the singers a look." We knew it was true. He'd been doing it for twenty-odd years. There were some decisions, he believed, that you just didn't delegate. More than most stars (not just musicians), Steve had spent his life combining celebrity with sanity and common sense.

So how was it that I was now planning to drag him to Essie's and disrupt his balance? Because Marilyn was weak? Because Steve was strong by contrast? Well, he was. The way I saw it, from the day of his fateful interview on *The Sonya Show* in the eighties, he'd been famous enough and strong enough to finesse whatever life handed him. Given the present circumstances, I certainly couldn't say the same for Marilyn.

It had been 1983 before Steve's life had finally taken its shape. He was forty-two years old, and in Detroit to tape a segment of *The Sonya Show* for USA Cable. While he was there, he planned to audition a girl named Kimberly O'Connor who aspired to become one of his shiksa princesses — a term he'd borrowed from Neil Sedaka to refer to his backup singers. The next day he'd fly back to L.A.

Steve always told this story with a kind of bemused wonder. He was picking out a tune on the piano in his suite at the Book Cadillac Hotel when the knock came on the door, so tentative he barely heard it. All he knew about the O'Connor girl was that his agent, Waldman, thought she might be all right. Steve always made the final selections himself. He chose the princesses leggy (like Sedaka's), and fair-complected since he himself was dark. Usually he picked blondes.

This one was a redhead. "Mr. Simple?" She was tall, white-skinned, very bright around the face. Hair wilder than he liked. A looker, though. He sensed the hairdo was not the result of a too-tight perm, but of natural curl.

"I appreciate your seeing me." She sounded more humble than her appearance warranted.

He motioned her in. She walked like a dancer, just the right sway of the hips under brown slacks, the right bounce of bosom under a beige sweater. In the show, the princesses wore neutral outfits, sometimes sequined, but always understated. Apparently she knew that.

Even so, she looked flamboyant. Her hair wasn't carroty but a true red. A neon sign, a focus. One thing he didn't need was a princess who upstaged him. Stick to blondes, Waldman said. "Blondes are safe, even when they're stunning. Chain of daisies on pale wallpaper."

Steve pointed the girl to the sofa. She

hesitated, then handed him a résumé. He hadn't expected that. Waldman already had one. Steve only wanted to get a look at her, talk to her. If she was good enough, he'd set up a session with the other princesses later.

But the typed pages threw him. He set them on the coffee table, stood awkwardly. If Waldman were here, he'd smooth it over. Read parts of her work history aloud. Let people see that Steven Simple's time was too valuable to waste on details. Good agents did such things. Sometimes Steve thought Waldman had figured out Steve couldn't read the résumés himself, but he didn't dwell on that. He'd been paying Waldman good money for over ten years. Besides, no one else knew; why should Waldman?

The girl was nervous, actually trembling, as if she knew the résumé was a mistake. "Really I only wanted to hear you sing," Steve said. He sat down at the piano, beckoned her over to stand beside him. Her hands shook, a pulse beat in her neck. She glanced at the closed door to the bedroom. Maybe she expected a come-on? He never messed with the princesses.

"Let's do 'Bus Ride,'" he said. If she knew anything, she'd know that one. As he began the intro, it struck him how much she reminded him of Penny: the red hair, the shaking hands, all but the voice. Penny had never been able to carry a tune. Suddenly he couldn't draw air. He hadn't seen Penny for twenty years and her double had walked into a Detroit hotel room. He stopped playing.

"I'm sorry," the girl said. "I guess I'm not good enough."

"No, it's my fault. Jet lag. Happens all the time." He put his hands back on the keyboard. The girl sang, but shakily. He didn't want her to break down in front of him. He knew something about breakdowns from Penny: how they could suck you in.

"Good. Now. Once more from the top." He smiled reassuringly and began again. Her voice improved as they went along.

"Mr. Waldman will get back to you," he said afterward.

"Don't call us, we'll call you," Kimberly whispered. Tears in her eyes now. What the hell did she expect? "It was nice of you to see me, anyway." Jesus. Penny had had blue eyes and Kimberly O'Connor had hazel, but the tears were identical.

"I'll tell you what," he said. "Let me hear you one time with the others."

She froze, a spotlighted animal.

"We're having a rehearsal at the studio at six, before the taping. I'll hear you then."

Usually he was not a sucker for tears. You didn't get this far if you were. When you could barely read, you learned to play for sympathy early and were suspicious of anyone else who did the same. Only a handful of people knew what a miracle it was he'd gotten through high school. He didn't con people because he wanted to; he lied because he had no choice. He wasn't sure if Kimberly O'Connor was for real or not, and he didn't mean to care.

But you never knew; the most innocuous things could throw you. In high school it had been the SATs. Who would have imagined? He copied all his tests from Bernie because Bernie was going with Marilyn and had to let him. For the SATs, the students sat every other seat in the Coolidge High cafeteria. Bernie positioned his paper carefully so Steve could see. Steve should have thrown off a little. It never occurred to him that Bernie's answers would let him do well enough to get into college in spite of his grades. His parents nagged him to go. He skirted the issue for a couple of years, claiming he was trying to make it with his band. Then his father said, "Son, you're getting nowhere. You want to end up like me, with a store that threatens to put you under every month?" His father worked twelve hours a day in his grocery store on Fourteenth Street. "At least get your education. Even if the band succeeds, an education won't hurt." So Steve spent a year at the University of West Virginia to appease him. He could no more have told his parents he couldn't read than strip in public. He still believed that if word got out, his star status would count for nothing, and the few people who loved him would be ashamed.

Even Essie Berman didn't know about his reading — Essie, who thought he was wonderful. Aware that Steve had heard music in his head since childhood, Essie proclaimed it amazing that he could play any instrument he picked up. Essie listened to any thought Steve wanted to share; she never told him his singing would come to nothing. Years later, she said, "See, all that time you sweated your grades, I always said in the end it wouldn't matter. It's a good thing you turned out a star because otherwise I never would have lived you down." For a long time, she was his sole adult support.

Not that Essie oohed and aahed. In his

early days, her grandest compliment was that his music "wasn't bad."

"What do you mean, 'not bad'?"

"Reminds me of soap commercials," Essie said.

"Soap commercials!"

"That's so terrible? They pay people good money to write soap commercials."

"Great. I barely pass the year, everybody looks at me and thinks, there's Ginsburg, the walking disaster. And you have me writing soap commercials?" This was at a period when his life caused him something close to physical pain.

"Artistically," Essie told him, "it doesn't hurt you later to have spent some time as a walking disaster."

A few years after that she said to him, "Competent, yes. Talent, yes. Staying power, that's another story. We might not know for a decade." So he went to college, even though Penny begged him to remain in D.C. When he decided he'd better drop out before he failed everything, he consulted Essie first. His parents would be disappointed, he told her, but book-learning leaked from his brain like water and left behind only his music. What else could he be but a musician?

"You won't be satisfied with just good,

it's genius you want?" Essie tried to stare him down, but Steve knew a few things by then and stared back at her. "Well then, you better be strong for it," she told him. "Genius has a black bottom to it."

Puzzled, Steve scratched a pimple at the end of his nose. He was twenty-two years old and still had pimples. They never covered his whole face, just appeared large and red in strategic places. He thought: red nose, black bottom — the lyrical possibilities. But coming from Essie, a black bottom was a dark, eerie, unfathomable place, and maybe he'd better not take it lightly.

Essie told him she had visited the Black Bottom of Her Soul once as a young woman. "Believe you me, even thinking back on it now still gives me the shivers."

Steve didn't have the faintest idea what she was talking about. Until years later, when he heard the story of the coyote, he didn't know what personal experience might have provoked such terror in Essie, and he certainly didn't know what any of it had to do with genius. Essie didn't offer any details. Yet the discussion armed Steve for everything. Having recovered from her own experience, Essie said, she was in a position to warn him. Imagination could take its flights; did he think the trip was always into the stratosphere? It could with equal ease dip into the depths of blackness, and only the very strong would recover. She was utterly serious. Steve nodded, baffled, and wondered what the hell was going on.

Then she'd said, "So sing your songs, Steve. With your grades . . . you think God has some other plan in mind for you?"

That day in Detroit in 1983, talk-show hostess Sonya Friedman had come into the dressing room while they'd been doing Steve's makeup. He recognized her from the tapes Waldman had sent. He always had Waldman send a couple of tapes so he could get a feel for the show before his interview. The truth was, he got a lot of his information from television. It was from a TV talk show that he'd first learned he couldn't read because he had a condition called dyslexia. Transfixed, he'd listened to a psychology professor explain exactly what happened every time he looked at a printed page. The professor described the dislocation of letters and words so matter-of-factly that it might have been a common experience, when Steve had always thought he was the only one. "It's very frightening," the professor said, "to look at a puzzle everyone else has figured out and not be able to make heads or tails of it."

Amen, Steve thought. He had been drinking coffee at the time, and he raised his cup to toast the TV. Dyslexia research was just beginning to unravel the tricks that could be played by the human brain, the professor said. "Some dyslexics can actually learn to read pretty easily. For others it's harder, but even then there's a lot of help we didn't have before."

Ah — help. Steve was beyond it. Penny had been too confused to care if he could read, and his sister and Barbara always kept it a secret, but his parents and fans and maybe even Waldman believed he was normal. He wasn't going to spoil a good thing by getting help. He dumped out the rest of his coffee and took a long shower to get himself back together.

As to *The Sonya Show* he'd seen last week — he'd liked it. Sonya Friedman was a cool, attractive psychologist, with a no-nonsense approach that reminded him of Essie. Walking into the makeup room to say hello to him, Sonya looked brisk and capable and, physically, much the same as she had on tape. That was in her favor. So many of them looked worse. She was wearing a red blouse and dark skirt that accented her thinness. She smiled, all confidence. "I'm Sonya Friedman," she said. The hand she offered him was cold as ice.

So were Kimberly O'Connor's hands, when she showed up ten minutes early for the rehearsal, looking beautiful but terrified. She calmed down a little when Steve sat at the piano, maybe because they'd gone through that part of the routine earlier. Penny, too, had always calmed down when he started playing. What was wrong with these beauties? In high school Penny was so good-looking you'd have thought she'd go through life strutting like a lioness. He knew Kimberly O'Connor must have her own share of admirers. And still she stood by the piano practically trembling, rubbing her hands together for warmth.

Then she started to sing. She sounded stronger than before, and her voice was sweet. But her looks were too flashy for a backup singer; there was a jittery quality about her that drew the eye. She made Carole and Francie look dim; she was like a fire burning between the two of them. Steve saw no possibility of toning her down, just as he'd never seen such a possibility with Penny. Both women had the whitest skin, the longest legs, the roundest breasts — and hands as cold as ice.

The routine ended. Kimberly O'Connor kept standing by the piano. There was no way Steve could use her, considering.

"You know, we're traveling the next couple of weeks and interviewing some other girls," he said. Kimberly stood still. Steve put a hand on her shoulder to guide her off the soundstage. Best to let her down easy, let Waldman give her the definite no. She walked with Steve to the waiting room, the green room, at the end of the corridor.

No windows here, just intense fluorescent lights and bright modern furniture. TV monitors on both end tables showed the soundstage outside. Francie and Carole stayed outside in the hall drinking Cokes, but Steve motioned Kimberly in. She sat on the royal-blue couch he indicated, following the motion of his hand like an obedient animal. It frightened him. He thought of Penny in her passive mode, waiting for instruction.

He began talking to her as idiotically as he once had talked to Penny, saying inconsequential things about his tour. Next to him, Kimberly O'Connor's body tensed into a knot. "We won't make an immediate

252

decision on another backup," he said finally. "Not for a couple of weeks."

"A couple of weeks . . . I see." She stood up, a wooden soldier, ready to go.

"You might as well stay for the taping, now that you're here. You could watch from back here or go up front with the studio audience." He couldn't make himself stop talking. "You ever see this show taped before?"

"No." She sat back down, stiffly.

"We're on last," he said. Sonya's audience would wait for Steven Simple, hang on through a diet expert, a couple of commercials, a *Reader's Digest* author. He was grateful. A month from now, a year from now, they might not give him the spot reserved for the star.

"Detroit your home?" he asked.

"No. Chicago. I've only been here a year."

She watched him closely, not at all unfocused now. "I saw you a long time ago in Chicago," she said. "It was before you got so famous. You had a whole different kind of style."

"I thought I was America's answer to the Beatles."

She laughed. Loosening up. He felt better.

"You must have been a little kid," he said.

"No, I'm twenty-eight." He was relieved that she was older than he'd thought. At the end, Penny had been — for a second he couldn't remember. Twenty-two? Twenty-three?

"I wrote a lot of my songs pretending to be a Beatle," he said. "Unfortunately, they didn't get an audience until I went solo, with just the piano. Did you know that?"

"Yes." Animated now, a little mischievous. "I do my research."

Francie and Carole came back in, shot him questioning glances, wondered why he'd invited the girl to stay. Good-mannered, they talked to Kimberly and at the same time watched the show on the monitor, which had started a few minutes before. "You married?" Francie asked.

"Was." A wry smile.

Steve kept his eyes on the TV, but listened to Kimberly's every word. She'd gone to Northwestern, majored in drama. Then the marriage. No kids. The divorce.

"I didn't do much with my singing until late." She spoke to Francie, to Carole, but kept her eyes on Steve. The girls were princesses and he was the king, the power source. He knew the look.

An assistant producer stuck her head into the door. "You're up next."

"Come watch us from out front," Steve told Kimberly. It would be more prudent to leave and come back to find her gone, but he couldn't bear it. "After the show we're all going to get something to eat," he said. "You can come with us."

"Thanks."

The princesses raised their eyebrows. Steve never did this.

Kimberly O'Connor fell into step beside him as they walked down the hall to the soundstage. He wasn't touching her, but he wanted to. He wanted to feel her relax, to tell her all his secrets.

He liked the sensation of standing backstage in a TV studio, on cold concrete, anticipating what would come next. The curtain in front of him hung from two stories high, chilly to the touch because of the air-conditioning that kept the cameras cool. In a moment, on cue, he'd step into the light of the stage, into heat, into brightness, and it would be like being born.

"Tell us about Steven Simple the person," Sonya Friedman had said. Usually in his mind it was clear what he'd answer, but Kimberly O'Connor was sitting in the studio audience and he felt reckless. He could give them more than the dumb-kid-who-makes-good story. He could tell them about his dyslexia.

Sonya was talking about the *Penny* album. A singer who'd gotten famous writing about a doomed young love made good patter. But Penny had been gone eighteen years, and Steve had been talking about her for ten, and the talk-show hosts had covered all the angles.

Of the *Penny* album he always said, "Well, she was a nice Jewish girl and I was a nice Jewish boy, but it didn't work out except that I wrote a lot of songs about her." Steve never said Penny slept with almost every male who asked her, or that she had instant, genuine amnesia about the acts they performed. He never hinted that Penny was not just disturbed but literally mad. He also never mentioned that he finally ran away from her with his band because the demands of her illness threatened to suck the music right out of him.

The talk-show hosts believed Steve wrote his songs out of grief. But Sonya Friedman was not going the sympathy route; she was after the shock tactic. "It's not many people who turn a real-life note into a song," she said.

"And not many people who write notes like that." He did not say he could never help the songs he wrote; he wrote what he heard in his head. He was sorry Penny's note had set itself to music, but it had.

I'm falling through the hole
At the bottom of my soul
And there ain't nobody to catch me.

Their friends had thought it a cryptic note, but Essie had understood at once. "You told her what I said to you that day, about the black bottom. I recognized it right away."

"Yeah, I did."

"I knew you might tell her. But who could predict she would find a hole at the bottom of her soul and not a shallow pit?" Essie put her hand on top of his and squeezed it. "Steve, a pit you can climb out of. A hole you can only fall through. It's not your fault."

But it was. If he'd stayed in D.C. and taken care of her, instead of going off to school, she might have been all right. For the next ten years, on the road with his various bands, Penny the person disappeared, and Penny the myth was born.

Steve began to think about her coldly, from a distance, the same way he thought about the other bald fact — he still couldn't read. About the time all the heat was drawn out of him, he got his chance to make the *Penny* album, with "Bus Ride" the second cut. "Bus Ride" made him famous. And that was that.

Kimberly O'Connor was looking at him. Staring worshipfully, as if he possessed something transcendent and had the power to impart it. Penny had given him that same look when she asked him to stay in D.C. and make her sane. He was tired of being worshiped. The truth was, all he could actually give Kimberly O'Connor was a job. If he were going to start something more, she would have to know all about him.

"Steven Simple the human being," Sonya was saying, stalling for time. "What makes Steven Simple run?"

He thought again of making a clean breast of it. *I can hardly read, even now.* Think of the youngsters he could save.

He opened his mouth, because Kimberly O'Connor's eyes were bearing down on him and Sonya Friedman was wishing the hell he'd get on with it. He wasn't sure he had the courage.

He cleared his throat, trying to dislodge the words that had been stuck there most of his life. Finally he said to several million people, "What makes Steven Simple run is that he could never learn to read. He can't read now." He cleared his throat once more and told the rest. His voice had been clear as glass.

CHAPTER 14

Return Trip

I raised a hand to fend off a plate of pastries Bernie was pushing in my direction. Marilyn stood, carried her soup bowl to the sink, then stretched and yawned. "Well, guys, this has been terrific. But now I think I'll go watch the tapes procured for me by a major Hollywood pooh-bah." She kissed Steve on the cheek. "Thanks for coming, Mr. Celebrity."

"I'm not leaving just yet. I expect you to entertain me in the morning."

"Count on it," Marilyn said.

Not wanting to be accused of mothering her too much, Bernie let Marilyn leave the room solo, but a moment later excused himself to see her safely tucked into bed. Steve and I rose to clear the table. If Bernie returned quickly, I wouldn't get to say a private word to Steve, so I spoke less tactfully than I meant to. "Marilyn told me the whole story about Essie Berman saying Penny had a baby. Marilyn's determined to track it down. What's going on, Steve? Why this big confession all of a sudden?"

Bemused, or maybe just surprised, Steve set a stack of plates on the counter and stared at me. "Oh, sweetie, I wish I knew." He stood agape for long seconds. "I wonder about it myself. I could hardly believe Marilyn was sick again. It seemed so impossible. We were both upset. It brought the whole baby thing back to mind — I don't know why. After all this time, maybe I figured there was no harm in telling."

"No harm? Did you know Essie Berman is still alive?"

"She's alive?" He looked bewildered. "I thought she'd been dead for years."

"I went to see her today," I said.

Slowly, Steve opened a cabinet drawer, rummaged until he came up with a roll of plastic wrap. In a low, controlled voice, he said, "And — ?"

"She got a little disoriented while I was there. Fell asleep, actually. She has diabetes. But she did tell me one thing. Did you know the baby was a girl?"

"A girl," Steve repeated. With great deliberation, he carried the plastic wrap to the table and began making neat packages of leftover Swiss cheese and roast beef. "I never knew. I always wondered."

"Penny named her Vera. I didn't tell any of this to Marilyn," I said. "Essie wouldn't say who the father was. She says if Marilyn wants to know, she should come with me to find out. I don't think she's up for the trip."

"No, of course not." Steve opened the refrigerator, nestled the wrapped cheese and meat inside, then said abruptly, "Essie told me about the baby on the condition that I didn't ask any questions."

"Marilyn told me."

"I think I could have asked anyway, but I didn't. Maybe it was just a good excuse not to know."

"You were just a kid yourself, Steve."

He pulled a plastic container from the cupboard and filled it with leftover soup. "Penny was always careful about birth control," he said. "Obsessive, even. Remember? I thought the only way she'd ever get pregnant was if she meant to."

"And even if it had been an accident and Penny was in a bad state mentally, her family would have told you, don't you think?"

Setting the soup inside the refrigerator, Steve turned to me with a sad, wistful smile. "Oh, no, sweetie. They thought I was a bad influence. I probably was."

I began loading the dishwasher. "None of it was your fault, Steve."

"The baby might have been," he said.

"But at the time, I was traveling with my band. I knew something was wrong when Penny dropped out of sight. But something was always wrong, and it was easier not knowing. Then, later, what struck me was the time frame. The way Penny went incommunicado just when she did. And the time frame between the bus ride and the end." He picked up the plastic wrap, replaced it in the drawer. "So I bugged Essie until she told me about the baby, and then I let her make it easy for me by agreeing not to ask any more questions."

"And you've been stewing over it all this time?"

"Only at first. I'd think how Penny had just time to have a baby and give it up and not be able to handle the fact that she'd given it away. Which was pretty much how Penny would react. It might even account for the grand finale. Although I'm not sure how." There was a cold clarity in his eyes, like a nub of melting ice.

"Steve, listen. If she got pregnant on that trip, it could have been the other guy's. It might not have been yours."

"I know that. But you know what? I never cared." After a long pause he added, "That bus ride — It was me she was coming to see."

I felt my throat close, my eyes burn, but I made myself focus and swallow. After more than forty years, Steve still sounded like the boy of fourteen who'd been left breathless by Penny's shy manner and red hair, like the young man of twenty still lovestruck in spite of the arc of destruction Penny had set out upon, and now the man of sixty still nostalgic in spite of Kimberly and their grown children. I knew something about the durability of first loves, myself. Maybe, whatever he learned from Essie, it would be better than nothing.

I crossed the kitchen, took his arm. "Let's go see Essie and find out what happened the weekend of that bus ride, Steve," I said. "We could go in the morning. What do you say?"

After a long, mute minute, Steve said softly, "Sweetie, I thought you'd never ask."

The next morning, after escaping from Marilyn on the pretext that Steve had to replace a pair of glasses, I drove south on New Hampshire Avenue once again, with Steve's famous "Bus Ride" lyrics playing over and over in my head: "Traveling, traveling . . . the Penny girl was traveling" — until I had to turn on the radio to make them stop.

"Bus Ride" had done so well, Steve always liked to say, because it had come out when Vietnam was ending and the country yearned to embrace the antithesis of a political icon — a song so sad and personal that it echoed the national mood without actually referring to it in any way. People liked that "Bus Ride" was a puzzle of a song. They hummed its sweet melody. They were bewitched by lyrics as vague and mysterious as Penny herself. And whether or not Steve's theory made any sense, it was certainly true that in 1975 his song fixed itself on the American consciousness as indelibly as another image had five years before, of a screaming, long-haired girl at Kent State keening over the fallen body of a classmate who'd been gunned down.

"Bus Ride" stayed at number one for twelve weeks, five weeks longer than it took "I Want to Hold Your Hand" to create the Beatlemania craze in 1964. When a radio station in Ohio held a contest for the best explanation of the events of that bus ride, and how they explained what happened to Penny later, twenty thousand entries poured in from all over the country. Like everyone else, I had always believed my own version of the story was the truth.

In the passenger seat beside me, Steve sat mute until south of University Boulevard, where the aging buildings must have begun to look familiar.

"I'm beginning to feel like someone in the twilight zone," he said.

"Nervous?"

"A little." He looked away from me, out the window at strips of tumbledown shops. "You know, I talked about Penny so much in the seventies and eighties that after a while it was like talking about somebody else. Somebody not real."

"Is that why you never told us about her having a baby?"

"Maybe. For a long time, it was as if she didn't exist, except in that surreal way. And the baby, too. Sounds like one of Penny's own tricks, doesn't it?"

"I can see you wanting to forget," I said.

"You know when I started thinking about it again? After I adopted my own kids. When you're young you don't have any sense kids are going to mean anything to you."

"And then you see that your children are going to be the best thing you've got."

"Exactly." Steve hunkered lower in his seat. "But I always felt a little guilty about the 'Bus Ride' story. Seems kind of mean-spirited to tell everyone in the country about it when you're not really sure what happened."

"You can't really have regrets. Not after all this time. You wouldn't have had your career. You wouldn't have drawn attention to how people can learn to read. You wouldn't —"

"Even before that bus ride," Steve said, "Penny used to tell me she didn't remember what she did with guys. I never believed her."

"And after?"

"I think it was true. She started remembering things on that trip and later remembered more. Not just what happened to her in the bus station. Things from way back in high school. Maybe even before that. It spooked me."

"Who knows what was going on in her head by then?" I said softly. "You had a right to be spooked."

Steve squeezed the bridge of his nose, then took his hand away from his face and smiled wryly. "Sometimes I think if she'd ever heard 'Bus Ride' she would have been furious."

"She would have been honored," I told him. For a long while, Steve had repeated obsessively the events of Penny's real-life bus ride every time the two of us had spent more than half an hour together. "But I didn't understand what was going on until later, after she'd wrote that note," he always said. "The note was the catalyst."

He had needed a long time to filter the events of those years through his mind. And then he had written his song. Like everyone else in the country, I had invented the story that went behind it. But unlike most of Steve's fans, I had known Penny and loved her, and I was pretty sure, even now, that my version was actually true.

Traveling, traveling . . . Penny Weinberg had been traveling without the knowledge of her parents or anyone else . . . traveling west, on a Trailways bus, to Morgantown, West Virginia, where Steve had been going to college. "That was the kicker," Steve always said. "I should have invited her. She shouldn't have felt she needed to surprise me. If only I'd known she was coming."

Three hours before, Penny had stepped out of her English class at the University of Maryland, the school she'd transferred to after she'd quit George Washington University. She stepped onto a campus of April-green grass and saw through the color into the idea behind it, the idea that green was the color of wellness. Penny would see Steve and be well. She started to walk into College Park to the bus station when a boy from the English class beeped at her from his car.

"You need a ride?" He looked at her with an expression in his eyes that meant he wanted to touch her, so she asked if he'd drive her to the Trailways station, and he did.

Pretty soon, she was on a bus speeding through the countryside, and a man was staring at her. Sitting across the aisle at the opposite window, he was only a couple of years older than she was, midtwenties maybe, wearing a short-sleeved shirt that showed muscular arms. His arms were suntanned; she could see that without moving her head. She didn't look at his eyes because Steve said not to; men's eyes would always be kind at first. Even Allan Kessler's eyes had been kind, all those years ago, before he'd called her a tramp and gotten her blackballed from the sorority.

Penny smoothed her skirt over her knees: a tan, perfectly ordinary skirt. She was perfectly ordinary.

Shifting away from the window, the man scooted across the aisle in a swift motion and sat down next to Penny. "How far you going?" he asked. She turned from the window. It would be impolite not to look at him now, not to meet his eyes. His face was smooth-shaved and open, with plain brown eyes like Steve's. "Morgantown," she answered.

"I bet you got a boyfriend at the university. Me, I'm going home for the weekend. I work construction in D.C. during the week, but I live in Cumberland." He was proud of that, she could tell. "Danny Sowers," he said, thrusting his long tanned hand out to shake hers.

She felt him touch her, noticing that her own hand was smaller and whiter than his, feeling their two hands move up and down together. Her eyes might have been a camera. She saw the pale brown freckles on her own, smaller hand, marring its whiteness. She took her hand away. "I'm Penny," she said.

"Nice to meet you, Jenny."

She could have explained it was Penny, not Jenny, but she was too ashamed of her hands. Outside the window, the light was fading. In another hour it would be dark.

They pulled off the highway and headed into a town. The streets grew narrow, lined by old brick buildings. People sat on the steps in front of the buildings. Most of the people were fat. "Cumberland," Danny Sowers said. The driver made a hard left into the bus terminal, pulled into a parking place. "Thirty-minute stop here," he said. "You got to change buses here, don't you?"

"I think so."

"You wanna have dinner with me before you go?" Danny asked.

Penny thought of the fat people on the steps of the buildings. This was a place where people got fat. Men were complete in themselves, but women were half, so they had to stay thin. Steve said there was no danger of Penny gaining weight, the way she picked at food, but she didn't like men to see her eat.

"I'm not that hungry," she said.

"Come on, at least have a cup of coffee. I know a place just up the street."

They got off the bus together. No one was staying on the bus during the long stop. In the parking lot next to the terminal, the light had gone gray and colorless. Only a little patch of grass out by the street had the last of the sun on it and was still bright green. Penny remembered she was going to Morgantown because of the greenness, the color of healing.

Danny had a duffel bag in his hand. His

arm beckoned her, its thick, tanned muscles rippling. "Come on."

She moved toward him. He touched a handful of her hair where it met her neck. Steve did that sometimes. "Your hair is some kind of red." In the dusk, everything had gone black and white except Danny's blue shirt and brown eyes like Steve's. He was the only thing in color. Penny let him lead her away from the bus station.

"Just let me drop my bag at my place." At the end of the block, he stopped beside one of the drab old buildings.

"Go ahead," she told him.

He said, "Come on up for a minute."

They climbed a wide wooden staircase that smelled of cooking. At the top, Danny opened a door into a small apartment. It had wood floors, but no rugs, and a few pieces of furniture that did not make it look less empty. It might have been a set for a movie.

"Come here," the man said. It was his place, not hers, so she had to go to him. There was kindness in his eyes, and that familiar expression of wanting her. Penny always thought the kindness promised something, that there was something on the other side.

It was Steve touching her, as always. He

touched her arms and breasts and any-where he wanted. Sometimes he was gentle and sometimes, like now, quick and rough because of wanting her so much. She didn't mind. Her last name was Weinberg and his was Ginsburg. Once after they started going together, Wish Wishner greeted them by saying, "Hi, Bergs," as if they were one thing. She saw this was true. She'd let other boys touch her so she could become whole, but it didn't happen until she was with Steve. Allan Kessler said she was a tramp. *Tramp.* An old, used-up word. It made her feel even less than half.

The man had taken off her blouse and was staring at her, in a disapproving way, like the man in the upholstery shop. "Don't," Penny said.

"Shut up," the man said. He held her by the wrist. "In there."

She let him lead her to the bedroom. She knew she had to. His hands were work-man's hands, thick and sandpapery. She watched through the cameras in her eyes. It didn't take long. It had been quick and rough.

Sometimes, she'd come up through an envelope of cool breeze and be as sane as anybody. "I have to make a phone call," she said to the man at her side. They were in the bus terminal. Yellow lights had been turned on; outside it wasn't quite dark. She'd been away from the bus station and now was back. She might have eaten, but wasn't sure. The important thing was: she had to let Steve know she was on her way to see him. He'd be finished with his afternoon classes and might have a gig that night. She needed to hear him play and sing. As long as he composed his songs for her, hearing him was the least she could do.

"You only wrote *one* song for me," she liked to tease him, pointing out that there was only one song actually entitled "Penny." Steve always replied, seriously, "Not just one song, baby. All of them." She didn't want to get to Morgantown without knowing where Steve was singing.

"You only got a couple minutes till your bus leaves." The man was fidgeting, eyeing the clock. "Maybe you better call from the next stop."

"No. I'll miss him if I call later."

"Yeah, well hurry up."

She had mostly dollar bills. "I have to get change." The man reached into his pocket and pulled out a fistful of coins. He looked annoyed. "Here."

She closed herself into the booth. The man stood outside, nervously checking the parking lot where the buses were waiting. Penny dialed. The phone rang miles away in Steve's dormitory, connecting them by wires through the night air. Someone answered. Not Steve. "I think he went out to eat," the voice said. The air crackled all around her. The voice said, "Hey, wait a minute, here he comes." Steve spoke to her and the air went still.

"Penny?" he said.

She told him she was coming. She told him what time. She had come up through a fine stream of air and was calm.

"Do your folks know you're coming here?" he asked.

"Oh. No."

"What about Dr. Novak?"

"No. Should I call somebody?" It wouldn't matter. Her father was dead, her mother didn't much care, her sisters were married and gone.

"No, never mind. I'll call. I'll fix it. You just get on the bus." Steve's voice was full and deep, the color of wine. When she hung up, a man was waiting outside the phone booth.

"You just got time," he said. The man had brown hair and eyes like Steve's, but she didn't know him. The man tried to take her by the arm. She shook her arm away.

"Hey, you okay? Jenny?"

He kept calling her Jenny. She walked out the door toward the bus. The man followed.

"You ever come through here again, you look me up," he said. Penny found her ticket in her purse. The man winked at her. "See ya, Jenny," he'd said.

The bus had turned on its headlights. Faint outlines of trees floated against the darkness, but mostly Penny saw her own reflection in the glass. She closed her eyes against it. Your reflection was your outside; it had nothing to do with your spirit.

The bus was speeding through the night. Steve said he didn't want Penny just for touching. He wanted her for more than her reflection.

Why had the man in the bus station kept calling her Jenny? He acted like he knew her. *Who was he?* He didn't even know her name.

Steve had never wanted to go away to college. He wanted to stay in D.C. with Penny and sing with his band. For three years, he lived at home while Marilyn went to college. His father said he was getting nowhere. He made Steve go back to school. "Just for one year. After that, you don't like it, fine. But for a year — try it."

So Steve came to West Virginia, where a family friend helped him get in. Fall and winter passed. Penny felt the sickness grow larger in her all that time. Now it was spring and the bus was speeding through the night. She thought of the color of the grass, the color of wellness.

At the terminal in Morgantown, Steve waited for her in a pool of light. She let him hold her, closing her eyes, leaning into his chest. Then he spoke. She recognized his words as truth, and remembered kissing the man from the other bus station, remembered the kindness going out of his eyes. She had let him do what he wanted, but he had not been kind. He was the same man who'd called her Jenny when she came out of the phone booth. It was not a dream. She was a feather dropping, falling in a spiral until she hit the bottom, falling from right now. It would take a long time before she'd be brave enough to do the rest. She didn't think of that yet. All she'd thought about in the Morgantown bus station was Steve holding her in his arms, rubbing her back, and saying in a voice that had been full of love, "Penny, you must be crazy to run away from home like this. You must be crazy, baby."

With an effort, I put aside my version of Penny's bus ride and the sadness it always brought me and turned onto Oneida Street.

At Essie's door, we were greeted not just by Taneka, but also by the bulk of Marcellus, who loomed in the entryway as if he meant to protect Essie from physical assault.

"She ain't used to a lot of company," Marcellus said, barring our way until the old woman, sitting in her chair by the window, barked, "I'm fine, Marcellus. Let them in."

"Good thing I could come over," Marcellus persisted. "Taneka got to go out pretty soon, and Essie got trouble getting to the door." He gestured toward her walker.

"Nonsense," Essie said, not budging from her seat. As Marcellus moved to let us in, Essie's gaze slid quickly over me and lit on Steve with an expression of such undisguised joy that I found it painful to watch.

"So," Essie said as Steve bent to hug her.

"Steven Simple. The important singer." Playfully, she patted his bald head and grinned. "The heartthrob singer becomes a middle-aged man," Essie teased, wagging a finger. Then her features grew rigid again, stern. "This isn't a social call, is it? You came to find out about Penny's baby."

Steve lowered himself into a chair, put his face level with hers. His confidential tone was soft and personal. "Barbara said it was a girl, Essie. She said Penny named her Vera."

Marcellus, who had situated himself on the sofa next to Taneka, got up and crossed the room to stand behind Essie's chair. Still grim, the old woman reached over and took Steve's hand. "Steve, believe me. I've thought about this. This is something you don't need to know."

"Tell me anyway."

Essie paused a moment, and I wasn't sure whether she was gathering strength or sizing him up. "Penny stayed with me while she was pregnant," she said finally. "I took care of her. I helped her with the adoption."

Steve lifted Essie's hand toward his chest, drawing her closer. "All those years ago, you asked me not to ask any more questions. I'm asking now."

Essie shut her eyes as if a great weariness had settled upon her. Marcellus placed his hands protectively on the old woman's shoulders. "Remember the first time you called me? That summer after the bus ride? I told you I didn't know where Penny was and I was telling you the truth," Essie said. "Penny wasn't in touch with me that summer. She came here in the fall. Right around this time of year." With her head back against the wing of her chair, Essie's fragile closed lids seemed nothing but a web of delicate purple veins.

"October? That was pretty late," Steve said. "Penny would have been pretty far along."

Withdrawing her hand from Steve's grip, Essie opened her eyes. "The baby wasn't yours," she said abruptly.

For a second, the room was perfectly quiet. Marcellus's hands began to knead Essie's shoulders. On the sofa, Taneka sat frozen.

Steve didn't flinch. He tried to stare Essie down, but finally gave up and dropped his head into his hands. "Vera was born . . . in January, right?" He studied the carpet. "I always thought it was January."

Essie reached forward and lifted Steve's chin so he'd have to look at her. Her voice was tender as lullabies. "Not January, Steve. April. April 16, 1964."

Marcellus walked around Essie's chair, stood in front of Steve. "What she's saying is, Penny didn't get knocked up the weekend of that bus ride — it happened later."

"I know what she's saying," Steve told him.

In my head, I was doing the math. Though it made no sense to me yet, a wave of light-headedness passed over me, clouded my thoughts.

"So it wasn't his, either," Steve said. "The guy on the bus."

"No," Essie said softly.

"She must have gotten pregnant in the summer," I muttered to myself. When I realized I'd spoken aloud, I felt stupid and slow. "She must have been with someone after she came home from seeing Steve."

For the first time, Essie turned her attention to me. "She stayed with some college friends in June." The old woman's expression was guarded, wily. "In July she took a little trip. For a few days."

"A trip?"

"To Camp Chesapeake," Essie said.

A knife blade of understanding sliced through me without cutting quite to my brain.

"Why would she go to Camp Chesa-peake?" Steve asked. "She hated camp even when we were kids." He turned to me. "You remember that year." To Essie he said, "The only ones who kept going as counselors were Seth Opak and Jon. Didn't Jon become swim director or some-thing?"

"Yes, he did." Essie's tone was so precise it was clear she'd been preparing for this. "Penny went to the camp to talk to him. To clear up some things that bothered her."

I felt the blood drain from my face and thought I might faint.

"Clear up what things?" Steve asked.

No one answered. I returned for a mo-ment to the summer of 1963, when I'd graduated from college and packed for Eu-rope and kissed Wish goodbye. I heard him say in the young, hopeful tone I would never hear again, "Don't worry, Barbara, you're in my heart while I'm eating, while I'm sleeping, even while I'm rescuing those nubile young twelve-year-olds from jelly-fish in the Chesapeake Bay."

I recalled myself laughing, saying, "Fat chance." Believing him all the same.

It had not made sense that the person who returned from Camp Chesapeake three months later was not Wish at all, but someone who called himself Jon and wanted to put as much distance between the two of us as he could.

"Oh, my God," I whispered.

"I'm lost," Steve said. "Does someone want to fill me in?"

"Jon," I gasped.

"What?" Steve's face was all bewilderment.

"The baby," I blurted. "She's Jon's, isn't she?"

Essie shrugged. "He may not even know it."

"Don't play games with me, Essie. He may not know about a baby, but he certainly knows if . . . if it's a possibility."

"Then he's the one you should talk to," Essie said.

"That's why you wanted me to bring Marilyn. To hold my hand." Until I felt the wetness on my cheeks, I had no idea I was crying.

"It's bad news, I know. But it's not the way you think," Essie said. "Ask Jon. Ask him what they talked about. Him and Penny. Before you do anything you'll regret, Barbara, think. Think how you and Jon started and how you ended once. Think if you want that to happen again.

Talk to him. There's more."

"More?"

Essie nodded. "Talk to him," she said again.

CHAPTER 15

Driving South

I didn't know how I managed to stand without my knees buckling, but somehow I did.

"You all right?" Taneka put a hand behind my elbow for support. I was too startled to pull away.

"I'm all right." Without willing to, I leaned on Taneka and moved toward Essie. The old woman also stood up, with agonizing effort and slowness, as if enacting some painful but compulsory ceremony.

"Thank you," I said, aware I was expressing gratitude for the worst moment of my life. I hugged Essie, though it was the last thing I intended. Inside the circle of her arms, Essie's bones were as birdlike and brittle as the illusions of my youth, and I resented them all: Essie and a thousand tarnished memories. If I got through this, I would never come back, not to Riggs Park and not to this house, not even for Marilyn.

When I released her, Essie said, "It will be worse when you see him. Don't give up on him until you hear him out."

"I won't, Essie." Without meaning to, without a shred of feeling behind the gesture, I smiled.

Steve said his own goodbyes, then tucked his arm around my shoulders. Marcellus and Taneka followed us out to the porch.

"You still glad you came around asking all those questions?" Marcellus asked me.

"She feels bad enough, Daddy," Taneka said.

"I told you it might be complicated. I asked did you still want to hear."

I stood up as straight as I could. "I wanted to hear. I'm not sorry."

"It's hard for her, too," Marcellus said. "She old. It's hard."

I was shaking too badly to drive. In a gesture of great tenderness, Steve plucked the keys from my fingers and slipped into the driver's seat.

Wounded and dull, I felt my mind move slowly, ineptly, like heavy boots through mud. "All this time, and I never knew," I said. "I'm actually living with him, and he never said a word."

"Maybe he doesn't know, either."

"You mean about Vera? He certainly

knows he slept with Penny."

Steve said nothing. Another thought crossed my mind. "Maybe Penny did go after Jon," I heard myself say. "Maybe it was the payback."

"You mean because you were in that sorority back in high school and she wasn't? No. She didn't hold it against you. All she wanted was to be your friend. Besides, that sorority business was — what? — six, seven years before all this happened. Penny loved you as much as she could love anybody. She certainly never cared about Jon."

"Then why did she go all the way out to Camp Chesapeake to see him?" Anger filled me like hot liquid, so searing that it finally cleared my head. "Why did she sleep with him?"

"That's the sixty-four thousand dollar question, isn't it?" With his free hand, Steve made as if to smooth the hair on his bald crown, but his expression was stony. He sat in a rigid posture I didn't recognize, and it finally dawned on me what strong emotion there must be behind that unyielding pose.

"I guess I'm having a real pity party here. Poor little Barbara. I'm sorry, Steve. What about you? Are you mad? Sad?"

"Just puzzled." A long pause. "Jon and

Penny? I don't get it."

I didn't, either, but the wound had become too raw to touch. "I mean how do you feel about the baby?"

"Relieved. Beyond relief. It's not something I'd want to have to tell my kids."

"I guess it's not something you'd want to have to tell Kimberly, either."

"Kimberly's not an issue," he said softly.

"What do you mean?"

"I was hoping this wouldn't come up this particular trip. I was going to wait until Marilyn was stronger." Steve watched the road, didn't look at me. "We're separated. Soon to be in the process of getting a divorce."

"Oh, Steve — *no.*"

"We've been keeping it quiet because we didn't want the media to know before the kids did."

"Well, sure. I just can't believe — I thought you were the perfect couple," I blurted. "I'm so sorry."

"We spent all that energy trying to have kids, and then adopting them, and then raising them. Once they moved out, there was nothing left." His tone was wistful. "It was one of those marriages that just wore itself out."

"Still —"

"You asked me before why I mentioned Penny's baby to Marilyn that day she called to say she was sick again. I think partly it was because I didn't want to tell her about Kimberly. Not with so much else on her mind. It seems pretty small now, but I thought the story would give her something to focus on besides herself. I didn't think she'd go anywhere with it. I didn't want to burden her right then with another family failure."

"It's not a failure. It's —"

"It is a failure, sweetie. When people break up it's a failure. For whatever reasons. It is."

We drove for a time in silence. In the distance, two dark clouds merged, heavy and smothering, and drifted across the blue clarity of sky. Steve watched the shadow cross our line of vision. Then the sight of a shopping center distracted him, pulled him back into the world, and he turned on his blinker to switch lanes. "We need some glasses," he said.

"Glasses?"

"To show Marilyn. Remember? You and I went out because I forgot my glasses."

"Oh. Right."

"And we'll get her some kind of gift. A get-well present. To cheer her up."

We ended up buying her a stack of CDs.

In the checkout line Steve said, "I'm going to stay a couple extra days. Push my trip to New York back to the weekend. I should have done that in the first place. That means you can go back to North Carolina and talk to Jon. That's what you want, isn't it?"

"I'm not sure 'want' is any part of it."

"Well, you've got to talk to him. Essie said there was more. Maybe there's some explanation."

"Whatever the explanation is, it won't change the fact."

The cashier was staring at Steve, trying to place him. I could almost see the thoughts racing through her head. *Steven Simple? No, it couldn't be. Well, maybe.* To her credit, the girl didn't say a word.

"Are we going to tell her? Tell Marilyn?" I asked.

Now it was Steve's turn to hesitate. "She wanted a niece. She doesn't have one."

The cashier counted change into Steve's outstretched hand.

"If it's not going to make any difference," I said, "then maybe we should wait."

I left Marilyn's house an hour later, having been more or less shooed out.

"Brother Stevie will take care of you," Steve told his sister. "I'm sending Barbara home so I can have you to myself. After all, you can see Barbara any time. How often do you get personal attention from an internationally acclaimed rock star?" Marilyn giggled, so enchanted by his attention she hardly knew I was there. Having a full night's sleep had restored her.

"Are you mad at me for hauling you up here and now sending you back?" she asked.

"Of course not, Marilyn." I hugged her gingerly, trying not to touch her face. "I have work to catch up on. But if you need me again — if you need anything — just say the word."

Steve carried my bags out, put them in the trunk. "Bernie and I will take care of Marilyn," he said. "You take care of Barbara, sweetie."

"I will." He seemed so solid that for a second I wanted to throw my arms around him and melt safely into his soft blue shirt. Instead, I opened the door and got in. Steve bent over and planted his usual sweet, chaste kiss on my lips, but held it so long it began to feel almost unbrotherly before either of us thought to move away. We were that rattled, that confused.

* * *

Southbound, homebound, I was so deep
into my memories that I hardly noticed the
gathering clouds or the beginning of a
steady, lulling rain. The gas gauge dropped
toward a quarter of a tank, usually my
signal to stop, but just then it was not
enough to concern me. With festering
anger I recalled our senior year. Ever since
our sledding accident, Wish and I had become a pair, but we'd been sly and furtive,
cautious as cat burglars. Wish was eighteen, old enough to have a girlfriend, but
too afraid of his father — who, everyone
knew, planned for Wish to become a
doctor and had been grooming him for it
forever. I must have been afraid, too. Carefully, we began to limit our "official" dates
to major events like Christmas night and
New Year's Eve and senior prom. The rest
of the time we went out with other people.
Or we went solo to parties where secretly
we could join up — but never freely, never
lightheartedly, always with an eye to
staying under Murray Wishner's radar. We
sneaked around.

All in all, I spent less time with Wish
than with Barry Levin, who for all his
beauty was never more than a casual
friend. I went out with Barry because I

knew word would get back to Wish's father, who always kept a sharp eye and tight rein on his son. Barry was handsome, witty and cheerful, a superb dancer, the perfect date to show off at a social function. Given Barry, why would Murray ever suspect my relationship with Wish?

But Barry was neutral. He gave off no fire. He didn't want a girl, he wanted to be a social director, and he used our many casual dates as opportunities to invite everyone to the parties he threw at his house. On those evenings, after his parents lost interest in chaperoning and he could dim the lights, Wish and I clung to each other during the slow songs, not dancing so much as simply hugging. It was as if Barry had been in league with me all along, orchestrating his parties exclusively for my benefit.

"Maybe he does," Penny mused once when I was spending the night in her dungeon of a bedroom. "Maybe it's — in gratitude. Sort of."

"Gratitude for what?"

Looking up from polishing her toenails, Penny seemed puzzled that I would need to ask. "For not telling anybody he's queer."

"Queer! What a thing to say!"

"Does Barry ever kiss you, Barbara? Or — you know. Touch." Penny lifted the brush from a painted toenail, cocked her head.

"Well —"

"I didn't think so." She placed the brush into the jar of polish, tightened the cap. "He'd die if he thought anybody knew."

"But *you* know."

"That's different." We didn't dwell on how Penny knew, or why. "It's nice the way you treat him. The way you never mention how he is."

"Well, thanks." But sometimes I wondered if Wish knew, too, and that was why he never seemed jealous. And sometimes I wondered if he conceded Barry to me because secretly he enjoyed the other girls he dated "casually" to keep his father in the dark. It was a stupid, stupid game. It had robbed us of a year.

Now I drove as if by rote and seethed with anger. I didn't notice that dusk had fallen, or that the rain was steady now, and pelting. I didn't see the Blazer pull around me, or register the puddle in the other lane. When the Blazer began to hydroplane, it came at me so slowly that I might have veered away as easily as Jon and I had once veered our sledding bodies to safety on Oneida Street. It would have been simple to pull out of the Blazer's path and drive on. In retrospect, everything is always simple. But I didn't see. I kept going straight just long enough to let the Blazer drift into me, starting the chain reaction that involved, finally, half a dozen cars.

CHAPTER 16

Beginnings

Fifteen hours later I jerked awake, aching all over, a sharp point of pain throbbing in the center of my head.

"Hey, you're all right. Just a little banged up." Jon's voice. Then Jon himself, his shirt wrinkled, face stubbled beneath the white mop of his head. He laid a cool hand on my arm to calm me. My eyes slid across the shadow of his beard to a clock on a strange night table. Ten twenty-three.

"A.m. or p.m.?" My voice hoarse, as if I had a cold. "Where are we?"

"A motel." Jon pulled back heavy curtains to reveal a bright sky outside. "A.m. You slept late because they gave you a sleeping pill before we left the hospital."

"Hospital?"

"The accident yesterday. Remember?"

Then I did. The Blazer first, the chain reaction. Cars skidding through the rain. Screeching brakes and clashing metal. In the end, dents and a few cuts, but amazingly, no one seriously hurt.

"Are you all right?" a policeman had asked.

296

"Yes. Fine." In the strobe effect of police cars and ambulances, I had stood dumbly, shivering with shock and disbelief.

"Is there someone we can call?"

Without thinking, I'd given him my number at home.

They'd made all of us go to the hospital. In the emergency room, I'd sat in the waiting area among the crowd, a bunch of bumped, bruised motorists, dazed and mute in varying stages of shock. That had been where Jon had found me four hours later. He'd gotten off his plane from Kansas City, driven to our house at the beach, and opened the door just as the phone had begun to ring. Without changing clothes, he'd left immediately for Richmond, where he found me at the hospital and brought me to this motel. I didn't remember the pain pills, but I felt too hungover not to believe I'd swallowed one. Maybe two.

"They took your car to a shop," Jon said.

"Bad, huh?"

"The back driver's side is pretty bashed in. And the passenger side in front."

I nodded. Jon looked awful. "You didn't get any sleep," I said.

"I did." He pointed to the other side of my bed. Rumpled. "A couple of hours."

I reached up, about to run my hand across his sandpapery chin when I remembered my purpose in making this particular trip. I drew my hand back as if it had been burned.

"You'll feel better after you take a shower," Jon said. "Then get dressed and I'll drive us home. They won't know more about your car for a day or two."

"You got off the plane and weren't in the house five minutes before you had to leave," I realized.

"I didn't mind." He touched what I discovered later was a purple bump on my forehead. "You're lucky you weren't hurt more. We're both lucky."

Were we? My limbs creaky and slow, I tried to swing my legs over the side of the bed. When Jon took my arm, I hadn't the strength to shake him off. "Not even sixty years old, and in need of assisted living," he joked.

I didn't smile. What I lacked, perhaps what I had always lacked, was a quality of mercy. I was annoyed that he was being so considerate, irritated at being beholden to him. I hated knowing I'd have to lean on him, at least until they fixed my car.

But by the time Jon had settled me in for the ride back to Wrightsville Beach, my bravado had vanished. I'd pushed around the food he insisted we have for brunch and swallowed the pain pills the emergency room doctor prescribed. "He knew you were going to be sore," Jon told me. But I wasn't sure whether it was my battered physical state or the medicine that made me feel so weak and confused and dependent. Lulled by the moving car and the warm sunlight coming in the window, I dozed and woke with a panicky start.

"It's okay," Jon said. "We just passed Roanoke Rapids. Go back to sleep."

When I opened my eyes again, we were another sixty miles down the road, and I was still so far into the twilight zone that it took me long seconds to adjust to the passing landscape. Then a more lucid moment came, when I registered a clear vision of Jon's profile as he concentrated on a nearly empty stretch of Interstate 40. He smiled wearily and reached over to pat my arm.

"Feeling better?"

"A little."

"Don't worry. Doctor Jon will take good care of you. Whisk you home and get you fixed up in no time."

Why did he have to be so kind? I closed my eyes to hide the tears that welled. *Re-*

member how you began once, and how it ended, Essie had said. *Think if you want it to happen again.* We had begun so many times. Which one was I supposed to remember? Then drugged oblivion claimed me again, dragged me back through the miles and years. Where had we begun, really? Which time?

It had been one o'clock on the afternoon of Penny's father's funeral — I could see the clock as clearly as if it were before my eyes — and Wish and I had been studying cat muscles in our zoology lab at the George Washington University in downtown D.C. Wish and I stood with our heads bent, pretending to be absorbed in our work, when uppermost in our minds was the fact that Sid Weinberg was about to be buried in Arlington National Cemetery and we'd better get going.

Our lab exam was the next day, and we were studying this extra hour because we'd skipped most of our classes while divers were searching for Sid Weinberg's body. Penny's father was one of nineteen navy bandsmen killed when their plane collided with a Brazilian airliner over Rio de Janeiro harbor, an event that seemed almost too distant and exotic to grasp. The band had been on a South American tour, flying to Rio to play at President Eisenhower's reception for the Brazilian president.

My hands trembled and my stomach hurt. I hated the idea of going to the cemetery with just Wish. Ever since we'd started school at G.W. the previous fall, I'd had another boyfriend, Sandy. Wish and I carpooled to school with Marilyn and Bernie and Penny, and we took some of our classes together, but we didn't see each other socially. Sandy would have driven me to the cemetery except that he had to work.

"We're going to have to get out of here," Wish said. "We'll be late." We'd skipped the service at Danzansky's funeral home, reasoning it would be a mob scene where we couldn't do Penny any good. We'd spent most of the last two weeks sitting in Penny's living room, where family and friends kept vigil, waiting for the bodies to be recovered.

"The ironic thing is, Sid didn't even want to go," Helen Weinberg sobbed day after day, dabbing at her nose with a flowered hankie. "None of them wanted to go." She had become too pathetic to hate.

Penny spent her days looking out the front window, her face as expressionless as if it had been shot full of novocaine. When the bodies were finally found, word came that the divers had recovered only *parts.* Helen sobbed so hysterically, and her three older daughters surrounded her with such tender ministrations, that you would have thought she was Mother of the Year. Penny kept looking out the window. "Parts," she said in a flat deadpan. "I wonder which parts."

In the zoology building, Dave Hochman came over, the lab instructor, short but handsome, with thick-lashed blue eyes. "You about finished?"

"Yeah, I'm afraid finished might be the word," I said, aware that Hochman had let us stay late so he could ogle me. He was going to the University of Virginia medical school in Charlottesville next year, which made him something of a catch. I pushed out my chest. My sweater was a bit tight, the only black sweater I owned.

"Come on," Wish urged. He shoved my book bag at me and more or less pushed me out the door. "You act like such a bubblehead around Hochman," he said.

"That doesn't stop you from using the extra lab time he lets me have."

"You know what? You're the smartest girl I know, and I doubt either Hochman or Sandy knows you have a brain in your head."

We came outside into cold sunshine — the pretty, deceptive cold of Washington in March. My dark skirt and sweater were too thin, my good coat was flimsy, and I had on high heels instead of my usual loafers, which let the wind wash over my feet. We walked west on G Street past G.W.'s parking lot, then down two blocks toward the river, to the construction site where Wish liked to park. I was shivering.

"I've never been to a burial at Arlington National Cemetery," I said. "We usually just take company there to see the tomb of the Unknown Soldier."

"Yeah, us, too." Wish had on his winter jacket and gloves. It had snowed the week before, and little patches of ice still clung to the grass by the river.

"Sandy can't make it to the cemetery at all," I said. "He's meeting us at Penny's house after."

"Yeah, well, thanks for telling me. That's a piece of information I especially needed to hear." Sandy was six years older than we were. A law student. An Episcopalian. I might never have met him if his father hadn't come to speak to my history class. Cornell Williams was one of the congressmen often asked to lecture at the university because their children were students. Sandy had come to hear his father talk.

Afterward, I went up to ask a question, not so much because I cared about politics as because Sandy was standing by the window with a bar of sunlight illuminating his blond hair — the same color hair as my own. He looked so handsome that I was drawn forward. He looked completely different from Wish.

Sandy said, "Is it anything I can answer?" and moved me away from the clutch of students around his father.

I was attracted to his sheer *difference*. In the first months of my freshman year, I'd gone out with Wish only once, in the safe company of Bernie and Marilyn, and then decided I was tired of being cautious because of Wish's father's expectations. Who cared? I dated two boys from the undergraduate Jewish fraternities and went to a few movies with my old pal Barry Levin, who was attending American University. All of these boys were Jewish. Before Sandy, I had never been out with a boy who wasn't. His Christian faith was part of his attraction. I expected my parents to object. My mother didn't disappoint.

"We scraped and saved so you could go to college," she said in a tone of uncharacteristic bitterness. "We were so proud of you. And the first thing you do is fall in love with a *goy*."

"Who said I'm in love? I'm going out with him, that's all. It's no big deal."

"No, and next week we'll see the engagement ring."

"Oh, mother."

"*Tikkun Olam,* Barbara."

"What's that supposed to mean?"

"It means an obligation. Repair the world. Fix the world. Improve the world. If you marry him, are you going to teach your children that? Oh, you might raise them Jewish, send them to shul —"

"When did *we* ever go to shul?"

"— but it won't take. Mark my words. What about your children's children? They won't know a thing about it."

It was a ludicrous battle. If Sandy became a congressman like his father, I argued, who was to say he wouldn't be engaging in *Tikkun Olam* himself?

"That's not the point!"

"Then what *is* the point, Mother? For heaven's sake!"

We shouted at each other for an hour, two nonobservant Jewish women acting as

305

if I were about to elope any moment with a young man I hadn't much cared about until my mother made him a challenge. We argued until we were both too exhausted to continue, and though no one won, we hugged and felt purged.

After that, my parents acknowledged Sandy's existence with grudging silence. Wish said my parents tolerated the guy because they admired Congressman Williams's politics. Sandy was going to spend the summer helping his father campaign for reelection. I announced to my friends — but not my parents — that I thought Sandy would ask me to join him.

"A summer in New England. It would be great, don't you think?" I had been in the back seat of Bernie's car on the way to school, crunched between Marilyn and Penny.

"Great," agreed Marilyn, to whom this was news.

"I wish it was me," said Penny.

Wish turned around from the front passenger seat to face me. "You know the first thing I noticed about Sandy? I noticed that the minute he opens his mouth, people know he started boarding school when he was five."

"Jealous?" I'd said, smiling.

Now, walking down G Street after studying, I blew into my hands to warm them. They smelled of formaldehyde, sweet but pungent. In the open air my queasiness was gone. Wish moved closer. For a minute I thought he'd put his arm around me, make me stop shivering, but he didn't. For months he hadn't touched me.

At the cemetery, cars were already parked all along the roadway. A huge crowd had gathered at the burial site — families of all the men, friends, the other hundred-odd members of the navy band who hadn't been on the South American tour. Wish drove up one hill and down another before he found a parking space.

The navy-band widows were seated in chairs by the caskets. So many caskets, draped with flags. Probably only part of Sid Weinberg was in there, and parts of the other men in the other caskets. I recalled our hours in Penny's living room, where every day we brought her assignments and pretended she was going to do them, to take her mind off things. She rarely did homework even when there was no crisis. Mostly, ever since we'd started college, she spent her spare time with Steve, unless he was off somewhere with his band. But this last two weeks, an occasional boy that none of us knew showed up at Penny's house, and if Steve wasn't around, Penny would go off with the boy for an hour and then return alone. It was sad to watch, but hard to blame her. Sitting around on furniture that had been placed into a circle for the guests, the dining-room chairs as well as the upholstered pieces, it was as if we were already sitting *shivah.*

Our friends from the neighborhood tried to lighten the mood by telling stories about our years at Coolidge High. We had graduated less than a year before, but it seemed longer now that some of us were at different colleges, making different friends. One evening, we were all laughing over one story, but when we turned to Penny her face was completely blank, and in the background Helen was crying.

Penny looked up as if she hadn't heard a word and said, "I'll probably drop out of school. It's been almost two weeks already."

"You don't have to drop out," Marilyn told her. "We'll help you make everything up." In a way, we missed tutoring Steve now that we were out of high school. We would have looked forward to tutoring Penny. We wouldn't have minded.

"I'm not sure I want to make everything

up," Penny told us.

A man began to walk along the line of widows, greeting each of them, the back of his dark head and black overcoat toward the crowd. When he reached Helen, she shook hands with him in a mechanical way. I recognized the jowls and the ridiculous slope of nose.

"Oh, no . . . not Nixon," I said. I leaned on Wish. He put his arm around me and held me against the cold.

"Eisenhower should have come to the funeral himself," I whispered. He'd gotten Sid Weinberg killed, but apparently didn't think navy bandsmen rated a presidential visit. Musicians weren't crucial to the running of the country; they were just background, just servants. I had always hated Sid Weinberg on Penny's behalf, because he'd wanted sons instead of daughters, but I didn't hate him then.

Nixon finished shaking hands, then moved away with his contingent of Secret Service men. He had a mean, mournful look on his face, like a parody of someone being serious, someone who really didn't care.

They folded the flags and handed them to the widows. The twenty-one-gun salute began. The crack of shots into the cold air made me jump. Wish let go of me. The guns were shooting and they were lowering caskets into the graves. Penny was clenching her teeth. Helen was crying and I was crying, too. I would never hate Helen again.

Afterward, I meant to ask my mother or Bernie for a ride back to Penny's house, but somehow I stayed with Wish. He'd also offered a ride to Paul Siegel, a boy I'd never liked. On the wet road going down the hill to Wish's car, my shoes were soaked through and I kept slipping. I could hardly feel my feet. Paul Siegel watched me with a menacing half smile on his face. I knew he'd love to see me go down on my can.

"Let me sit in the back," I said when we got to the car. "My feet are all frostbitten. I can't even feel them. I need a little room to stretch."

Paul slid into the front seat next to Wish.

I pulled off my shoes and started rubbing my feet.

"So where's the lawyer?" Paul asked, referring to Sandy.

"Sandy won't be a lawyer until he graduates in June." With Paul it was always the lawyer this, the lawyer that, like I was dating some octogenarian. Under my stockings, my feet were an unnatural white.

"He'll never practice law. He'll go right into politics." Paul made *politics* sound obscene. Even Essie Berman said, "People like Sandy have nothing to do with people like us. We work for the government and they come down here to *be* the government."

In the rearview mirror, Wish looked at me rubbing my feet. "You okay?"

"Yeah, I guess." A little sensation was coming back into my toes, the feeling of pins and needles.

"You should've worn boots," Wish said. "A heavier coat, too."

At Penny's house, Paul got out of the car, but didn't push his seat release to let me out of the back. As I leaned forward to do it myself, Wish said, "Here, get out my side," and offered his hand.

I started to put my foot onto the street. When it touched the ground, I couldn't feel a thing. I might have been trying to stand on a pile of marshmallows. My knee buckled and Wish caught me.

"I don't think I can stand up," I said.

"It's okay, probably just frostbite." He motioned me to sit down in the car again, and he got back behind the wheel.

"Hey, where're you going?" Paul yelled from the sidewalk.

"She forgot something," Wish said, and drove up the block to my house.

My heart was pounding fast. I had a picture in my mind of white hospitals, white ice, my white toes.

"Give me your house key," Wish said. My father was at work and my mother would go right to Penny's. Wish parked at my curb and got out. "Here, hang on to me." Still wearing his gloves, he pulled me from the car, onto my feet. Before my legs could give, he caught me under the knees and was carrying me — into my house, through the living room, and up the stairs to the bathroom, where he sat me on the edge of the tub. I didn't know if anyone had seen us. I didn't care.

He took my shoes off and yanked at my stockings. While he was pulling my stockings down he was running water into the bathtub. "What's going on?" Wish was undressing me right across the street from the funeral where everyone in the neighborhood had gathered, but I didn't really care; maybe I wasn't fully conscious. I wanted to close my eyes and sleep.

Next thing I knew, I was sweating. Wish stuck my bare feet into the water in the bathtub. The water was cool, but against my feet it felt warm.

"You all right?" he said. His words came at me from a long way off.

"Yeah, I guess. What're you doing?"

"I'm thawing out your feet."

"I thought you were undressing me."

"No, not now. Maybe some other time." He knelt on the bathroom floor next to me. "I think we're supposed to rub them until the feeling comes back," he said. "You rub one and I'll do the other."

We bent over, heads together. Any other time I would have felt foolish, but just then I didn't.

"You feel anything?" he asked.

"A little."

We kept rubbing. The unnatural pallor of my feet began to give way to a pinkish color under the water. Then the pink turned bright red. My feet itched something terrible.

"This might be worse than the numbness," I said.

"Don't scratch. Here." Wish handed me a towel. "The itching is normal. Dry off and I'll wait for you downstairs." He went out of the bathroom.

"How do you know the itching is normal?" I asked when I got to the living room. I had put on dark stockings and closed pumps, because my feet looked like I'd stuck them under a sun lamp. I kept rubbing my toes together to control the itch.

"I don't know, I must have read it somewhere." Wish sounded tired, or maybe embarrassed. "Come on, let's get back to Penny's before they miss us."

Everyone from the cemetery had arrived, leaving no parking spaces anywhere on the block. We were walking down the hill, when Sandy came up the street toward us from wherever he'd left his little Triumph. He took my arm.

Inside the Weinberg home, the mirror by the entryway was covered by a black cloth for the mourning period. Sandy pulled himself up like someone at attention and led me to a place against the dining-room wall. "How was the funeral?" he asked.

"It was all right." I wanted to tell him about my feet, but people were standing on both sides of us and the subject seemed too private.

We were crushed against the wall by a woman who pushed past us with a platter of whitefish and bagels and lox. There was deli and rye bread on the dining-room table, and people were bringing cakes and strudel.

"Nixon was there," I told him. "I think Eisenhower should have come."

"Traditionally the vice president represents the president at funerals," Sandy said.

People jammed the whole downstairs. Bernie and Marilyn were squashed against the far wall, eating. Helen sat on the living-room couch, receiving whoever came in. I didn't see Penny.

"Let's get something to eat," Sandy said.

"I'm not hungry. You go ahead."

As Sandy disappeared into the crowd, my mother came toward me, holding an old lady's hand. "This is my daughter, Barbara," she said. "Barbara, you remember Mrs. Ades, Francine's grandmother."

"Oh, of course." I didn't.

"All grown up," Mrs. Ades said. "I remember when you were this high."

For just a minute my line of vision cleared and I watched Penny sit down next to her mother. Helen didn't notice. Helen was talking animatedly because so many people were around her, wishing her well. No one was talking to Penny just then. Her face was vacant, and I knew she really was going to quit school.

My mother and the old woman moved

away. I remembered all the nights from third grade on, teaching Steve. I'd miss having the chance to tutor Penny. I'd miss carpooling to school with her and seeing her after class. After the cold outside, it was too warm in the house. I scanned the room for Wish. I wanted to tell him how sad I was that Penny was quitting school. How sad I was that Penny was sad. I wanted us to cheer her up. We would tell her my feet had frozen at Arlington National Cemetery, and Wish had thawed them out in a tub of water, though he'd never thought to stoop so low as to rub my feet. "Other parts maybe, but never her feet."

Penny would laugh, and even if she quit school, she would come back next year, or go to American University or the University of Maryland instead, and she would be as well as she could be. This was what we had planned, maybe without ever talking about it. One of the young men at the table caught my eye. It took me a minute to realize it was Sandy, standing among all my dark-haired friends eating bagels and lox. I smiled at him, though there seemed no point to it. He had nothing to do with me, not really, not now.

When I broke up with Sandy a few days

later, I was careful not to tell my mother my reasons. Let her think, if she wanted, that I gave him up because he wasn't Jewish. Let her think she'd won. I didn't tell her my decision had nothing to do with religion and everything to do with being in love with Wish. But my mother already knew that, and so did everyone else.

This time, Wish was strong enough to stand up to his father. He was a college student, mature enough for a girlfriend. He'd made dean's list and seemed on track for medical school. For the most part, Murray left us alone.

We made love for the first time a few months later, in a rooming house at Rehoboth Beach. We spent the entire afternoon in the bedroom while Marilyn and Bernie and Penny and Steve were out enjoying the ocean. A breeze blew into the open window as Wish took off my clothes item by item, careful not to hurry. He kissed me everywhere, and did not stop kissing until I moaned and came and sighed. After a while he started kissing me again. He guided my hand to his penis. By the time he entered me, I was so wet, so stretched, so ready, that it did not hurt. I was surprised, afterward, to see blood on the sheet.

We lay there until the sun dropped behind the trees to the west, dozing and waking and talking. "I've waited for this since forever," Wish told me in a raspy voice.

"Since the day we fell off the sled," I added. I traced the line of his injured shoulder with my finger, amazed that at last he was mine to touch.

When the others returned, everyone knew what must have happened. Wish and I didn't care. We had waited and were not sorry. This, both of us had known, was for the rest of our lives.

CHAPTER 17

Explanation

By the time Interstate 40 ended and dumped us onto College Road in Wilmington, I was finally waking up. The medicine had worn off. A slow ache crept up my spine and fanned out into all my limbs. When Jon looked over and gently asked me how I felt, I avoided his eyes, steeled myself against softness. I let the pain remind me I'd been left bruised before, and not just physically. All I needed now was the resolve to confront him. Traffic mishaps aside, there could be no more diffidence or hesitation.

In our driveway at last, Jon opened my car door and reached in to help me. I pulled away. "I'm not an invalid." Ignoring his puzzled expression, I wriggled out of the car, marched up the steps as fast as my gimpy limbs allowed, and waited in the living room while he carried my bag to the bedroom.

"Now we'll get *you* tucked in," he said when he came back, humoring me in a voice laced with an exhaustion I tried not to hear.

"I'm not ready to be tucked in yet."

"Barbara, what's wrong?"

I opened the sliding glass door to the deck, to the sight of a gray and foamy sea. Although the breeze was not balmy as it had been a few days before, I ignored the chill and willed the sound of the ocean to drown out the blood beating in my ears. "Sit down, Jon." In a voice more modulated than I expected, I told him everything. He listened in stunned silence until I got to the part about Penny having his child. Then I saw by his expression that he was not surprised.

"You knew all the time," I accused.

"I didn't know 'all the time.' I didn't know until five years ago. Right before my father died."

"Who told you?"

A solemn stillness dropped across his features. "It's not the way you think it is, Barbara." He took a long breath. "However you imagine it, it's worse."

He told the story almost in a monotone. I had the feeling he'd memorized the exact words, bled all the emotion from them. I had the feeling the task had taken most of his life.

When Penny had shown up in the Camp

320

Chesapeake dining hall on a Wednesday evening in July 1963, Jon said, at first he'd been puzzled. The camp was a far more glamorous place than it had been eleven years before when Penny had endured the fateful camping experience from which she'd finally escaped. There was now an Olympic-size pool; the cabins sported ceiling fans and window air conditioners; a lighted tennis court sat next to a newly paved parking lot. Even so, Jon didn't think Penny would be curious to see the improvements. Her memories of the place, he imagined, were still unpleasant enough to keep her away.

His next thought, as Penny scanned the room and stopped when she spotted him, was that something had happened to me. After graduating from G.W. in June, Marilyn and I had gone to Europe for a long-anticipated, long-saved-for fling. Penny would have come with us, but she still had another year at the University of Maryland, where she'd enrolled a year after her father's death, and didn't have the money. Watching the grim, set line of Penny's jaw as she made her way through a dining hall full of campers, Wish knew I must have been hurt. It would be like Penny not to want him to hear by phone. Why else would she drive all the way to southern Maryland to seek him out like this?

Penny said no, she hadn't come because of me. "It's something else. Is there somewhere we can talk?" The dining hall was sweltering, but Penny crossed her arms tight over her chest, and when Wish touched her elbow to lead her out, she was shivering.

They sat atop the bluff overlooking the Chesapeake Bay, on a blanket Wish had grabbed from his bunk. "This is no friendly social visit," Penny said. "I came to tell you what happened in your father's upholstery shop that summer after eighth grade."

Already wary, Wish decided the best thing to do was suggest that, whatever had happened that terrible summer, it could no longer be as important as she thought. "That was a long time ago," he said.

"It could have been yesterday," Penny told him.

The hot, pretty day was dwindling into a long, green twilight. A few perfect white clouds floated over the silty brown water. Penny did not seem to notice.

"I was only fourteen," she said softly.

"I know. That's what I mean. A long time ago. It was bad, but it's past."

Penny shook her head. "When I got to the shop after my dentist appointment, my sister was out on an errand. Just like I told them. There was nobody there except for one person. I told them that, too. But the person wasn't the laborer," Penny said. "You know who it was?"

"Who?"

"It was your father," Penny told him.

"I don't believe that." Wish's mouth went dry, and a buzzing started inside his head.

"You do believe it." Penny held him with a steady gaze. He was the one who broke eye contact first.

"He invited me to wait in his office," Penny continued. "I thought he was being nice. It was the only air-conditioned part of the shop. When he closed the door, I thought it was so he wouldn't let out the cool air. I sat down on the — You know that couch he used to have?"

Wish nodded.

"He kept some magazines on the end table. I started reading one. Your father was at his desk doing some work. I could tell he didn't have his mind on it. He kept looking up at me. Studying me. Frowning. Finally I asked him what was wrong.

"He kind of smiled. Not quite." Penny's

voice grew clipped and mechanical, as if she'd rehearsed. "He said, 'You're an *ugly* cunt, aren't you?' I thought maybe I hadn't understood. Mr. Wishner wouldn't talk that way. Yet — I thought, well, it was true: I *was* ugly. I didn't know the word *cunt*."

Penny sat hunched over, hugging her knees to her chest.

"Your father had this way of sneering. Just a kind of — a little lift in the corner of his upper lip. He said to me, 'Yeah, an ugly cunt, no kidding. Too ugly to stick a dick into.' I was — in shock, I guess. I said, 'What?' He kept sneering. 'You heard me,' he said."

Her voice was a tiny thread now, so soft Wish had to strain to hear. "I just sat there. I was too scared to move. By the time I bolted for the door, it was too late. He was right behind me. He caught me by the arm and turned me around to face him. His face seemed — magnified. He smelled like onions. He said, 'Yeah, way too ugly to stick a dick into. I guess I'll have to let you blow me.' "

Slowly, Penny turned to look at Wish. "I was just fourteen. I didn't know the term *blow me*."

Wish looked down at his fingers, the

blanket, a clump of grass growing in the sand.

"So your father showed me," Penny said. "He told me if I bit, or if I told anyone, he would cut off my breast."

"I don't believe it," Wish muttered, though both of them understood that he did.

"That's exactly what happened," Penny told him. "I've never told anybody about it till now." By the time Penny got home that afternoon, she had developed a befuddled but complete amnesia about what had happened. She hadn't remembered any of it until recently, the weekend she went to West Virginia to see Steve.

"Why do you think it came back to you then?" Wish asked.

Penny shrugged. "Who knows? All I know is, now I remember everything." She didn't elaborate, but both of them knew she meant not just Murray Wishner but everything that had happened since, and that it was a heavy burden to bear.

Penny and Wish sat for a long time in silence. "Why did you tell me this?" Wish asked finally. "What do you want me to do?"

Penny said, "Your father did me wrong. I want you to do me right."

That night, the waters of the Chesapeake Bay stretched to the horizon in a white path of moonlight. The main thing Jon remembered afterward was that the air had been hot and so close it had been hard to breathe. The humidity must have been a hundred percent.

Goose bumps rose on my skin as soon as Jon started to speak, but it didn't occur to me to close the door to the deck. Nor later, when the daylight faded and the room grew shadowy, did either of us think to turn on the lamp. As far as I knew, the lights had dimmed everywhere, and it seemed fitting that they should. Even at a remove of all this time, I couldn't bear to see Jon's face.

"I had no idea she was trying to get pregnant," Jon said. "I didn't know about the baby. I just thought it was —"

"You thought it was just a little old roll in the locust leaves." I kept my eyes downcast, stared at my hands.

"I have no excuse, Barbara. I wasn't drunk."

"You knew she was crazy. You used to say she was pathetic."

"She *was* pathetic. But also . . . I was angry at her for telling me. Even though I believed her. Especially because I believed her. I wasn't nice. Then she started to cry. She said the only way she could make it right was to do . . . to do even more with me than she'd done with my father. Only to do it gently. If I was gentle, it would make up for what happened before." Jon ground his hands into fists, opened and closed them. "We were sitting on the blanket. She moved over toward me. And I was so mad. I can't explain it. I thought, 'Okay. Okay, you asked for it.' And I did what she wanted. Only I wasn't gentle. I was like my father." His voice was less than a whisper. "I didn't know I had it in me to be like that."

"And then you came home," I said. "And you didn't tell me."

But Jon seemed not to be listening. "The worst part was . . . Afterward Penny got up and she — She *thanked* me, for Christ's sake. *Thanked* me."

"I knew her pretty well," I told him. "Maybe I would have understood."

"Maybe."

"But you just ran away." Even now the memory filled me with equal parts fury and pain. When Jon had returned from camp in August, and I'd returned from Europe, we'd flown into each other's arms with such passion that I'd thought nothing had changed since we'd parted in June. During that first embrace, our future unfurled in my mind like a bright flag over our pending engagement, his first year of medical school, my first job. Then he let go of me, and I knew something was wrong. Within minutes, he picked a fight about something so meaningless, so petty, that I could never remember what. We argued for what seemed like hours.

"Wish —" I finally said. "This makes no sense."

"Don't call me Wish!" he shouted then. "Wish is a word that means something you hope for but probably won't get. It isn't my name, it's only the story of my life."

"Wish —" I was as bewildered as I'd ever been in my life.

He leaned close and whispered in a voice bordering on contempt (whether for me or for himself I was never sure), "Not Wish. I was never Wish. My name is Jon." Then he'd slammed out, and except for a brief moment at a funeral when we'd both been too upset to talk to each other, we hadn't seen each other again for more than thirty years.

Now, sitting in the chill, dark echo of the ocean, I said again, in what came out as a tortured rasp, "You didn't even have the decency to tell me."

"No. I acted like a shit." His voice ached with bitterness. He knew exactly what he'd done. Knowing Penny was helpless, he'd taken advantage of her. Loving me, he'd screwed around with my friend. He was his father's son. He did not deserve the happiness he had planned for himself. His nickname, Wish, seemed a special irony. As for Murray, in Jon's view he did not deserve happiness at all. If Jon's going to medical school would please him, Jon would not go.

"I was running away from my father," he said. "I was doing you a favor."

I swallowed hard. "Not a favor. Not even close."

Outside, an undecided rain began, fell in fits and starts onto the roof and into the ocean. Jon reached over and switched on a lamp. It shed the kindest, gentlest light.

"The irony," he said, "was that except for losing you, my life was better. I would have been a lousy doctor. I would have hated being around sickness and death. I liked writing about sports. Maybe I would never have been a world-class swimmer anyway, but after I broke my shoulder I missed it. Writing about sports was like a way of having it back." He leaned toward the coffee table that separated us. "But Barbara — I missed you every day of my life."

I felt myself softening, then caught myself. "Don't be melodramatic," I snapped. "How did you find out about the baby?"

"From my father. A deathbed confession. He probably would have told me a lot sooner if I hadn't been avoiding him for twenty years."

"Your father knew?"

"Penny told him," Jon said. "She told him the day she walked back into his shop with that gun."

"Oh, my God."

"I told you it was worse than you thought."

I understood everything then, even before he told me the rest. I had known much of it before; all Jon had to do was fill in the blanks.

Of course, I kept thinking. *Of course*.

Penny had gone into Wishner's Upholstery Shop for the second and last time in October 1964, six months after the birth of her daughter. On this visit, as opposed to the previous one, she came armed with a pistol she'd bought at a pawn shop the week before. It was late on a sunny, crisp afternoon. She waited outside until all the employees had gone home, leaving only Murray Wishner in the office. Penny was wearing black slacks and a black sweater, colors she never wore because with her red hair she believed they made her look washed out. In her pocket was the poetic note Steve would later put to music.

Later, Murray told the police Penny had come to the shop looking for the laborer who had assaulted her back in the fifties. "Of course we'd fired the jerk right away. Years ago. He would have been arrested except that Penny clammed up. Who knows where the guy is by now?

"Penny knew that laborer wasn't at the shop anymore," he'd said angrily. "It was crazy. *She* was crazy."

Not until his final day of life, confessing to the son who'd fled from him after Penny's visit to Camp Chesapeake, did Murray amend this story. Jon had come to his father's bedside only because his mother begged, and he was not prepared for what he was about to hear. But Murray had been in the final stages of congestive heart failure and had had no reason to lie.

"He looked like — Terrible. Dying," Jon said. "But I didn't care. I told him what

Penny had said about him. He didn't deny it. I told him I figured Penny had come to his shop to kill him and I was sorry she'd lost her nerve." Jon extracted a small whorled cowrie shell from a bowl on the coffee table and turned it over and over in his hand. "You know what he did? There he was, so sick, a tube in his nose, gray skin, he could hardly breathe —" Jon rubbed the shell as if it were a charm. "You know what he did? He smiled. Not a sweet smile, either. He said to me, 'Yes, but it was your kid she had.' "

Jon turned the shell over one last time and then placed it gently back in the bowl as if trying not to harm it. "I didn't want to believe him. But you know, the minute he said it, I knew it was true."

I closed my eyes.

According to Murray, Penny hadn't come to his shop to kill anyone except herself — not the innocent laborer, long ago fired in disgrace, or guilty Murray, still prospering from his business. Unaware of that at first, Murray was afraid. He didn't know Penny was pointing the gun at him only to make him sit down and listen.

"I came to tell you I righted your wrong," Penny told him. "You did me wrong and now I've made it right."

"Put the gun down," Murray cajoled. "Put the gun down and then we'll talk."

"You took advantage of an innocent child," Penny said as she aimed the pistol at his chest.

"Listen, I know what I did to you. I've felt bad about it all these years," Murray lied.

"You haven't felt bad," Penny told him. "It doesn't matter how you feel."

Murray held out his hand so that Penny could give him the pistol.

"You know, for years I didn't even know what happened or who did it," she said as she raised the sight to his head. "I blocked it out. People said it was the laborer, so I figured it was. Then last year I remembered. I remembered what happened with you, and I remembered what happened with a lot of guys." She aimed the pistol at the center of Murray's face. "If it weren't for you, I wouldn't have done anything I needed to forget."

"I just wish I could make it up to you." Murray made his voice as smooth and soothing as he could. "Maybe I can still make it up. I have money."

"You think I'm here for money?" Penny curved her lips into an icy smile.

"If not money, what? Let me help you, Penny."

"You know what I learned? I learned you have to help yourself. When somebody does you wrong, there's only one way you can live with it. You have to make it right."

"So you made it right, did you?" Murray was humoring her. He would have said anything.

"The Wishners aren't all bad," Penny told him. "Your wife Pauline, for example. When we lived in Riggs Park she was always nice to me. She acted like a lady. And Wish is okay. There's a good part to the Wishners. The good part is what I used to make things right."

With typical Penny-style logic, she outlined for Murray how she'd known that in order to survive she would have to create something more precious and good than his act of violation had been evil. She would have to create a new life. A child. She would not come back to Murray for that; he was too vile. But it was important that the positive thing come from Murray's own flesh. She would use the unspoiled part of him that he had left behind. Jon. She had gone to Jon at just the right moment. She had always known when she was fertile, she said. That's why she'd been so careful about contraceptives for so many years. She'd always known it would be easy to have a child when she wanted one. It had happened just as she'd planned. Penny even told Murray her daughter's name: Vera.

She thought the birth of the child would mean a new beginning for her, she continued, trancelike now but still pointing the gun. Giving up Vera for adoption had been hard. Penny had managed because she knew her mind was too tangled to make her a good mother. She had put Vera in a good home. The evil that Murray had put into motion had been appeased. Penny would never again need to say yes to every man who wanted to touch her. She would never again need to forget, immediately afterward, what she had done with those men. Her confusion would go away.

"But it wasn't like that," Penny told him. "It was like, now you've done what you were here for, sister. That's all there is."

Murray made what he thought were calming clucking sounds. "It's certainly 'all there is' if you do something you'll be sorry for," he crooned. "You're only — what? Twenty-three?"

"Twenty-three can be a lifetime," Penny had replied.

Hearing this, knowing what was coming, I caught my breath. I hadn't eaten all day, but the hollow in my stomach felt like it belonged to someone else. "So that accounts for the note," I said. " 'I'm falling through the hole/in the bottom of my soul —' "

" 'And there ain't nobody to catch me,' " Jon finished. He took a long, slow, thoughtful breath. "You know what else? I think she figured splattering herself all over my father's shop would reflect badly on his business."

"Jesus Christ," I said. That was precisely how Penny would have seen it: that leaving a mess in Murray's office would condemn him.

When Penny stuck the pistol in her mouth, Murray claimed he tried to stop her, with talk at first and then, seeing talk was fruitless, approaching her and holding out his hand. Jon didn't believe him. Murray was a strong man, and Penny was a small woman with the power to ruin him.

Everyone knew the rest. Penny sat down in a chair in the middle of Murray Wishner's office and pulled the trigger.

With the evidence of Penny's suicide note in her pocket, Murray was never suspected.

Jon sank back in his seat, his olive complexion sallow as wax.

"My God," I whispered.

"You think you aren't going to live through things," he said. "And then you do. All those years passed. By the time I saw you on TV in the hurricane, Penny was dead such a long time, it was such ancient history — You forget you're ever going to have to deal with it again. You think you won't. I know I should have told you."

"But you didn't."

"I'd just spent a couple of years trying to find Vera. All I found out was that in adoption cases the search can only be instigated by the child. If the child wants to find the parent, okay. But not the other way around. I went to Penny's sisters. If they knew anything, they weren't saying. Actually, I think hearing about a baby shocked them. I'm not sure they believed it. Going to Essie Berman never occurred to me. I was running into nothing but blank walls. Finally I just wanted it to be over."

"So you came to North Carolina and started this — Started us. And still didn't feel like you had to tell me."

"I was happy," Jon said quietly. "I didn't want to spoil it. After a while, I stopped thinking about Vera. Everything was better than it had been for a long time. Except the times when . . ."

"What?"

"When Robin came to visit."

"Robin!"

"She's just a few years younger than Vera. Every time I saw you with Robin, it brought it all back. I guess, in my mind, Robin and Vera were the same."

I was momentarily dumbfounded.

"So that's why you were so solicitous to Robin?"

"I hadn't thought about it. I guess so."

"I was beginning to think you had designs on her."

"On Robin?"

"Well —"

"The only one I have designs on," Jon said softly, "is you." He leaned across the coffee table toward me, but I froze, unable either to shrink back or to move forward toward him. Now the mysteries were stripped away. Now everything was clear. How like Penny to assume the sins of the father could be erased by the infidelity of the son. How like Penny never to imagine a quickie with Jon on the shores of the Chesapeake Bay could ruin our friendship, any more than the sorority had back in high school. Friendship was precious, inviolate;

sex was fleeting and cheap.

Jon, on the other hand — Jon could have said no.

For a long time I didn't move. Jon got up, went to the kitchen, came back with a glass of water and one of my pain pills, which I took. I wasn't grateful. I was cold. I shivered. Finally, I made myself get up, walk to the sliding glass door. The rain had stopped, but the air felt damp and raw. I shut the slider against the steady, rhythmic breathing of the sea. I closed the curtains and sat back down.

Jon got up, paced. "Listen to me," he said. "I love you. I loved you when I was fifteen and I loved you when I was forty-five and I love you now." He sat next to me, grabbed my arm, held it immobile. "I've made some horrible mistakes. I've run away from them. When I came to North Carolina, I was going to make up for everything and didn't. I handled everything badly. But I love you. I was hoping to spend the rest of my life here with you, whatever's left of it. I still am." Aware that he was squeezing, he dropped my arm. The indent of his fingers remained on my flesh. "I'm sorry," he whispered. His eyes were black as olives, lambent and sober. He hung his head in a posture of capitulation. "It's your call, Barbara. What do you want?"

"I don't know. I really don't know. Some time to think, maybe."

"Then as soon as you're better, tomorrow or the next day, I'll go."

"Go where?" My voice felt far apart from me. Nothing felt real.

"A motel, I guess."

"This is your house. Your office." I rubbed my hands together, trying to bring feeling into them.

"It doesn't matter. I'll be okay. Take as much time as you need."

And the next morning, after spending the night in his office, checking on me every hour, he was gone.

CHAPTER 18

Limbo

The next month was among the strangest I ever spent in my life. That first night, I huddled under every cover I could find, trying to stop chills that shook me like a carnival ride. Having asked Jon for time to think and being rewarded with his going, I no longer felt righteous. I felt abandoned. I tossed and shivered. Toward dawn I fell into a deep, heavy, dreamless sleep from which the phone jolted me a few hours later, with Steve and Marilyn talking at the same time on two extensions, telling me that Steve had told Marilyn everything.

"Oh, Barbara, I'm so sorry," Marilyn gushed. "Lucky for you I'm a woman with great largeness of heart, phoning even after you ran off without telling me about the baby. And Jon! What a bastard. I had no idea."

I sat up in the bed, feeling every bone and muscle groan. "I'm a woman with great largeness of heart myself," I said, "coming to D.C. even after you kept your cancer secret for a week."

"So how are you, sweetie?" Steve interrupted. "I tried to get hold of you yesterday, but no answer. Did you have your talk with Jon?"

I told them about the accident, and how Jon had come to get me. I told them what Murray had done to Penny, and her trip to Camp Chesapeake. I told them Jon had moved out so I could think. It was a good thing both of them were on the line at the same time, because I couldn't have related the story twice. I insisted I was fine.

"Fine," Marilyn growled. "Oh, Barbara."

"Well, if it's not true now, it will be," Steve asserted with such confidence that I believed him. "If you need anything, give Uncle Stevie a holler. Or call Marilyn. Anytime, even three in the morning. Promise us, sweetie. Now I'm going to let the two of you talk."

"I'm coming down to be with you," Marilyn said as soon as he hung up.

"That's ridiculous. The best thing you can do for me is get better."

"I wish you'd told me about Jon and Penny before you left," she said.

"Too upset. Besides, you sounded like you really hoped Steve and Penny had a baby together. Aside from everything else, I thought you'd be disappointed."

"Disappointed!"

"I thought you wanted a niece. So you could find her and be nice to her. Make it up to Penny, somehow, for not always treating her very well."

"Make it up!" She paused long enough to reconsider this. "Well, if I did, this cured me. Anything we did to hurt Penny, she certainly went us one better. Now, none of us needs to feel guilty about Penny anymore. Not you, not me, not Steve. It's a big relief for all of us." Then she caught herself. "I don't mean it's a relief that you got hurt in the process, Barbara. Never that."

"I know."

"Let me help you. What do you want to do, Barbara?"

"Right now? Just lick my wounds a little."

"At least promise you'll call every day. Promise you'll check in."

"Of course," I told her. As if I, not she, were the ailing patient.

During the short time I'd been gone, the season had moved decisively from summer to fall. A run of warm, dry days and cool, clear nights replaced the sulky heat. Temperatures dropped to the seventies, the ocean grew jewel-toned, the sand golden in the angled light. Seized by an unexpected inertia and ambivalence, I wandered mechanically through the fine bright days, toying with a small research project, cleaning my computer, staring at the indigo sea. I thought very little about Jon. I thought very little about anything.

I didn't come out of my daze until the fourth morning, when Jon showed up at the door.

"I know I said I wouldn't bother you," he said, looking sheepish, "but I need some clothes." He was wearing the same shirt he'd had on when he left. As I opened the door, I was aware of his physical beauty as I hadn't been since our first months together, if the term *beauty* could be applied to a man approaching sixty.

He disappeared down the hall and returned with a pile of clothes and a stack of files from his office. "This should do it for a while."

"I've kicked you out of your own office," I said.

"I have my laptop. The motel is cheap this time of year. I meant what I said, Barbara. Take as long as you like."

"Have you been wearing that shirt every day?" I asked.

"I took advantage of the sale at Redix."

Redix was a store just east of the draw-bridge, which carried everything from fishing gear to fine clothing, and had excellent sales at the end of every season. Knowing how much Jon hated to shop, I couldn't help the smile that tugged at the corners of my mouth.

"If you need anything, call me. I mean it. Errands you need to run. Groceries —" He stopped. We'd always gone to the super-market together on Thursdays. "Anything."

I remembered then what we were about. "I won't need anything," I told him.

But that night my bed felt deserted. I felt sorry for myself. In a way, I even felt sorry for Jon. When Penny had told him about his father, how horrified he must have been. Had his first reaction been disgust? Repugnance? Shock? Surely shock. He'd been away at camp when Penny had been molested at age fourteen and hadn't re-turned for a month. He had no reason not to believe the story about the laborer. If he'd had sex with Penny all those years later, while he was still stunned with the horror of his father's perversion, he'd also had the decency to part from Penny full of self-loathing, believing his behavior was a mirror of his father's, knowing that in some vile way, he would never escape the taint of being Murray Wishner's son.

No wonder he hadn't told me. No wonder he'd fled.

But still.

What I didn't forgive was that he'd left in order to keep his secret, and in the process robbed me of half my life.

I tossed in the bed, unable to get comfortable with so much empty space beside me. Had he really *robbed me* of half my life? Too melodramatic. I had *had* a life. After Jon's desertion, I'd suffered grandly for a year, creeping through days dry and featureless as a slab of concrete. Then I'd discovered that the young body is a hungry, fickle beast, yearning so urgently for pleasure and joy that it usually gets it. A year after Jon left, I put my youthful angst aside and fell in love with Wells. A dentist, no less! A man out to repair the teeth of the world! *Tikkun Olam.* A son-in-law even Ida would approve! The navy had paid his way through dental school, so he owed them eight years. Amazingly, he was never sent to Vietnam, only all around the States: Carlsbad, California, where our apartment looked out to the Pacific Ocean; Tucson, Arizona, where the sharp desert air was always too hot or too cold, the sun a bright white fire; Pensacola, Florida, near the lush, humid, semitropical Gulf.

I loved each new assignment, until after Robin was born, and Wells decided to make the navy his career. By then we'd acquired so many *things* that moving began to seem a chore. I was tired of making friends and leaving them, getting established and moving on.

When Robin was ten, Wells returned from one of his six-month floats and I, throwing my arms around him in greeting, realized I was not glad to see him. And vice versa. Our life together had unraveled so gradually that neither of us noticed until it was too late.

We didn't get around to divorcing until Robin was a teenager. After a hard first year, I found single life exhilarating. I worked for a small research firm, then a larger one. Eventually I started my own business. By the time Robin was grown and gone, I realized I could live anywhere. One thing the navy had taught was that if I didn't go to the sea now and then, ill will would fill me and make me miserable. Walking by the ocean was the only cure. I found Wrightsville Beach and calculated I could afford a house in Wilmington, fifteen minutes away. I could breathe the sea air whenever I liked. Except for the loneliness that drifted through me now and then like a chilling shadow, I knew I'd come home.

How could I have thought, even for a minute, that Jon had robbed me of half my life?

I let the image of him go, sift out of my mind like dust. When finally I dozed off, there was nothing left. I dreamed instead of Penny, amnesiac and confused after the incident in Murray's shop, baffled by her growing fascination with men, in the bus station, pregnant . . . dead.

I couldn't be angry with her. I had loved her. I was only sad.

The next day, I was able to work again. In just over a week, my life had fallen back into some kind of routine. I could do without Jon. This proved it. Of course I could.

Then the garage in Richmond called to say my car was ready. Jon wanted to drive me up there to get it. I didn't really have a choice.

It was a beautiful day, crisp and clear and invigorating. We opened the windows and shouted to each other over the breeze. By the time we reached I-95, we'd closed the windows again and fallen back into our easy pattern of speech as if nothing had interrupted. I found myself telling Jon about my visit with Essie Berman (no matter that she was the source of our current troubles) and with Marcellus Johnson. "No kidding, Jon," I told him. "He's the only person I ever met who had a different set of grammar rules for every listener and every mood."

After that journey, Jon showed up at the house more frequently — to pick up his mail, to search for his files, to rummage through his clothes. He insisted he was fine working at the motel on his laptop, but he'd appear at least once a day, sometimes twice.

This went on for more than two weeks. Did he know his comings and goings kept me in a constant state of agitation, listening for his car in the driveway, his key in the lock? Was he keeping me off balance on purpose?

"This is insane, Marilyn," I finally said in one of our frequent phone calls.

"So? I don't see you doing anything to change it."

True enough.

"Get over it, then. It will resolve itself soon enough."

"I suppose." I didn't see how.

A dark silence filled the air, hovering

until I thought we'd lost our connection. "Marilyn, what's wrong?"

"That's just the trouble. Nothing's wrong. I feel good. I'm even starting to look good. My jowls are gone. My turkey neck is gone. I look better than I have in years."

"But that's wonderful."

"It means I have no excuse to delay my treatment," Marilyn said. "Then I'll probably feel like cow plop. I'm tired of feeling like crap."

"Oh, Marilyn."

"Don't 'oh, Marilyn' me. People are always 'Oh, Marilyn'-ing me. Be glad all you have to worry about is kicking out some guy because he acted like an asshole half a lifetime ago."

"Half a lifetime ago. You make it sound like — like *nothing.*"

"Well? Isn't it?"

"Maybe by comparison, but I thought you'd — Why are you defending him?" A chill skittered across my collarbone, up my neck. "What's eating you, Marilyn?"

"Cancer. A numb face. All kinds of things. And you know what? You're not twenty-one anymore, either. You think this big dark secret is the worst thing that can happen? Fine. Kick Jon out for good.

You're healthy right now, so why not? You figure you can have any life you want. But I'll tell you what — you're no spring chicken and neither is he. You don't know how many good years you've got left. Take it from the voice of experience. Why would either of you want to spend them alone?"

Why, exactly? Given a chance to love someone, to make a life together — rare enough — why would you run away? That was the question I'd posed to myself when I was twenty-one, and now again, the question of the moment.

I was healthy. I'd been happy. Could I run away because, as Marilyn put it, someone had treated me like crap half a lifetime ago?

Yet in spite of all the reason I tried to put to it, there were moments when knowing Jon's secret still filled me with the same slicing anguish I'd felt at twenty-one when he'd first walked out on me. The same breathless, paralyzing anguish.

"Listen," Marilyn said. "I don't mean to pass judgment. It's just that — Betrayal can be a snaky, easy kind of thing. Sometimes it's over even before you realize what you've done."

"As in screwing Penny?"

"Yes. But also — the wretched way he

stomped away and disappeared without explaining anything. And you were stubborn, too. You probably could have found him and made him confess. But you didn't. Not that I blame you. But it was —" She stopped. "It was a snaky, easy thing for both of you," she whispered.

I felt as if I'd been slapped. After all, I *hadn't* run after him. Too proud. Too hurt. Too stubborn. After all: Who had betrayed whom?

"And speaking of betrayal," she said, "if you're so angry at Jon, why aren't you angry with Penny, too? I'll tell you why. Because you see Penny as wounded. Not weak, but wounded. Why can't you see Jon that way, too?"

"Because I know better. And so did he."

"All right. Even so. You think you were betrayed? Everybody betrays you. Penny betrayed you whether you like it or not. Even your own body will betray you someday. I know all about it. But you don't abandon it. You try to make it well. Because you want to live there. Because it's your life."

I was taken off guard, floundering. "What's all this about, Marilyn? What's going on?"

She said nothing for a minute, then let

out a long sigh. "I'm just out of sorts. Call me tomorrow. Okay?"

"Take care of yourself, Marilyn."

"You, too."

I hung up, shaken. I needed to see her, to touch her. I didn't trust what I could only hear from three hundred miles away. The next morning, when the phone rang just as I was brushing my teeth, I knew there must have been a crisis. At that early hour, who else but Marilyn could it be? I almost tripped over a throw rug as I bolted across the bedroom to answer.

"Barbara? Phyllis Levy here." The smoky voice belonged to a woman I'd met at the Temple of Israel, where Jon and I occasionally went to services. "I called to remind you about the *oneg* tonight."

"The *oneg?*" My stomach twisted into a knot. Months ago, I'd signed up to provide refreshments for the social hour after the Friday-night service. I had completely forgotten. It was too late to back out.

Three hours later, Jon showed up with coffee and found me in the kitchen, making a pumpkin roll to serve. "I'll go with you."

I whirled around, flailing floured hands. "You knew!"

"I remembered when I saw you baking."

"Jon, this makes no sense. You moved out, but you're here every day. We're trying to resolve things, but nothing is resolved."

He handed me a roll of paper towels. "For me it is," he said softly. "For me, everything was resolved the day I got off the plane in Wilmington."

"Jon, don't." I couldn't stand another dose of his charm. "Exactly what is this going to accomplish — your going to temple with me? Are you trying to keep up appearances?"

"No, I enjoy it." How could I argue? He *did* enjoy it. His one marriage, five years in his early thirties to a woman named Denise, had broken up after a long haggling about whether they would go to church or synagogue with the children they ultimately never had.

Driving into town that night, Jon sat at the wheel looking upbeat and sporty in a tweedy gray jacket and bright tie, and I sat beside him with the pumpkin roll on my lap, too unsettled even to make small talk.

During the service there was, finally, no need for us to look at each other, talk, pretend. The familiar prayers still calmed me, soothed me the way the tunes from *Peter and the Wolf* had once soothed me when my mother tested her reeds at bedtime.

Not a very religious notion, I supposed, but for me prayers and music had always been, equally, lullabies for the soul.

Then the service was over and I was downstairs in the social hall, setting out pumpkin roll, cookies, foam cups for coffee. As other congregants began to drift in from the sanctuary, I found myself greeting people, socializing, behaving as if the evening were perfectly normal. As I watched Jon talking to friends across the room, tears stung my eyes at the idea that our breakup would force us to leave behind not just each other, but also the braid of life we had begun to plait together, almost unaware.

I hurried to the kitchen on the pretext of getting more coffee creamer and stood clutching the cabinet door, trying to compose myself. Maybe this was why, for a whole month, I had done nothing. Marilyn was right. I was no spring chicken. Why would I leave Jon to face the coming darkness alone? But how could we live breathing the tainted air that now hung over our every common action — even this lively social hour with people we liked? Setting a jar of creamer on the counter, I thought bitterly of the false calm that had infused me just a few minutes ago during the service: all that illusive sense of peace. Did it solve anything? Not at all. We were still in limbo.

And then, the next day, in a white FedEx envelope bearing Marilyn's return address and marked for Saturday delivery, came the tape.

CHAPTER 19

Videotape

I held the package in my hand for a long minute before ripping it open. If Marilyn hadn't mentioned it beforehand, and then spent the money to have it delivered on the weekend, I probably had every right to be scared. Inside, a note read, Don't call me. Watch this first. It was a gift from Essie. With shaking fingers, I closed the drapes and slid the tape into the VCR.

It was a short clip, less than a minute, meticulously edited so as not to give too much away. In the weight room of a high-school gym filled with bench presses and free weights, a female reporter was interviewing a boy who'd been named High School Athlete of the Week. The camera moved in close, no wide angle that might reveal a banner with the name of the school, an emblem, anything to suggest their whereabouts. Even the mikes were attached to their collars, not the handheld kind imprinted with the station's call letters. The boy was shy, the reporter poised as she presented him with his plaque.

There was more to the segment, but the film editor had cut it short, let the tape revert to static and snow.

I pushed the rewind button, played it again. By the third viewing, my heart had stopped slamming against my chest and my breathing was less ragged, but my mouth had turned to sandpaper. The reporter, of course, was Vera.

For the past few weeks, I'd been certain that, if I ever got a glimpse of Jon and Penny's child, even from a distance on an unfamiliar street, I would know her instantly. It wasn't so. The reporter was a mature woman rather than the girl I'd pictured, and not a clone of either parent. The high cheekbones might have come from anywhere; the bouncy hair, reddish but darker than her mother's, was closer to mahogany than auburn. Though Vera's complexion was fair, it was not as fair as Penny's, and there was no sign of Penny's trademark freckles. More telling, the crinkly lines around Vera's eyes were deep enough that even makeup didn't hide them, when Penny hadn't lived long enough for crows' feet. Older than her mother had ever been, Vera was a woman past thirty-five, probably a mother herself. And a sports reporter like her father.

Was her choice of a profession coincidence? Irony? Or somehow programmed into her genes?

I ran the tape a fourth time, a fifth. In Vera's short-cropped, carefully cut hair, I began to notice the suggestion of Penny's unruly mane; in her thick, dark eyebrows an echo of Jon's. The hints of her breeding were like occasional whiffs of familiar perfume: Penny's slightly backward thrust of shoulders, Jon's inflection of voice. Who would have thought a child would inherit that?

By the time I turned off the VCR and slipped the tape back into its jacket, my right leg was numb from sitting on it.

A sharp flame of anger leaped into the hollow of my gut. What was the point of this? If Essie had this tape, why give it to Marilyn rather than Jon or me? And what was Marilyn up to, sending it to me like this? I had had enough drama lately. When I called her, she answered on the first ring.

"I know. You're mad at me. I'm sorry. I just didn't know what else to do."

"You could have told me this was coming, for starters," I said.

"Oh, Barbara, I wanted to bring it to you in person. But Bernie and Steve said you'd need to show it to Jon and I'd just be in the way."

"If the point was to show it to Jon, why all the middlemen?"

"You know how high-handed Essie can be. I never even talked to her in person. She sent the tape to me via her personal messenger, Taneka. And then your friend Marcellus called to give me Essie's instructions."

"Instructions!"

"A whole list of them. She thinks it's time Jon met his daughter. She's arranging a meeting. She says Jon didn't know Penny very well, so it's up to you and me to fill Vera in about her mother. Steve should stay out of it since he isn't the father. And by the way, in case I die from cancer before all this comes to pass, it's mainly up to you."

This was exactly the sort of thing Essie would be brazen enough to say.

"She says she knows we cared about Penny," Marilyn said. "She knows we'll put her in the best possible light."

"The nerve! Never mind that Vera was conceived during an act of betrayal that changed my life!"

"Essie was always pretty shameless."

"But I, on the other hand, should be big

enough to tutor Jon's child about Penny's merits?"

"Essentially, yes." Then Marilyn whispered, "But first you have to show Jon the tape."

"Like hell I do."

"I'm sure Essie knew that was exactly what you'd say. I'm sure that's why she made me the intermediary."

"Well, Jon's in Charlotte, so forget it." He was more meticulous about giving me his schedule now than he'd been when he lived with me. Before dropping me off after temple, while I was debating how to make a clean break from him, he'd told me he was leaving this morning to do an interview, and gave me all the numbers where I could reach him before he came back tomorrow.

"He won't be in Charlotte forever," Marilyn said. "Show it to him when he gets back."

I saw there was no getting out of this. "So when is this meeting?" I asked.

"Taneka says Essie will let us know. I think they're planning some kind of big party. Taneka made it clear we're supposed to be patient and not ask."

"Lovely."

"Listen, I thought it was as hokey as you

do. I tried to call Essie and talk to her myself, but Taneka wouldn't let me through. First Essie was asleep. Then she was out. I said, for an old woman who can hardly walk, it's amazing how much she goes out. Taneka said, she goes out more than you expect. Finally I thought, well, I'll just go over there. Then Steve said don't, it'll just make her mad. I spent two days thinking about nothing else. Finally I just gave up."

"And took the tape over to FedEx," I said.

"Listen, I know it was crappy to send it to you with no warning. I just couldn't see what good warning you would do. And I wanted to give you — I don't know. Maybe some time alone to take this in."

"This is why you changed your tune the other day about Jon being the rat that he is, isn't it? You didn't just 'give up,' you switched sides on me, didn't you? You and Essie. Let's help the little man meet his daughter, let's help the little man tell the girl about her mother, since the only time the father was ever alone with her was the half hour they were screwing."

"Don't," Marilyn whispered.

"You know what? I think I'll take that time alone now. I think I'll go for a walk."

"Yes. But Barbara, call me later. Promise."

I hung up. After flinging the tape onto the coffee table, I stomped the pins and needles out of my sleeping legs, and ran down to the beach.

The glorious weather mocked me: warm breeze, blue sky. I took off my shoes and walked the length of Wrightsville Beach, more than three miles, all the way to the southern end. By the time I reached the bottom tip of the island, my head was clear. I turned and started back, the whoosh of rolling surf and the strain of exercise momentarily wiping my mind free of Jon's infidelity, Essie's dramatics, Marilyn's complicity. When another subject entirely popped into my head — the subject of Barry Levin — it seemed so unrelated that I didn't make the connection, until it was too late.

Even after Jon and I had become an official couple our freshman year in college, Barry and I had stayed friends. We could talk on the phone as easily as Marilyn and I did, and sometimes we'd go to movies that Jon didn't want to see, often with some of Barry's new friends from American University. It was after one of those films, while driving a boy named Neil home to the other side of town, that Barry had to stop to fix a flat tire on a winding road in Rock Creek Park. As he bent over the trunk trying to retrieve the jack, another car came around the bend and, before the sleepy driver thought to swerve away, rear-ended Barry's car. The impact shoved Barry into the open trunk and nearly severed both his legs. He bled to death in the ambulance on his way to the hospital, surrounded by medics, with Neil holding his shattered, bloodied body in his arms.

At the funeral, even Neil's inconsolable grief did not give Barry away. Anyone who'd lived through such a night with a friend would react like this. Nobody suspected love between the two boys, and certainly not sex. On the way home, Penny smoothed the lap of her black dress and said, "It's better Barry died this way. It would have been worse if he'd lived for people to find out. You should never tell anyone, Barbara. I won't, either. Some people, you have to protect them even after they're gone."

And except for confiding to Marilyn, I had heeded this advice. In a cruel, ironic way, Barry had been spared what to him would have been the supreme disgrace of revelation. Even now, when coming out of the closet was perfectly acceptable, I wouldn't have told. And as I paced the beach I'd hoped would offer me comfort, Penny's words seemed especially loaded: *Some people, you have to protect them even after they're gone.*

As now, it seemed, Essie was asking me to do for Penny.

Without realizing it, I had reached the other end of the beach again. The sun had disappeared into a cloud bank beyond the marsh; the air was chilly. I knew now what I would do. Tomorrow when Jon returned, I would take the tape to him. This was Jon's business, not mine. Let him deal with it. Let it be over. Anything was better than this.

I limped toward the house, so distracted that at first I didn't notice the car in my driveway — and then didn't register that it was a car I'd never seen before. Upstairs, the drapes I had drawn were open, and in the living room someone had turned on a light. What the hell — ?

A fair-haired woman appeared on the porch and waved to me.

"Mom!"

"Robin!" I took the steps two at a time. I hugged my daughter as if clinging to a life raft.

"Mom, are you all right? Aunt Marilyn

said I needed to come — this wasn't optional. You won't believe how I got here. Uncle Steve rented a *private jet.* What's going on?"

I didn't mean to, but I laughed. "Marilyn arranged this? Steve rented you a plane?"

Robin flung an arm around my waist as we walked into the house. "They told me you weren't sick, but I didn't believe it."

"Heartsick is all."

She looked around. "Where's Jon? Is this about Jon?"

"As you film people well know," I said, "a picture is worth a thousand words." I put the tape back in the VCR.

Robin watched attentively, polite but puzzled. "I expected something more shocking," she said when it was over. "The woman looks a little like Jon. One of his relatives?"

"His daughter."

"He has a daughter?"

"I found this out a month ago. He had a baby with a woman who was my best friend except for Marilyn."

Her mouth actually dropped open.

"Maybe you better sit in a more comfortable chair," I said. I explained everything but the part about Murray Wishner, which I couldn't bring myself to repeat.

"You mean all these years and you didn't know?"

I shook my head.

"What are you going to do?"

"I feel like such a fool. Buying this house with him. Making it all so complicated. He's been staying in a motel. Giving me 'time to think.' Making me feel — Anyway, when the tape got here this morning, I guess that clinched it."

"Clinched it how?"

"Essie thinks I can just forgive everything. Just like that!" I snapped my fingers. "And Jon! He's been so nice about everything. Making all the right gestures. Being so *understanding*."

"Is it really that bad?"

"What am I supposed to do, Robin? Condone this — this pattern of deception? Just because he turns on the charm?"

"You know what you should do when something like this happens?" Robin said. "Get drunk. Then you'll feel better. I know."

"The only person I get drunk with is Marilyn. Now that I'm older, I don't even enjoy that. I have two drinks and suffer for it all the next day."

"Then at least let's go out to dinner. I'll treat."

We ate at The Oceanic, on the windowed second floor that overlooked Crystal Pier and the beach. For all my distress, I was famished. I'd eaten nothing since morning and had done more exercise than I usually did in a month. After growing tipsy from my first glass of wine, I switched from alcohol to bread as Robin sipped her second Cosmopolitan.

"So Vera's a sports reporter," Robin mused. "Seems kind of eerie, doesn't it? Like father, like daughter."

"When I was young we all wanted to be doctors and lawyers and professors. In your generation everyone wants to be in the entertainment business."

"Thanks, Mom."

"I didn't mean it as an insult."

"None taken." Robin reached across and squeezed my hand. "Let me tell you a happier story. Even if I weren't in Wilmington now, I'd be coming in a couple of weeks. I'm coming back for this independent feature a bunch of us have been developing for two years."

"Two years?"

"I didn't want to say anything because it was so iffy. Getting financing for something like this — Usually it just doesn't happen."

The arrival of our meal gave me time to tame my dueling emotions: pleasure at seeing Robin so happy, irritation that nobody ever told me anything until after the fact — not Jon, not Essie, not even my own daughter.

"We've even got a distribution deal," Robin said as she lobbed butter on a baked potato. "Distribution is so critical."

"And you sound like your old self again."

"Oh, I am." Robin winked. "If this thing goes, I'll be financially independent. Well, not exactly. But I'll be in a position to get money for other projects."

"Good. Put on your list of projects supporting your mother in her old age." I lifted a forkful of grouper to my mouth. I was amazed at my own appetite.

All through dinner, Robin chattered about her movie — a coming-of-age story for the twenty-first century, she called it. She sounded so carefree that her divorce might never have happened. She even looked different. Her hair had been layered into a short, geometric cut — a shelf of hair above her ears, a triangle of sideburns. Robin's hair was too wiry to lie flat, so it puffed up all around her face, creating an unintentional and original effect that made

Robin look exactly as she should.

After the waiter cleared our plates, we drank coffee spiked with Kahlúa while she finished her story. I hadn't eaten so much at one time in a year. By the end of the meal, I felt calmer than I had in a month.

It was a lovely thing to have a grown daughter, especially if she was paying for your dinner. So what if she didn't tell you about her movie until it was about to go into production. It was a lovely thing simply to know your daughter existed; to know she was walking somewhere in the world.

Even Jon deserved such a thing.

This, I realized, was why Marilyn had not come to North Carolina to watch the tape with me. This was why Steve had rented a jet to bring my daughter to my doorstep.

"Mom?" Robin asked.

I made my eyes focus.

"You okay?"

"Just full." But I felt suddenly sober. This was what Marilyn had known and I had not: that whether we died before sixty or lived until ninety, at some point we belonged to the generations and not just ourselves. Penny was our history and our duty was to pass it on. If it would be kindness to sugarcoat the story a bit, we had to do that, too. Feeling as I did about Robin, how could I do anything else?

I'd read somewhere that when something was inevitable, you ought to embrace it. But no one said you had to do it gracefully. By the time I got Robin settled into the guest room, I was too tired to do anything but fall into bed and sleep like the aging, snoring, overfed dowager I was.

In the morning, I followed Robin to the airport to drop off her car, then took her to breakfast before her private jet whisked her back to her Pennsylvania film shoot.

"See you in a couple of weeks," she said. "I'll be here before you know it." The wind lifted a tuft of her short hair in a cheerful salute as she marched out to the tarmac, expectant and hopeful.

It was another beautiful morning, the landscape dominated today by the bright Chinese tallow trees, their small triangular leaves an autumnal patchwork of red and gold, purple and orange — a stunning display. And Robin's life, right now — who knew for how long — seemed filled with exactly such colorful breathlessness.

A small plane lifted into the clouds above me — Robin's jet, surely. *Fly safe,* I thought. And then, unbidden: *Life will not be as you imagine, child. Enjoy this now.*

Then my mood went from Technicolor to black-and-white. I drove straight home, called Jon's motel and left word for him to come by whenever he got in.

It was full night before he arrived. For half an hour I'd been standing on the chilly deck, watching a shifting path of moonlight arc across the sea. He ran up the stairs. "I didn't leave Charlotte till two," he panted. "What's up? Is something wrong?"

"It depends on how you define the word." I slid the tape into the VCR. "I was just going to drop this off to you," I said. "Call me a pushover, but I thought it would be too hard to be by yourself when you saw your daughter for the first time, all grown-up."

He stiffened but didn't say a word.

We watched the clip. "She's so much — herself," he said at last. "Herself and not me. I guess I didn't expect that."

"She looks like you a little. Sounds like you a lot. I couldn't get over it."

"She sounds pretty sane, doesn't she? Pretty together," he said. Try as I would to remain aloof, I couldn't help returning his grin at the idea that Vera's sanity would be uppermost in our minds.

"Why do you think Essie sent it? Why not just call and tell us where she was?" he asked.

"I don't know, Jon. From here on out, I don't think it concerns me."

He acted as if he hadn't heard. "I think it's because if there's going to be a meeting, she wants to orchestrate it herself. Old as sin and still wants to run everybody's life." He paused. "Maybe I should call her anyway. Thank her for the tape. Sort of — hasten things along."

"Call her in the morning," I said. "It's too late now."

He arrived the next day at six, but I was already awake. We drank coffee, flipped through the morning news shows, fidgeted until it seemed a decent hour to phone. When Taneka answered, she told Jon that Essie was sleeping.

"At 9:00 a.m.?"

"She gets up at the crack of dawn and takes a nap later," Taneka explained. "She's old. Old people need a lot of sleep."

Jon phoned again at noon. No one answered. "Maybe they went out to lunch."

"You mean, out to a restaurant? No chance," I said. "Essie can hardly walk."

"Maybe she had a doctor's appointment."

"Maybe she just doesn't want to talk to

you any more than she wanted to talk to Marilyn. Maybe she wants all of us to be patient. She said she'd let Marilyn know as soon as she set up the meeting."

"And how long should that take?"

"Look, Jon, I don't know. I'm not sure it matters. After thirty-six years, what's another couple of days? But if you want me to call Marcellus, I will."

I thought he'd have the grace to say no. He didn't. And Marcellus, unlike Essie, was more than willing to talk.

"Essie don't want some man Vera never saw drop by one day and say he's her father. She wants it to happen by plan," he told me. "That's why I had my man edit the tape. Pretty good, wasn't it?"

"Very anonymous," I said.

"Essie wrote Vera. Said Vera's mother stayed with her when she was pregnant. Asked Vera to write back if she wanted to know more."

"And did she?"

"Yeah. They still writing."

"Just writing? Why not talking on the phone? Why not — ?"

"Essie got to do it her own way," Marcellus said. "You know how she is. When she's got it all worked out, she'll get in touch."

The next day, Jon moved back into the house. We didn't discuss it, but both of us felt there was a momentous task ahead of us that made this all right. Tactfully, he put his clothes in the guest room. We avoided physical contact with the zeal of recent converts to celibacy. I was sure if I let him touch me, he'd be thinking not of me but of Penny, of her pale skin and fiery hair; of the supple body — not mine — with whom he had created a life. All the same, I felt every moment that we'd soon end up in each other's arms.

Three more days passed. I spoke to Marilyn every day, but she seemed to have lost interest, or at least passed on the responsibility for the meeting to me and Jon. She cut our conversations short. If I'd been paying more attention, I would have said she sounded weary, or even sick.

We spent most of our time in the house, trying to work but actually waiting, waiting, waiting for the critical call. If there were errands to run, only one of us went out. Our nerves were thoroughly jangled. "This is ludicrous," Jon finally said the third day after we'd cobbled together a lunch from the meager scraps left in the refrigerator. We decided to go out, as we used to do, to stock up on groceries.

Less than an hour later, we pulled back into the driveway, and Jon, three plastic bags in hand, bounded up the stairs to check the answering machine.

"You're supposed to call Marilyn's," he called down.

I hefted my own bags higher in my arms and took the stairs two at a time. "I talked to her just a couple of hours ago, so this must mean she's finally heard something about the party! She promised she'd call the minute she heard from Essie."

"It was Bernie on the tape. Not Marilyn. Maybe it's something else."

"Bernie?" Alarm rang in my ears, the food in my stomach coalesced into a lump. I had thought we would be driving to D.C. for a party. Bernie's calling couldn't be good news. But even then, as panic began to bubble in my blood, it didn't occur to me that we would be going for a funeral instead.

CHAPTER 20

Reunion

We stood in the cemetery just outside the tent top that had been raised over the newly dug grave. Jon started to guide me toward the folding chairs set up beneath the tent, but I shook my head and stayed where I was while his hand rested on my elbow, its pressure welcome through my jacket. I didn't want to get any closer to the rent-a-rabbi droning on at graveside, a short young man with a beard that looked like an affectation and a high-pitched, irritating voice. I resented his ease at eulogizing someone he didn't know, had never seen. My whole body tensed as I waited for him to segue out of his sermon into the final prayers.

An overnight rain had left the ground soggy and the air bitingly wet, with the kind of poisonous damp that seeps through the clothes and under the skin, that plants pneumonia deep into the lungs. After the stuffy funeral home, I thought being outside would be a relief. But it was worse.

Earlier in the day, Jon and I had sat in

the Waxmans' kitchen still in shock, bleary from the early morning flight that had gotten us to D.C. in time for the traditional Jewish funeral, within twenty-four hours of the death. Steve's plane landed just before ours did, so Bernie collected all three of us at the airport and brought us to his house to change clothes. Sitting in the kitchen, I cupped a mug of coffee in both hands for a long time, trying to get warm. "When I saw her she seemed so healthy," I heard myself say over and over. "Or at least relatively healthy. Despite all her problems, I honestly thought she was okay."

Steve reached over and put his hand on top of mine. "I did, too. I never thought she'd die on us."

Jon had said almost nothing since we arrived. He lifted his coffee, cold by now, and swished it around in its cup.

Bernie cleared his throat. "She wasn't healthy, no matter how she seemed. We should have known that. It isn't unusual for people to have a stroke."

For a long beat, no one responded.

"When somebody's old or sick and it's not a gunshot wound or a traffic accident, nobody should be surprised," Jon put in, his voice dragging like a heavy weight pulled from his chest. "But so much was going on, I guess we weren't prepared."

"With all this talk of a party —" I stopped. Jon stared at the table.

"Everyone was distracted, of course we were," Steve said. "We thought things were moving along."

Sipping a cup of tea, silent as fog, Marilyn had listened to the conversation for half an hour without saying a word. But I had seen her flinch at Bernie's assertion that "she wasn't healthy, no matter how she seemed." The remark might have applied to Marilyn herself. Her post-surgery swelling was gone, her jawline smooth, her skin unwrinkled. The only real indication of illness beneath the freshly refurbished face was the dark smudges under her eyes, not quite hidden by her makeup. Yet for all that, she seemed exhausted.

I hardly dared look openly at her after Bernie's "not really healthy" remark, no matter how much I wanted to. How often, these past few weeks, had I pretended not to hear the fatigue that laced her voice? How often had I pretended she was "coming along" because I couldn't concentrate on anything but myself? She sat straighter in her chair, leaned in my direction, and whispered conspiratorially, "Thought it would be me, not Essie, didn't you?"

I was so shocked I found no words to defend myself. Marilyn chuckled. "Close your mouth, Barbara. Bugs are going to fly in." And then she said, more softly, "I forgive you."

Abruptly, Bernie stood up and said, "We better get going or we'll be late." We all rose at once as if jolted by electricity.

At the funeral home, Marcellus and Taneka were sitting in the private wing reserved for family, where we greeted them before the service started.

"Thank you for coming," Marcellus said after Jon and I offered our condolences. "Thank you both." I heard warmth in his voice I hadn't expected. "We'll talk more later. To clear up — everything." He turned to Jon. "I'm sorry this is how we had to meet, man."

"Me, too," Jon said.

Then someone else came up, and after the haste with which Marcellus turned away, I didn't think we'd really talk.

The funeral service itself was more like a PBS documentary than a religious event, the young rabbi alternately mumbling in Hebrew and explaining in English the various parts of a Jewish service. This approach continued when we got to the cemetery.

By the time the final prayers were recited and the casket lowered and the traditional handful of soil thrown on top, I realized I'd been clenching my jaw so tightly that it hurt to open my mouth.

Marilyn and Bernie and Steve emerged from under the tent and caught up with us as the crowd dispersed. "Know any of these people?" Marilyn gestured at the retreating backs of the few white mourners headed to their cars: a middle-aged couple walking arm in arm; a youngish man opening a car door for a much older one; a hugely pregnant woman, nearly hidden by the folds of a hooded cape that must have been the only garment that still fit her, leaning on the arm of a man who guided her protectively toward the road.

"Nobody I've ever seen before." Essie's circle of friends was an enigma, just as Essie herself had always been, a repository of intrigues and secrets — including those about Vera she had apparently taken to her grave.

"I'm sorry, Jon," Marilyn told him. "I really thought there'd be a meeting."

"I guess not," Jon said in a tone that closed the case.

After sidestepping a puddle gilded by weak sun, I turned one last time toward the tent where workers were already re-moving the folding chairs. "Bye, Essie," I mouthed silently. For a moment, my mind reeled back to other funerals, sadder ones — Barry Levin's, Penny's — and then to a time before any funerals at all, when Marilyn and I had viewed death as an exotic, impossible concept.

We were headed — as if the funeral thus far hadn't been bizarre enough — to what had been described as "Marcellus's church," where food and strained fellowship would be waiting.

From behind us, Marcellus's voice startled me. "Barbara and Jon, how about riding back with me." It was an order, not a request.

I climbed into the back seat of the chauffeured car between the two men. Even before the driver turned on the ignition, Marcellus began to speak, so rapidly that I wasn't sure whether he was anxious to unburden himself or simply wanted it over with.

"Number one, Vera sent Essie that videotape over a year ago. I just had it edited so you couldn't trace her. Number two, it wasn't Essie's first stroke that killed her. It was the second." He turned to me. "She had the first one a few days after your visit.

She knew she was dying. She knew it wouldn't be long."

I gasped. Jon said nothing.

"I know we weren't straight with you, but it was what she wanted," Marcellus said. "She never stayed in the hospital but two days. She was home. The reason she wouldn't talk to anybody was, she couldn't talk."

"So she was never planning a party," Jon said woodenly.

"Nobody ever said a *party*. She said a *meeting*. Listen, man, she was a proud woman. She didn't want you to think she was —" His face glistened with a thin veneer of perspiration. "Nobody likes people to know they can't talk. That they're all crumpled up." His voice nearly broke. "She couldn't talk but she could write. She'd been in touch with Vera a long time. She wrote her about the meeting and told her what to do. It took all her energy." Again his voice grew throaty with emotion. "When you have a stroke, it wears you out. Essie knew she was dying, you know what I'm saying?"

I had no idea.

"Me and Taneka, we got that tape to you. And when Essie passed, we did what she asked." Marcellus leaned back in his seat.

"So there's still —" Jon cleared his throat. "There's still a possibility of a meeting?"

Marcellus turned toward us again, miraculously recovered. "*This* is the meeting, man. Essie told Vera to come to her funeral. That pregnant woman at the cemetery? You already seen her, man. You already seen her, and you're about to see her again."

But Vera was not at the church, where a buffet had been set up in the social hall. We filled our plates, nibbled nervously, watched the door.

"It's sick, planning a meeting like this at a funeral," I said to Steve, who stuck close to me while Jon paced.

"It's quintessential Essie." He bit into a pastry. "She probably figured it was the closest she could come to being here herself. Not to mention an occasion none of us will be likely to forget."

I would have said more, but a stream of people began approaching Steve and introducing themselves, saying how much they liked his songs, sometimes asking for an autograph. Marilyn and I ended up sandwiched between a wall and the coffee urn, musing at how funeral receptions often turned cheerful, unless the deceased was young or the circumstances tragic. "Like Penny's funeral," Marilyn said.

"It was awful." Penny's funeral had provided me with my first glimpse of Jon after our breakup, and my last for another thirty years. Jon and I had made a point of staying far enough away from each other in the crowd that we wouldn't have to talk. It had been one of the most difficult days of my life.

An old lady with hearing aids in each ear pulled on my sleeve and began a monologue about having been Essie's neighbor. "Only white woman I was ever friends with," she declared. She fixed her gaze on me and then on Marilyn, as if awaiting a challenge.

"Mrs. Brown, Keisha's looking for you!" Taneka rushed toward us in a black sheath that showed off her ample curves. "Keisha thought you wandered off outside."

"That girl!" the woman said, and hastened off.

"Tough couple of weeks, huh?" Marilyn asked Taneka. "Barbara says you took real good care of Essie."

"Thanks. I tried."

"I hear you're at the University of Maryland. Have you been able to keep up with your classes through all this?"

Taneka nodded. "When Essie couldn't talk she wrote me a note. She said no matter what happens, I damn well better stay in school."

We all smiled at the image of Essie doing that. "What about the house?" Marilyn asked. "Will you stay there?"

"Probably for a while."

"I guess Essie will leave it to you, anyway," I said. "Or to your dad."

"Oh, the house isn't Essie's. It's Dad's. Has been for a long time."

"You mean she gave it to him?" Marilyn asked.

Taneka's vivacious tone grew measured and cool. "No, of course not. He bought it."

"Bought it?"

Taneka examined the skirt of her dress as if looking for a stain, then took a breath and looked up. "He bought it because Essie ran out of money. I don't know all the details. He bought it so she'd have some place to live."

"Oh." Trying to suppress my surprise, I spoke more to myself than to Taneka. "I guess she paid him rent."

"She did," Taneka replied shortly. "In case you're curious, her rent was a dollar a month."

"I didn't mean —" I felt the hot blush spread over my face.

"I guess he'll sell it now. Sooner or later. Too many memories. Sometimes it's better to start fresh." With less than tactful deliberateness, the girl excused herself and caught the attention of a woman pouring coffee.

Across the room, Jon was pacing back and forth in front of the entry door, a plate of uneaten food in his hand. *I should go to him*, I thought, but didn't move. His tense, preoccupied expression made it clear he didn't need me.

"You know what? I think I better sit down," Marilyn said, her face draining of color.

I guided her to one of the chairs lined up at the edges of the room. "I'll get you a drink." I bolted to the buffet table, grabbed a glass of water, thrust it at her. Her pallor was alarming.

"This is how it always happens. Okay one minute and zonked the next," she muttered.

"I thought you were going to start treatment."

"I was. I am. Most of the time I feel all right, just tired the way you always are after surgery."

Bernie had spotted us, was coming over.

"Listen," Marilyn said, "these little spells are nothing. It's been a long day. Don't tell him."

"Let him take you home, then. Jon and I can go with Steve."

"Are you kidding? You think I'm leaving without getting a glimpse of Vera?"

As if on cue, the door opened and inside the doorway, recognizable for the first time as she slipped off the hooded cape that had hidden her face, there she was. Jon stood an arm's length away from her, staring. In person, she looked more like Penny than she had on the tape — not her features so much as her questioning, unsure expression as she scanned the room for the face that belonged to her father. Following Marilyn's gesture that I should go, I made myself move toward Jon.

But in the end it was Marcellus who took Vera's hand and brought the young couple over to where Jon and I stood, immobilized, and made the courtly, formal introduction. "This is Vera Silverman and her husband, Ed," he told us. Then, to Vera, he said, "Vera, I want you to meet your father."

The four of us stood in the center of the room after Marcellus walked away, staring at each other like tongue-tied adolescents.

"I hardly believe this," Vera said finally.

Jon coughed, cleared his throat. "Me, either."

"We wondered when you were going to get here," I said, resorting to small talk to defuse the charged air of emotion.

"We were late because we don't know the area. It's so easy to get lost," Vera said.

Ed nodded. "We were lost and Vera was so hungry we had to stop for a snack."

"I feel like I'm eating for three or four instead of just two." Vera's face flushed, as Penny's used to do, and I noticed the pale sprinkle of powdered-over freckles on her nose.

"Twins?"

"Oh, no. Just one."

"You came from out of town?" Jon asked. "I guess you know Essie sent us a tape, edited so we couldn't figure out where you were from."

"Cumberland," Ed told them. "No secret." It was in western Maryland, less than three hours away.

Vera laughed. "Essie was pretty protective, wasn't she? Did you know she kept track of me from the time I was born?"

At six foot three or four, Ed hovered over his wife like an umbrella. When he took Vera's arm and guided her to a chair, Jon and I trailed them like shadows.

Settling herself the best she could, Vera looked first to Jon, then to me, careful not to let her eyes linger longer on one than the other. "I guess we better get to the point." She switched into her reporter's voice. "I always knew my mother was dead. My adoptive mother told me. But I never knew anything about my father."

"And you wanted to?" Jon asked.

"Oh, always. After I got out of college, I went through channels and got the birth certificate. The reason my mother never told me anything was because she didn't know. In the place for the father's name, it said unknown."

"I see."

"I was curious about my father because I really never had one. My adoptive parents divorced when I was three. I was one of those kids who were supposed to save the marriage but didn't."

"I'm sorry," Jon said. "I guess you could have used me to be around."

"It's okay. I turned out pretty normal." A slow grin lit Vera's face, then an out-and-out flash of merriment. "It would have been complicated, if you'd actually showed up back then."

As Jon tried to hide his embarrassment, Vera patted her stomach. "Maybe it's not too late. The baby could still use a grandfather."

It was then that I stopped fearing Vera would somehow be the ghost of her mother, haunting us every time her name came up or she walked into a room. In person, Vera had more sense of humor than Penny had ever had, and none of her mother's neediness.

Jon and Vera both looked at me beseechingly, wanting to be left alone. Ed said he was going to get something to eat. An empty space opened before me as some of the well-fed mourners departed for home, and, for a moment, it was as if the tumult of the room had dimmed and the faces of the guests fallen out of focus, a feeling I'd had many times when after the busyness of the day I returned, always, to the solid nub of loneliness that had been my life. I felt truly bereft.

Then a reassuring hand plopped itself onto my shoulder. "Don't feel abandoned. Uncle Stevie's here to see you through your time of need."

"Thanks, Uncle Stevie."

"This is going to turn out to be okay," he said.

"Is it?"

He eased his arm around me, pulled me close. "Maybe not today. Maybe not tomorrow. Maybe not the way you think. But yes. Sure."

Something in me shifted then. The shelf of the world readjusting itself. A seismic correction. I wasn't sure what it meant, didn't much care. It was Steve who sheltered me like an oak tree, Steve I leaned on while Jon got to know the daughter who in a better world might have been from another union entirely. Steve who turned me away from the sight of them and escorted me across the room. "Let's go say goodbye to Marcellus," he said.

Shaking hands with people heading out the door, Marcellus seemed to be having a good time. "Well, how they doing?" he asked, gesturing in the direction of Jon and Vera.

"They seem to be doing fine," I said without looking.

"Well, I thought they would. Good."

"I would never have expected this," I told him.

"You weren't supposed to."

"I mean, your following through on Essie's idea of a father-daughter reunion — I wouldn't have expected it — under the circumstances."

"What'd you think, that after all this I would disrespect Essie? She was more a mother to me than my own mother was."

"I know she was. I saw how you tried to protect her. And how much she cared about you."

"She liked you, too."

"Not really." I tried to sound flip, but it was as if someone were squeezing my heart. As a child I'd resented Essie not making more of a fuss over me, pampering Penny and Steve instead. I'd never quite gotten over it.

"She liked you more than you thought," Marcellus said. "She said your big problem was, you worried about how you looked. You were smart, you had a nice family, everything going for you, and you worried how you looked."

"I did. I still do." Marcellus's words brought my sense of humor back. "Major character flaw, huh?"

"She said you'd always look all right. You had good bone structure."

"She said that?"

Marcellus shrugged.

"She always told me looks were temporary. Not to count on them."

"Yeah, well — Somebody could have hit you upside the head. You could have gone through a windshield. She was probably preparing you for that."

"I wouldn't put it past her."

Marcellus backed up slightly, studied me through narrowed eyes. "Of course now that you're an old broad, looking just like any other old broad —"

I laughed.

Marcellus held out his hand to say goodbye. I meant to take it, but instead I moved forward and gave him a hug. It startled us both. Unpromising as our start had been, somehow here we were, making jokes like old friends. Confusing as this was, I had no intention of analyzing it. Sometimes the best policy — as I had lately learned — was simply to be grateful.

Across the room, Jon was shaking hands with Vera and Ed. *Kiss her,* I wanted to say. *Kiss your daughter.*

"Don't rush him," Steve told me. "There'll be time."

"What's this? Are you reading my mind now?"

"I've always been able to read your mind, sweetie. Ever since you came to my house wanting to quit piano lessons." He bent over and softly kissed my cheek.

In the plane on the way home, Jon said, "The baby's due in a couple of weeks. Vera isn't really supposed to travel, but she wanted to meet me."

"Are you flattered?"

"Very much."

"This is going to be good for you, this late-blooming fatherhood. It's fine not to have children, but if you don't, there's a big chunk of your heart you just never get to use. Trust me on this."

"I believe you. But what about her saying the birth certificate lists the father as unknown. Do you think maybe I'm not?"

"Not her father? No. Just look at her — those eyebrows! That voice. Of course you're her father. I think Penny didn't put your name down because she wanted to protect us. If somebody got hold of the birth certificate later, she wanted to be sure you couldn't be traced. Because she thought you were going to marry me."

Jon drew a deep breath. "And will you?" he asked.

CHAPTER 21

Wrightsville Beach, NC

February 2001

On this warm February day, the seascape is all pastels, sand the palest possible beige, sky and ocean identical shades of blue, shot through with wisps of thin clouds. In the surf, something wonderful to eat — the gulls circling, diving, making a racket; the pelicans bobbing on the swells like ducks, reaching down for occasional nibbles.

I took my shoes off, waded into the icy tide for the ritual of exposing my toes to the ocean, then sat down on the soft sand above the tide line.

A month ago, in January, I'd flown to Washington for Marilyn's son Andrew's engagement brunch, and as I scanned the water, my thoughts were dragged back to that now. Robin had come from Los Angeles, partly to meet Andrew's fiancée but mostly to see Marilyn, who was in the middle of her treatments. Jon was in Texas doing interviews, but Marilyn had invited Vera and Ed. "Trying to make them feel like family," she'd said.

The young couple had showed up early, toting their six-week-old son.

"So you named him David." I let the baby's name play on my tongue as I helped Vera arrange her diaper bag and other baby miscellany in the bedroom where she could nurse him and let him nap. "You named him after your mother, Davidina."

"Yes."

"Penny was supposed to be a David herself, but turned out to be a girl. Did Essie tell you that? Essie was the one who gave your mother the nickname, Penny."

Vera shook her head. "I didn't know that."

"I'll tell you the whole story," I said. "Lots of stories. Essie's last request."

With the weary slowness of the sleep-deprived, milk-engorged, garment-stained new mother, Vera lifted the baby to her shoulder. "This will be hard for you, won't it? Essie told me you and Jon had been engaged and out of guilt he ran off. She told me you never knew the whole story until last fall. If I found out Ed had a baby with a friend of mine, I don't think I'd ever forgive him. Or her, either."

"You might surprise yourself," I told her.

"So you don't mind telling me about my mother?"

"There was a time when I would have. Not now." It seemed an age since Jon and I had returned from Essie's funeral and had the long-overdue talk that finally erased my reticence about Penny and so many other things. Would I marry him? Probably. But first we needed to know each other without the burden of secrets hanging between us like a shield. After thirty years, why not take a few more months to be sure? In the end, Jon took an apartment and rented his share of the house to Robin, very cheaply, while she was in Wilmington working on her film. Even after she left, we kept "dating" with a kind of tenderness neither of us had expected. We wouldn't have forever to make up our minds. But we had now.

There in Marilyn's guest room, I ruffled the baby's soft hair as he lay with his head on Vera's shoulder. Little by little, David's eyes drifted shut and his forehead furrowed as if he were deep in thought, bringing together brows already black and sleek as a seal's. "If your mother knew she had a grandchild named after her," I said, "she would have been honored."

"You think so?"

I nodded. "I'm sure of it. I feel honored in her behalf."

I hadn't expected the seesaw of emotions that gripped me that weekend. Talking to Vera brought more pleasure than I'd bargained for, but seeing Marilyn was a painful, ongoing shock. She was frighteningly thin, thinner than during the brutal days of chemo years before. Her clothes hung on her, even the slim jeans she wore the afternoon I arrived. In the two months since Essie's funeral, she must have lost fifteen pounds. How was that possible?

Seeing the look on my face, Bernie cornered me in the kitchen as soon as Marilyn went to get a tablecloth out of the dryer. "It might be nothing," he said. "She has her scans next month and then we'll know. She's always a little peaked in the winter. The treatments were tougher than she thought."

"She did this to spare the hair," I said bitterly.

"She's glad she spared the hair, she's just tired. It takes a little while to make a comeback. Not that anyone was ever optimistic."

"Not optimistic?"

"This was a recurrence. A recurrence is never good news."

"But these new treatments —"

"It's not just the treatments that have

her down. It's everything combined. Waiting for the fatigue to go away. Numbness from the face-lift —"

"She hasn't said anything about fatigue or numbness since Thanksgiving!"

Marilyn appeared just then in the doorway, the tablecloth clutched to her scrawny chest. "I didn't want to worry you, that's all."

"I thought we were friends! I thought we were finished having secrets!" I felt on the verge of hysteria.

Making his escape, Bernie fled into the den. Marilyn took my arm.

"Come outside for a minute." She got our coats and gestured toward the screened porch in back. "My current condition is nothing to get excited about. Come on, sit down."

We dropped into chairs and looked out to the frostbitten yard, bleak in the pale afternoon light. A gusty wind growled in the bare trees and rustled the bushes. "Okay, here's how it is," Marilyn said. "Sometimes I feel like I'm on a roller coaster. I keep trying to get off, but I'm never sure if I have. Sometimes I'm up in the air and sometimes the ground feels solid. Listen, don't be upset with me for not telling you before. You can't blame me for not wanting to spill my guts while you and Jon were reorganizing your lives."

"And why not, Marilyn? Why the hell not?"

She ignored that. "Anyway, I can't control it. Being tired. Having no appetite. You have no right to be angry with me for something I can't control."

"Sure, put me on a guilt trip," I shot back, but had to pretend it was the wind that was making my eyes water so.

At the back of the yard, two cardinals, a male and a female, sat on the branches of a holly bush, fluffing their feathers. Marilyn hugged herself into her coat. Dwarfed by the high-backed chair, she seemed already insubstantial, as if she'd been whittled away by the pumice stone she used on her nails, rubbed down until soon even the nub would be gone, her features wavering and indistinct through my tears, her flesh so soft that at any moment she might liquefy and drift away.

"Don't think such morbid thoughts," Marilyn said.

"How do you know what I'm thinking?"

"If you could see your face, you wouldn't ask. Keep in mind that it's uncharitable to put me in the grave before I'm actually dead."

"Don't talk like that."

"Why not? You don't really think it's going to happen to you. That you'll get that old or that desperate or that sick. Or be that unlucky. You don't ever really believe it."

"I guess you don't." I swallowed my grief and made myself meet her eyes.

"You know what I always thought I'd do after the kids left?" Marilyn asked. "Promise you won't laugh. Run for office."

"You still might."

"No. I would have hated it. People calling all the time to complain. No privacy. It would have been awful."

As if everything were settled. As if everything were past. Inside the house, beyond the sliding glass door, someone on the TV was laughing. "Do you feel bad? Are you in pain?" I raised my voice against the wind and the TV and the jumble in my head, and realized I was shouting.

"No pain, just achy. Like I have the flu."

"Maybe you *do* have the flu."

"Maybe." Marilyn didn't smile. Already something permanent had changed, the relentless cheeriness had gone, she'd dropped the mask she'd been wearing and let me see her raw and genuine self for once, not upbeat, her face tight with fear.

I will love this Marilyn better, I thought. *I will love her better if I get the chance.*

At the brunch, Marilyn was a perfect mask again. "Wouldn't have a clue my sister sleeps fourteen hours a day, would you?" Steve asked. He had flown in just for a couple of hours.

"Is she as sick as I think she is?" Robin wanted to know. "Tell me the truth, Uncle Steve."

"No way to tell when people are having cancer treatments," Steve told her. "Until they're over, you just hold your breath." He put one arm around me and one around Robin. "Listen, sweetie, if your Aunt Marilyn can be perky today, so can we. Let's go congratulate the bride and groom to be," he instructed, and herded us into the room where Andrew and his fiancée, Dee Dee, were holding court.

Before I left for my evening flight home, Marilyn made me walk with her around the block in the frigid air. Her face was flushed; she was still on an adrenaline high even though the party must have worn her out. "Here," she said, taking off her necklace. It was the pearl on a thin gold chain her mother had given her the day of our Sweet Sixteen. She'd worn it on special occasions, for luck, ever since.

"I can't take that."

"You can. I want you to have it. Who else from our Sweet Sixteen can I foist it on?"

"No!" I insisted. "It's like — a last offering. Give it to me another time. Next trip. I'll be back."

"Just in case," Marilyn said, and folded it into my hand.

We pretended nothing had happened. We walked back. Made the usual small talk. Laughed. But when Bernie opened the car door to let me in, I flung myself into Marilyn's arms and burst into tears and held tight. "When will I see you again? I want to know exactly. Let's make plans right now."

"Why, at Andrew's wedding," Marilyn said without hesitation. "In April." Her tone made me feel that in spite of her pale translucent skin and the fine blue vein that beat beneath the skin of her temple, she might be right.

All the same, it was Marilyn who had to extricate herself from my embrace. I couldn't let go of her, didn't see how I ever would.

Now, a month later, I felt rather than heard Jon and Steve approach me on the beach, and drop down onto the sand on either side of me. I didn't look at either of them, only felt the pressure of Jon's hand on top of mine, pleasant and somehow binding, and the teasing nudge of Steve's shoulder, pushing me closer to Jon.

"Gentlemen, I appreciate this," I said, "but all this attention is almost too much." I got up, brushed sand from my clothes, and walked down to the tide line. Marilyn stood with her toes digging into the wet sand, watching a noisy gaggle of gulls make a commotion and then fly off. What luck, not to have to wait until April to see her! She greeted me with a slow smile. "Who would have imagined this? Short sleeves in the middle of February, and not even in Florida."

"Seventy-three degrees. And just when you and Steve could visit." Steve had been working in New York lately so he could spend a day or two each week at Marilyn's, but this was the first time she'd been strong enough for him to bring to North Carolina.

"Look at us," she said, opening her arms out to the nearly empty stretch of sand. "Just two old ladies on the beach."

"Old! We're not even sixty. You think we're old?"

"It's all relative. Depends on how old you expect to get."

"Don't talk like that! I've told you before!" I batted my arms at her, not seriously. She was a feather, too weak to run away.

She linked her arm in mine, leaned on me a bit as we headed back toward Steve and Jon. "Guess what? Andrew and Dee Dee are pregnant."

"And still unmarried until April? I'm scandalized!" I laughed, then echoed what I knew she was thinking. "See? Maybe, after all, you'll get your little girl."

She paused just a beat too long. "Let's hope so."

I pretended not to hear her hesitation. "I'll have to give the necklace back, won't I? You'll want it for your granddaughter."

"I might."

"Indian giver," I said.

Back above the tide line, I flopped down between Jon and Steve while Marilyn lowered herself slowly, gingerly, as if all her bones were sore.

"Tired?" Steve asked.

"A little," Marilyn said. "Not much."

Jon took my hand and clutched tight, as if to squeeze out my sadness. "What are you thinking?"

"I'm thinking," I said slowly, "that as far as I'm concerned, we can sit here the rest of the afternoon. Sit here till darkness falls."

"And freeze our butts," Steve said.

"Sit here till the tide comes in. Till waves of age wash over us. Waves of infirmity. Till it carries us away."

"I think you *are* carried away," Marilyn told me.

"Not that we're complaining," Steve said.

We did sit for a long time, looking at the wide swath of beach, balmy between cold snaps, the shore of the new century and our old age, the shore of our last pilgrimage. Fine with me. As long as they were along for the journey. As far as I was concerned, we were still at the center of the complicated tapestry that had been our lives: love and treachery, the wail of babies, the rustle of falling leaves; friends, torrential snowstorms, humid heat — a cloth of different colors, woven, textured, rich. The calendar said winter, but maybe not. As far as I was concerned, we were still at the very core of autumn, the blazing sunset before the dark, old enough to look back, young enough to look forward. And oh! it was dazzling.

READERS GUIDE

DISCUSSION QUESTIONS

1. Like many people, Barbara and Marilyn have a nostalgic view of the "old neighborhood" where they grew up. How does this change when they revisit Riggs Park many years later? Is it altered more by what they see there, or by what they learn about events that happened there when they were young?

2. *Riggs Park* is a novel about women's friendships, and particularly about the lifelong bond between Marilyn and Barbara, as well as their early friendship with Penny. Was each one always the kind of friend she wanted to be to the others? What are some of the sacrifices they made for each other? Were there times when they could have done better?

3. Essie Berman makes many decisions that affect the lives of the children in Riggs Park well into adulthood. Are they wise ones? Should she have done some things differently?

4. In what ways is the Jewish concept of *Tikkun Olam* — fix the world — important to Barbara's not-very-religious parents and later to Barbara and Marilyn themselves? Are they serious about "fixing the world," or just conveniently adapting the idea to fit their lives?

5. As a result of their experiences and life lessons, some people "mellow" as they grow older, while others grow bitter. How would you characterize the changes in Marilyn and Barbara and Jon — first, over the years of their lives, and second, as a result of what happens during the months of the story?

For more discussion questions, visit www.readersring.com

About the Author

Ellyn Bache began writing freelance newspaper articles when her four children were small. As they got older and gave her more time, she turned her hand to short stories. It took her six years to get her first one published. Then, for many years, her fiction appeared in a wide variety of women's magazines and literary journals and was published in a collection that won the Willa Cather Fiction Prize. Ellyn began her first novel, *Safe Passage*, the year her youngest son went to school full-time. That book was later made into a film starring Susan Sarandon, and Ellyn went on to write other novels for women, a novel for teens, a children's picture book and many more stories and articles. There's more on her Web site, www.ellynbache.com.

The employees of Thorndike Press hope you have enjoyed this Large Print book. All our Thorndike and Wheeler Large Print titles are designed for easy reading, and all our books are made to last. Other Thorndike Press Large Print books are available at your library, through selected bookstores, or directly from us.

For information about titles, please call:

(800) 223-1244

or visit our Web site at:

www.gale.com/thorndike
www.gale.com/wheeler

To share your comments, please write:

Publisher
Thorndike Press
295 Kennedy Memorial Drive
Waterville, ME   04901